CW01032826

I KNOW YOUR SECRET

J.M. O'ROURKE

INKUBATOR
BOOKS

Published by Inkubator Books
www.inkubatorbooks.com

ISBN (eBook): 978-1-83756-152-0
ISBN (Paperback): 978-1-83756-153-7
ISBN (Hardback): 978-1-83756-154-4

Previously published by the author as Jess Roy in 2021.

PROLOGUE

It's a nightmare many experience. A nightmare you know is a nightmare, but you're still living it, in real time, behind closed eyes, locked into a virtual-reality world of boundless, infinite terror. It's a nightmare so real your brain can't always differentiate between the two: fall from a great height, your heart can stop; believe you are drowning, you can't breathe.

This is the world where she had been taken, a world of utter darkness, a world of monsters and demons, where she was tethered to a wall in a chamber of blood-curdling echoing screams, her breathing short and desperate and burning hot in her chest.

But for her there was no relief. There was no waking up to realise it had all been a dream, no crying into a pillow with relief that she was safe in her own bedroom, in her own bed, that it had all just been a horrible dream.

No, for her there was no relief. Because this horror was real.

Her eyes flickered now, the lids parting slightly, the

grey black smudge filtering in. A man was skirting the edge of her nightmare, both separate and part of it at the same time, yet always there. Malevolent, evil, she could hear his footsteps, she could not see him, but he was always there. Fading now, the sound of those footsteps, slowly disappearing, but never quite gone. It petrified her. Her dream burning onto her consciousness like a sudden bright light, wanting to shade her eyes against it but unable to move her hands. Realising, in all its brutal reality, that this was no dream. She cried out, from shock, helplessness, fear. As he put his hand in there, cold and soft, yet the movement rough, his nails pinching her, his flesh dragging across her sore, raw crotch. He mumbled something, his voice muted, distorted, of throwing off metaphorical shackles, freeing himself from himself, unleashing the barbarian.

And then he was before her, stepping out of the shadows.

Amanda screamed.

He wore a mask; it stretched over his face, cling-wrapping his ears and nose, buttressing his lips, cobwebbing his eyes behind a fine mesh.

For a moment she could not breathe, her inhale catching at the back of her throat, stuck fast. She gagged a couple of times, her eyes so wide that all it would take was a little squeeze on either side and they might pop out, her face turning crimson, her tongue hanging, curling, desperate for air, but nothing happening, the sound like a suction pipe in a dentist's surgery. Then she retched, once, twice, expelling a yellow mucus that dribbled down from the corners of her mouth. She lay there then, breathing again, frantic, its sound filling the room, before she opened her mouth wide and screamed, a scream of hopelessness, a scream of the trapped animal, a scream she would never have guessed she was capable of making. It was desperate and primal. And utterly useless.

1

Dr Amanda Jackson emerged from the revolving doors of the White Rock Medical Clinic and walked quickly towards the private hospital's car park. It was just after four thirty, but the early September sun was still hot in a clear blue sky. In a corner of the car park, where a sign said 'Staff Only', she pointed her key fob, and a lime green Mercedes in the second row of vehicles made a squelching noise in return and blinked twice.

She crossed to it and got in, pulled off her high-heel leather pumps and threw them into the passenger footwell, took a deep breath, held it, closed her eyes, and exhaled slowly before repeating the process. She did her potato sack routine, imagining on each exhale potatoes, which represented thoughts from her busy day, running out of a bag. When the bag was empty, in theory, her mind should be empty too, leaving her to refill it with happier thoughts. It usually worked.

With her eyes still closed, she pressed her feet on the hard rubber grooved pedals and rubbed them across, the rough sensation soothing in a way, further removing her from her head. Then she imagined pouring herself a gin and tonic when she got home, plopping a slice of lemon into it, raising it to her lips, taking a sip... hhmm. That was better.

She opened her eyes and placed the key in the ignition, turning it, firing the engine into life, flicked the car into gear, and was about to move off when she noticed it. Tucked beneath the driver's windshield wiper directly in front of her was a white envelope.

Didn't whoever placed it there know that unsolicited material is strictly forbidden within the hospital and its grounds? Even staff members couldn't promote anything, not even charity events. She thought of Nurse King, with her lucrative sideline business selling expectant mums and dads coloured images of their babies in the womb. Even she wasn't allowed to advertise.

Amanda cursed under her breath, tempted to activate the wipers to try to brush the damn thing away. But she was a little curious too. Because who went to the trouble of placing a flyer inside an envelope? It didn't make much sense. The flyer maybe. But inside an envelope?

She opened the door and stretched out a hand. The thing was just beyond her reach, so she was forced to get out, feeling the gritty tarmac through her nylons. She snapped the envelope out from under the wiper with a thumb and index finger and held it gingerly, like a sample just taken from a patient. She got back into the car and threw it onto the dash, noticing it was sealed shut. She leaned forward and picked it up again, turning it over, like a curiosity in an antique shop. There was nothing written on it. Carefully, she lifted the edge of the seal and peeled it back just enough to place a finger inside and tear it open.

It was not a flyer, she could see that straight away, but a sheet of plain white paper. As she touched it, it felt thicker than standard copy paper, but not quite board paper either. It felt somewhere in between, like a type of card paper maybe. Amanda pried it from the envelope, it had been neatly folded in three, and opened it out. As she stared, her mind scrambled for meaning.

Was this a joke?

But as she read, her blood ran cold.

No. This was not a joke.

2

I KNOW YOUR SECRET

She stared at the words printed on the sheet of paper in her hands, her eyes going over each letter, noting the curve of the S, the squat bluntness of the I. Fifteen letters in total, combining into four words, combining into one sickening belly punch.

She released it and watched it float down, coming to rest on her lap, touching her like a burning ember. But she ignored it, because at that moment a memory came crashing into her consciousness, sweeping all else before it...

Of a sliver of grey light seeping around the edges of the large curtained window next to the bed she was lying on. And a smell, of wood polish and soap, mixed with alcohol and sweat – male sweat. She was petrified, too petrified to move or to make any sound, to even breathe. From outside, she could hear the occasional swoosh of a passing vehicle. The air against her skin was sharp and cold. She realised then she had no clothes on, and her arms, painful and heavy, were like leaden weights. She forced herself to try to move them. But she could not, and immediately she understood why. Her wrists were tied to the headboard. She opened her mouth, heard the loud shrill noise, realised it was that of her screaming.

I KNOW YOUR SECRET

AMANDA CLUTCHED THE STEERING WHEEL, tighter and tighter, a low croaking noise coming from her throat, her breathing rapid. She could feel her nails digging into her palms. But she welcomed the pain because it diverted her attention from her rising panic.

I KNOW YOUR SECRET

Who knew her secret?
Her mind whirled.
Who?
She looked ahead, completely still, a tsunami of fear devouring her.

3

She drove home in a blur, her hands shaking on the wheel. Once or twice she was tempted to pull in, that she couldn't go on, her mind churning the words over and over: I know your secret, I know your secret...

Oh, Jesus!

She slammed on the brakes at an intersection as she noticed almost too late the traffic lights had turned to red. The driver behind her honked his horn. She dropped her head into her hands in desperation. What was she going to do?

Tell Edward. Of course! He'd know. He'd know what to do... well, wouldn't he? Her husband was a doctor too, a consultant at one of the largest public hospitals in the country. Yes, Edward would know. Calm, practical, completely unflappable, her Edward... oh, get a grip, who the hell are you bloody well kidding? Edward...? I don't think so. The driver behind honked again, longer this time, more insistent. She glanced in the rear-view mirror, saw him gesturing wildly with his hands as he pointed.

She looked and saw the traffic lights had turned to green. She moved off quickly, keeping her eyes straight ahead as the car shot from behind into the next lane and overtook her.

As she continued, she realised she'd been fooling herself for so long. Long enough that the reality had almost escaped her. She mulled it over, a large white colossus looming up out of the corner of her vision. She glanced across, saw that there was a huge juggernaut alongside, and she was too close for comfort. She yanked on the steering wheel, the car wobbling momentarily as it righted itself.

Okay, she told herself, relax before you kill yourself, take a breath, nice and slow...

WHEN SHE GOT HOME to Ocean View House, she made herself a stiff gin and tonic and gulped it down, made another and sat in the drawing room sipping on it, staring across the room through the French windows of the big old house to the garden outside, but seeing absolutely nothing at all. Her mind began to reach back through the years, dredging through time, trying to make sense of it all, trying to find an answer to that one question: who? Who knows my secret?

'There you are.'

She looked up, startled.

'Is everything alright?' Her husband was standing in the doorway. 'You look like you've seen a ghost. Really.'

Is everything alright? A memory sprang to mind, of being asked the very same question by someone many years before.

'What time is it?' She glanced at her watch. 'Oh, I didn't realise... I'll get something on... are you hungry?'

Edward Jackson dropped his case. 'Maybe later.' He came and sat next to her. 'Tell me, how was your day?'

She felt his hand on hers and looked down at it. It was such a slender hand, a pianist's or a surgeon's, and there was a time when its touch could have made her scream, could have sent her wild. But not anymore. She looked up into his face, such a handsome face. One time she'd thought he might be everything she had ever dreamed of. A horrible sense of shame and self-loathing crawled through her as she stared at him silently, unable to speak.

'Well,' he said, tapping his knee and pointing to her glass, 'I'm going to get one of those. I don't think you need another; you've already had your quota for the day in that one, I'd safely say.'

The alcohol, which had initially given her a warm glow, was now leaving her system, leaving her feeling even more hopeless than before. She would like another gin and tonic, and maybe another one after that too, enough to send her to sleep and to not have to think about any of this until morning. But Edward would tut-tut and tut-tut and tut-tut about it for days. It was better just to go along and keep him happy. Anyway, he was right, she had reached her daily alcohol quota in that one glass, so it was probably all for the best.

'Really,' he said, smiling. 'You don't look so good. I should know. I'm a doctor.' It was an attempt at humour, about the limit of his grasp of the subject. Normally, Amanda might force a chuckle at a time like this; instead now she sat there stony faced as Edward placed a palm against her forehead. 'No temperature,' he said, his expression earnest, and added, 'Seriously, darling, is everything alright?'

It was all a charade, of course. This polite, happy domesticity that usually passed unnoticed and invisible between them. Now she felt she couldn't take it any longer. She wanted to curse and scream, to jump up and shake this man and reveal to him her terrible, dark secret. She wanted him to come and protect her, to rescue her, to be her knight in shining armour.

But she knew that was impossible.

'How was your day?' she asked instead.

'How was my day?' He looked at her strangely. 'You wouldn't be trying to change the subject now, would you?'

This time she forced a chuckle. 'Of course not.'

They were silent, a silence she felt would suffocate her, would drown her, a silence that had a sound all of its own, like a feral scream.

'I'm going to lie down for a little while,' she said. 'I won't be long. There's some lasagne in the fridge; just pop it in the microwave.'

His expression changed, and she realised her mistake. She might as well have mentioned one of the ten best ways to catch the bubonic plague as mention the microwave. The only reason the appliance was even in the house was because it had come free with a kitchen refit. While Amanda used it occasionally, she was always careful to clean it afterwards and have it look spick and span like it had never been used in the first place.

'The microwave?' Edward said. 'The microwave? Tell me you're not using that.'

'No, well, very rarely... sometimes, if I'm in a rush.'

He pursed his lips.

'Please, Edward, don't give out, not now. I don't feel so well.'

She could tell he was debating whether or not he would. He opened his mouth and closed it again. For a moment he said nothing, then: 'You go and have a rest. I'll check on you in a little while.'

She smiled, a genuine smile, one of relief this time.

'But what's brought all this on?' he asked. 'I know something's up.'

She leaned forward and kissed his lips.

'Nothing's brought this on. Don't you ever have a bad day?'

He arched an eyebrow, an expression she found irritating.

'Well yes, of course, everybody does.'

'A lie-down,' she said, 'that's all I need.'

'A good night's sleep is what you need,' he answered. 'Really, I think you should stay in bed until morning.'

She nodded. 'Yes, maybe I will.'

She left the room, feeling his eyes following her every move. She went quickly up the stairs to their bedroom, into the en suite, locked the door and crossed to the toilet bowl, crouched over it, and vomited.

4

1994

She screamed until she could not scream any longer, and once, when she opened her eyes, she wondered if it hadn't all been a nightmare, that she really wasn't tied to a bed, this bed, and that she had not been screaming. But then she tugged on her arms and realised she was wrong; she really was tied to the bed. She ran her tongue over her dry lips and swallowed, her throat so sore and raw the effort made her wince, as she realised that yes, she really had been screaming. Her fear morphed into an altered state of reality, one that she was both a part of but separate from at the same time. The swooshing sounds of traffic were more frequent, and once or twice she could hear voices, loud voices from somewhere outside, somewhere below, bringing with them a reassuring sense of normalcy, blunting her fear just enough for her to think rationally for the first time.

Her mind filled with images, a jigsaw of random memories, frozen snapshots without any order or logic. She forced herself to concentrate, picking up a piece of the jigsaw and peering at it, picking up another, trying to

put the two together, discarding it again when they didn't
fit, picking up yet one more, and starting all over again
until eventually... Click, a piece finally fitted with the one
she was holding, snapping into place. She looked at the
two images newly joined together, smiling faces, hers and
Fiona's...

Of course. Yes, she and Fiona.

She quickly selected other pieces, knowing what she
was searching for now, found them and pushed them
together, click, click, click...

She considered the enlarged image. It was of the flat,
hers and Fiona's. Okay... they were in the flat. She ran her
eyes over the remaining pieces of jigsaw. What now? She
picked up more pieces, but nothing would fit this time.
She picked up more still, becoming frantic, trying to force
them together, desperate to find meaning, but nothing
was making sense, her memories were even more
confused... then, click, as two more pieces fitted together.
She stared, her breath quickening, a hollow sensation in
the centre of her chest. Two dull orbs floating on a brown
sea beneath a diffusion of colours. She concentrated on
them, bringing them into sharper focus, everything crys-
tallising, becoming familiar, the orbs – brass handles; the
brown sea – wood panelling; the diffusion of colours – an
abstract of coloured glass... Yes, yes, that was it. The door
to the pub. The Merchants. She and Fiona had gone there.
Yes, yes, yes. She remembered, a complete section of the
jigsaw coming together all by itself. The image came to
life. Stepping in from the cold, from the miserable night
outside, a wave of heat washing over her as they began to
push through the thick forest of people, the band on stage
tuning up, 'Testing, one two three...' reaching the bar and
Amanda leaning over, her eyes sweeping across the faces

of the serving staff, catching the eye of a barmaid, a girl with a crew cut and huge doe eyes that reminded her of Goldie Hawn.

'Two bottles of Pils.' Having to shout because the band had suddenly launched into their first song, 'Dirty Old Town'.

As if by magic it continued, the jigsaw pieces moving of their own accord through the air, criss-crossing, seeking each other out in correct order. Everything came back to her until there were no pieces left. But yet, but yet, the puzzle was not complete. There was still a blank section, like a great big bite had been taken out of her conscious-ness, her reality tapering to the jagged edges of a black void.

Panic began to rise in her again; she realised she was never going to make sense of this. Of how she had come here, had ended up this way. And where was Fiona? Where the fuck was Fiona?

She opened her mouth to scream again, but all that came from it was a muffled croaking sound.

5

She did indeed stay in bed as Edward had urged, sleeping initially, but then waking up, lying as still as possible so as not to wake her husband. He hated being woken, yet still insisted they sleep together in the same bed. At the very least, twin beds would suit Amanda much better, but as with everything, she went along with it because she felt she had to. So for much of the night she had lain still, her mind churning as she fought against her thoughts, not allowing any to fully develop and consume her, which they would do, an endless battle against half-formed images, many too shocking to even contemplate. When the dawn light finally seeped through the curtains, she slipped out of bed and went to the en suite, turned on the shower full power, stepped in, hoping she could wash her exhaustion away. But when she stepped out again and wiped the condensation from the mirror to look at herself, she knew it would take much more than that, much more. 'I look dreadful,' she muttered, two bloodshot, black-ringed eyes staring back at her.

This was bound to happen. She'd been fooling herself to think her past would just go away, disappear. Even after all this time, all these years. She thought of Edward. She really wanted to love him, but the man made it just so damn near impossible. 'The microwave,' she mimicked. 'Tell me you don't use that.' She covered her mouth. My God. Had she really just mimicked her husband like that? What did that say? Was she coming to hate him now?

She shook her head. Focus, she told herself, and opened the cabinet above the sink. Make-up and eye-drops, that was what she'd need, plenty of both to get her through this day.

When she went into the bedroom again, Edward was sitting on the side of the bed, naked. One time she might have taken this as an invitation, but not now.

'Are you feeling better?' he asked.

'Yes,' she lied, 'I didn't sleep very well, but apart from that, I feel fine now.'

He stood, gave her one of his searching looks. 'It's hard to feel good when you don't get a good night's sleep, I know.' He passed her, heading for the en suite, and added, a crust to his tone, 'You have far too much bloody make-up on, by the way; it doesn't suit you, makes you look cheap.' Then she heard the en suite door bang shut.

But she could not compromise on her make-up, and it would remain. They ate breakfast – wholemeal bread, boiled eggs and avocados – in near silence, Amanda merely picking at her food. When she rose to take her plate and clear it into the sink disposal unit, Edward stared at it, then looked up and stared at her with an expression she considered to be one of disgust. She felt an almost irresistible urge to fling the plate at him. How would he like that? That would shatter the charade between them once and for all. But then she thought of her secret – her secrets – her past like a great monster that had suddenly reappeared, trailing along behind her, growling, snarling, full of menace. She felt sullen and dirty. What man would have bothered with her had he known the truth? She cleared the plate into the sink, turned, told Edward she was sorry for upsetting him, lowered her head and left the kitchen quickly, denying him any opportunity to reply. Because she had to be first to leave this house, she couldn't risk another note being left on her car, and worse still, of Edward finding it before she did.

SHE STEPPED out of the house and stood on the porch. The day was cloudy, but the breeze was light and cool on her face. She looked down towards her car parked a short distance away next to Edward's big, staid Volvo. She put a hand to her mouth, felt like throwing up again, took a deep breath and swallowed, felt a little better. She stepped onto the gravel driveway, hearing it crunch beneath her feet as she walked towards the Mercedes. And with it a weakness came over her, and she began to stumble, just getting to her car in time to reach out and lean against it and stop herself from falling. A line of tall privet bushes shielded her from the house, so she knew if Edward was standing by a window looking out, he would be unable to see her. She closed her eyes tightly, waited a moment, then slowly opened them again, took a couple of tentative steps forward until she had a view of the windscreen. She stared at it and blinked...

·   ·   ·

'YOU HAVE A FULL SCHEDULE,' Amanda's secretary said
when she got to her surgery, handing her a clipboard with
a printout of names, times and other details on it.

Amanda looked it over quickly and turned away,
started walking towards her surgery on the other side of
the reception area.

'Dr Jackson.'

She turned. 'Yes.'

Her secretary pointed to the fawn leather handbag
with its gleaming brass buckles resting on the counter.

'Your handbag.'

'Oh.' Amanda felt herself blush, but knew this couldn't
be seen under all the make-up she had on. There was an
awkward silence as she stepped back and reached for the
handbag, meeting the questioning gaze of her secretary.
Amanda took great pains to present an image of professional, efficient detachment – at all times. She was not the
type to forget a €5,000 Pierre Zuzo handbag. And she
knew her young secretary knew this too.

'Thank you, Layla,' she said, picking it up.

She walked across the plush carpeted reception once
more, feeling Layla's eyes burning a hole into her back.

For the most part, her surgery did not look like a
surgery, being predominately all dark wood panelling and
soft lighting, with a large bay window to one side looking
out onto the car park and the green area behind it to, off
in the distance, Galway Bay. To maintain the relaxing
aesthetic of the office area, the actual surgery was hidden
behind a remotely controlled privacy screen that divided
the room in two. Her surgery, or medical suite as it was
known, was one of a number at the White Rock Medical
Clinic, all offering a particular speciality. Hers dealt
mainly with referrals from insurance companies for long-

term illnesses and injuries, as well as interactions with corporations, usually via Skype or Zoom, on health and safety policy.

Amanda dropped the clipboard and her handbag onto her desk, went and stood by the window, folding her arms, staring out, her mind churning again like a rough sea, but just that little bit calmer now. Because there had been nothing there, on the windscreen. She had circled the car, making sure there was nothing lying on the ground either. Then she had thought: what about under the car? She had hitched up her skirt with one hand, had been about to get down onto her knees to have a look, then realised the pebbles would probably tear her tights. She had unlocked the car instead, sat in and started the engine, moved it forward a short distance, got out again and inspected the ground it had been parked on. If Edward had seen her, he would have come out demanding to know what she was up to. But she didn't care, because it didn't matter, nothing was there.

Nothing was there.

She could have whooped for joy. Because if a note had been there, it would have meant, of course, that someone had breached her world, not just the physical high walls of her home, with its automatic gates, but also her immanent world, someone had violated her. With no new note today, it allowed her to think: maybe this had all gone away?

Now, standing by the window of her surgery, she allowed herself another thought: what if this was all a coincidence? A crazy, unlikely coincidence for sure, but that's what coincidences were, weren't they? Definition of coin-

cidence: a remarkable occurrence of events or circumstances without apparent causal connection. Of course,
even taking that into account, this one was an extreme
freak... but nonetheless possible. Well, wasn't it? Yes, she
decided. Yes, it was. That note, it could be anything. She
relaxed. But then another voice spoke: no, no, no, it's not
possible, it couldn't be anything, that would be too much,
way too much of any kind of coincidence; you're just
trying to fool yourself, couldn't happen, couldn't
possibly...

Or could it?

She refused to discard that hope, clinging to it,
holding it close, willing it to be possible, willing it to be a
way-too-much-couldn't-possibly-happen-freakish-coinci-
dence coincidence. It was possible. It was. She gave a
nervous laugh, then laughed some more, a little harder
this time, and was soon doubled over, clasping her hand
tightly over her mouth, trying to stifle the sounds. If Layla
heard her, she would definitely think something was not
quite right with her for sure.

The landline phone sounded on her desk. 'Dr Jackson.' Layla's voice through the intercom. 'Your first patient
has arrived. Shall I send Mr Henderson in?'

Amanda quickly gathered herself. She hadn't even
looked at her patient list yet, but there was nothing she
could do about that now. When she spoke, her voice was
surprisingly bright, cheerful, hopeful.

'Yes, Layla. Send Mr Henderson in, please. Thank
you.'

BY LUNCHTIME, she was ravenous. Her two o'clock client
had cancelled. It was a pet hate of hers when a client

cancelled without giving the required twenty-four hours'
notice – unless the situation was completely unavoidable,
of course. But today, when Layla told her her two o'clock
appointment had cancelled, she just thought: Thank God.
With the extra time, she pondered going into town for
lunch. But as she did, it came back again, the fear, her
belly tightening, her anxiety levels rising. That would
mean taking the car. And now she could picture it,
walking to the Mercedes, her heart pounding, and flickering in the wind beneath the windscreen wiper, there it
would be – another note. She hadn't thought about it for
the past few hours, she'd been too busy. But here it was
again. Oh, God.

The hospital had an excellent canteen; she'd eat there
instead, sit in a corner, her back to the door; no one would
notice her; she didn't want to talk to anyone, didn't want to
see anybody. Oh, God. 'A coincidence, that's all,' she
muttered to herself, 'just as you said earlier. Go into town,
because you can't live in fear like this, with your imagination running wild; go down to your car, there's nothing
under that windscreen wiper, you'll see, that's never going
to happen again, a coincidence, that's all; go on, go into
town, go...'

She left the hospital, people she knew passed her by,
they spoke to her in greeting, and she replied with a 'hello', her voice a robotic drone. Outside, the wind was
strong, scattering her hair about her face, but she scarcely
noticed. She was aware of a sensation inside her chest,
like the galloping of horses, and a loud cascading sound
in her ears. She knew it was a rush of epinephrines, better
known as adrenaline, causing her heart to beat faster,
increasing the blood flow...

Her hand was clammy as she raised the key fob and

pressed it. The car made its familiar squelching sound and blinked twice, just as it always did. She realised she had unconsciously lowered her gaze so that she could not see above the line of the car's headlights. Slowly she raised her head to take in the windscreen.

Oh God, please, please, don't let there be another note.

6

She stood, frozen, staring. Beneath the windscreen was... nothing.

Nothing!

She giggled with relief and took a slow, tentative step forward, then another, and when she reached the car, slowly began to walk around it.

'Did you lose something, Doctor?'

She was at the driver's door now and looked towards the sound of that voice.

The security officer was standing a few feet away, in his uniform: blue jacket, flannel pants and shiny brown shoes. Amanda thought it required only the addition of shoulder tassels and a bicorn hat to complete the parody of a naval officer. In the White Rock staff bulletin the head of security had boasted the uniform represented both a sense of chic and understated authority. To Amanda, she thought the uniform looked silly, like something out of a fancy dress shop.

'No, Bill, just checking my tyres; it felt like one might have been a bit flat on the drive in this morning.'

Now, just toddle off and mind your own bloody business, will you, Rear Admiral?

But she realised her answer had not been the correct one to achieve this goal.

'Let me have a look at it for you,' he said instead, stepping forward.

'No. It's fine, Bill. Thank you. I know a flat tyre when I see one.'

He stopped.

'I'm sure you do, Dr Jackson. Aye, I'm sure you do. Sorry.'

'But thank you anyway,' she said, softening her tone. 'I appreciate it; it's very thoughtful of you. Now, I'd best be on my way.'

She opened the door and was about to get in, but could see from the corner of her eye that he was lingering.

'You know,' he said, 'there was someone at your car yesterday...'

Her body tensed, and with it an invisible hand reached inside her chest and squeezed – hard.

'What?' she said, suddenly breathless.

'I saw them from the main door. The policy is strict, Doctor, as you know, no flyers or promotional material of any kind. So, of course, I rushed over immediately, but they were gone before I got here. I noticed an envelope under the wiper, didn't know what to think, so thought I'd best leave well alone, didn't consider it an emergency, said to myself I'd tell you when I saw you. I hope that's alright. Is it?'

She was silent, her mind spinning, clogs engaging, trying to work it out. Someone was at my car.

'Who?' she demanded. 'Who? I mean, a man? A woman? Them? You said "them". Who's them?'

She could hear the frightened urgency in her words.

'No, not them,' he said. 'It was a man, looked like.'

'A man,' she repeated, 'young, old, what?'

The security man looked uncomfortable.

'I dunno, Dr Jackson, too far away to tell.'

'What was he like? Old, young, slim, fat, black haired... what? Tell me.'

'He had a hat on. I didn't...'

'What type of hat?'

'Red. A beanie hat. That's all I know. I'm sorry. He was too far away to tell anything else.'

'Okay. Okay. His build, surely...'

'Tall, okay, Doctor. Really, that's all I can say.'

'Then how do you know it was a bloody man...?'

She realised she'd gone too far.

'Sorry. Sorry, Bill. That was uncalled for. Totally uncalled for. Really. I'm sorry.'

His expression hardened, and he said nothing for a moment, like he was calculating his best response. Then a trace of a smile cracked his thin lips.

'And I know a man when I see one,' he said, savouring the retort. 'What I'd like to know is: what should I do if it happens again? Call the police? I mean, we have CCTV. I could give it to them. The hospital takes this seriously, the thin edge of the wedge and all that.'

'No!' She practically shouted the answer. 'I mean, from what you tell me, sounds like a, well' – her mind scrambled for words – 'a former patient, yes, it's why I was so insistent on a description, sorry, because it's a very delicate matter, um, this person, this former patient has... issues, that's all.'

His expression became earnest as he nodded.

'I don't want to take any action if at all possible,' she

added. 'It's just a difficult period for, um, him, one that needs my complete understanding. So we need to keep this discreet, between ourselves. Yes?'

He nodded again, energetically this time. She took this as confirmation of his complicity in keeping this grave professional matter secret.

But he would have a different opinion if he knew the truth, a very different opinion indeed.

She summoned up a wide smile.

'Would there be any chance,' she asked sweetly, 'you could let me look at that CCTV?'

His expression gave nothing away, but then the Rear Admiral nodded slowly, and she promised herself never to call him by that name again.

THE SECURITY OFFICE was just inside the main door to the hospital. Another officer was sitting at a desk, watching a bank of monitors. He turned as they entered.

'Everything alright?' he enquired, looking at her.

'Yes,' she said, glancing to his name tag, 'everything is fine, Peter, thanks.'

Peter was older than his colleague, bespectacled, with white hair.

Bill spoke. 'Dr Jackson just wants to look at some CCTV. See if she can identify the person who left an envelope on her car yesterday.'

'Someone did that, did they?' Peter said. 'And what was that about? Everything alright, I hope?'

'A delicate matter,' Bill added, lowering his voice, the holder of a great secret.

He had not closed the office door. Amanda could see

out to the busy foyer. She turned her back in the hope that anyone looking in wouldn't recognise her.

'Can you bring up yesterday, Pete? Now, what time was it 'bout? Four o'clock, I'd say, yeah, four, I was just coming back from the canteen then... bring up the staff car park, Pete, about four o'clock, yeah?'

'Righteo.'

Peter pressed on a keyboard and indicated with a nod of his head to a monitor a little further along the desk. 'Monitor three, Bill.'

They stepped over to it, images of a hospital corridor flickering and disappearing, replaced by those from the car park outside. They stood silently watching for what seemed like forever to Amanda but was in fact mere minutes, before a person appeared, striding in from the bottom of the screen towards the rows of vehicles.

'Freeze it, Pete,' Bill said. 'There, Dr Jackson. That's the person, right there.'

Amanda stared at the screen, her belly tightening. She leaned in for a closer look. The person was too far away to see very much, but the gait and posture told her it was probably a male, tall, wearing a red hat – a beanie – and dark clothing, possibly navy-blue jeans and a fleece.

'Can you get in close, Pete? Thanks,' Bill said.

The images on the screen magnified.

'A couple of cameras are down for maintenance, Bill,' Peter said. 'This is the best I can do. Not great.'

The images continued to magnify until they eventually pixelated, the person in the beanie hat becoming a mess of charcoal strokes against a lighter bubble wrap background.

'Whooo,' Bill said, 'hold it, zoom out again, Pete. Play it once more, normal resolution, please.'

The screen reverted to normal resolution and began to play. Amanda watched as the person walked, a little hesitatingly to begin with, by the first row of vehicles, almost to the end, where he stopped, walked down between two cars to the second row. There, she was surprised to see, he walked away from her car, but only a couple of paces, before he stopped and retraced his steps, stopped next to the one alongside hers. There, he reached into a pocket and took out the envelope, his head turning both ways before settling on the Mercedes, like he was inspecting it, finally stepping over to her car and placing the envelope beneath the wiper. Something about his gait and stature seemed vaguely familiar to her.

'The car alarm should have gone off,' Bill said, 'you'd think, though he seemed very light of touch about it... Now, as you can see, he's walking away, heading for the shortcut through the bushes onto the road outside. No cameras out there, I'm afraid.'

'He knows the area, then,' Amanda said. 'Would you think?'

Bill shook his head.

'Everyone knows that shortcut; it's no secret.'

'No, it's not,' Amanda agreed.

She straightened and felt, well, strangely relieved. The person she had just witnessed didn't seem very threatening to her. Indeed, she had the feeling they didn't know exactly what they were doing, seemed uncertain of the car they were looking for.

'Sorry? What did you say?' She realised Bill was speaking to her.

'Anything else we can do for you, Dr Jackson?'

'No, Bill.' She followed up with another radiant smile.

'Although, I need to apologise for my being a little offhand with you earlier.'

He waved a hand through the air.

'Don't mention it, pressures of the job and all that. I understand. Anything any of us can do here at security for you in the future, don't hesitate to ask.'

'Thank you,' she said, turning, 'to both of you. And I won't. You've been very kind.'

She left the security office and walked away quickly, realising she was sweating, emerging through the revolving doors into the daylight, the breeze like a soothing balm against her skin.

Her mood lightened, and she suddenly felt like some company. Who was available at such short notice for lunch?

7

She parked in a multi-storey at the rear of Shop
Street close to the heart of Galway City, having
played out everything in her mind on the short
drive in. Now that she had witnessed the person actually
place the envelope on her car, she felt not only the relief
of earlier but also a reassurance. Because someone had to
have placed it there; it couldn't have got beneath the wiper
all by itself. And now that she had seen this person, she
felt the same about this whole business as before: that it
was just a coincidence. It could be anything, a prank, a
joke, someone just happened to place the envelope onto
the wrong car, that was all. Well, it could. She didn't know
why. Whatever the reason for it was, she didn't care, just
so long as she was left alone in the future. Matter resolved,
stamped 'Coincidence' and filed away for incineration.
Yes, it was a coincidence, because she needed it to be a
coincidence. She would not start dwelling on this again. It
was over.

Though, while Amanda would be the first to call out

someone who was simply fooling themselves, she couldn't see this in herself now.

But was she fooling herself?

She'd soon find out.

THE DAY FELT MORE like one in July than it did September. Normally, she enjoyed walking through the old, narrow streets of Galway City, at this time of year still packed with locals and tourists alike. But not today, today it just didn't feel the same.

Pri was waiting in the small fish restaurant just off Shop Street, at a corner table towards the rear.

'Thanks for meeting me,' Amanda said to her friend, taking a seat. 'I didn't think you'd be able to.'

'Well, you know me,' Pri said with a laugh, 'any excuse for a good lunch with a good friend... you had a cancellation, right?'

'Right, Pri, I had... Look, I really need to talk.'

Her friend's expression became earnest. 'What's up?' she asked, lowering her voice.

Amanda felt her eyes start to well up, and she blinked back the tears, her positive conviction of just a little earlier deserting her. 'Oh, Pri.'

The waiter appeared, stood for a moment by the table before silently withdrawing again.

Pri reached for Amanda's hand and held it in hers. 'Come on,' she said. 'Tell me. What's up?'

Amanda took a breath, steadying herself. She looked at her friend and considered that she looked tired, drawn. Was it fair to burden Pri with her problems?

She hesitated.

'Go on,' Pri prompted, 'tell me.'

'A note,' she replied flatly. 'On my car. I know your secret, that's what it said. Pri, my secret. Someone knows my secret.'

'Amy, you're not making much sense. A note? On your car? I know your secret. What secret? You never told me. Anyway, we all have secrets, don't we?'

'Yes,' Amanda agreed, fumbling in her handbag and taking out a tissue, dabbing her eyes with it, 'but not like this.'

Pri raised her eyebrows. 'Really? Come on, Amy, how bad can it be? Have you spoken to anyone else about it? A problem shared is a problem halved, you know.'

Amanda shook her head. 'No. I haven't.'

'When did you get this note, by the way?'

'Does it matter? Yesterday, when I was leaving work.'

Pri's eyes widened.

'Yesterday. Why didn't you ring me before now? You could have come round. I had the house to myself. We could have talked.'

Amanda took a breath.

'I couldn't. I was in shock. Anyway, Edward likes me to be home when he gets in, you know...'

'Yes, I know...'

Pri's tone said it all.

There was silence for a moment.

'Do you want to talk about it?' Pri asked.

Amanda considered the question for the first time.

'Yes. Of course I do. Not now, that's all. Not just yet. I'm not ready. What I need right now, Pri' – she could feel tears welling up again – 'is to know that someone is there for me, that's all, someone I can trust, that's what I need. Right now.'

Pri smiled. 'Oh, Amy, you know I'm here for you. I'll

always be here for you...' Her voice dropped as she added, 'You were there for me, remember?'

Amanda remembered. Outwardly Pri was the polar opposite to Amanda, gregarious and with a wide circle of friends, yet it was to Amanda she had turned that time.

'God. I nearly left my husband for him,' Pri said before pausing, glancing over her shoulder, then continuing, 'Like, really? That'd never have worked out. Thank God you talked me out of it. I mean... ugh.' She squeezed Amanda's hand. 'That's it for me. I'm never having an affair again.'

Amanda couldn't help but smile.

'Really,' Pri said, 'I'm not. But maybe...'

'But maybe what?'

Pri gave her a long, searching look.

'But maybe you should.'

Amanda felt a jolt.

'What?' she spluttered. 'I couldn't. I love Edward.' A silence descended again, heavy this time, a silence that she couldn't stand, that she needed to banish. A kaleidoscope of thoughts flashed through her mind, each one separate and distinct, of her father, past boyfriends, of crying alone, abandoned, unloved, unwanted. 'You see,' she said quietly, the words escaping as if of their own accord, without any conscious effort on her part, 'I could never please my father. All my life I sought acceptance, approval, attention... from men. This may sound strange, Pri, but when I got it, and I did get it, I felt unworthy, undeserving, and then I moved on.' She paused, took a deep breath before continuing, the words tumbling out. 'It was when I found a man who didn't give me what I wanted, what I thought I wanted, attention I mean, well, I stayed in that relationship because then I had to strive to convince him that I was worthy, just as I had with my father. I'm an only child, so everything was magnified, but if I could convince a man to treat me how I wanted to be treated, if I could change him, then, in my mind, I might have been able to change my father too...'

Pri cocked her head to one side, like she was trying to make sense of what she was hearing.

'... to have him love me,' Amanda added, her voice faltering. 'Of course, I never could convince a man to change... pathetic, really, that I thought I could, and it's a mistake many women make, I think, which is also why I'm in this situation, with my marriage, I mean. I know it, but I don't want to change it. Edward loves me, I know he does... in his own way.'

'In his own way?'

'Yes. I know that sounds stupid, and I feel stupid too for saying it.'

Pri smiled. 'You shouldn't be so hard on yourself.' Her voice was soothing. 'And, you, stupid? Come on. You're one of the smartest people I know. How can you even think like that? Please don't think like that. I forbid it, you beautiful, intelligent person you.' Pri stretched her hand out onto the table, peering down at it before looking up again as she asked, 'How long is your dad dead now, Amy?'

'Twenty years, almost. Mother, three. She was a drinker, as you know, which didn't help matters.'

'No,' Pri said, a sudden vacant look in her eyes, 'it never does, does it? Now. Come on, let's eat.'

As they sipped on coffees afterwards, everything seemed to have melted away, and Amanda felt renewed. The conversation while they ate, after the initial heaviness, was light and distracting, with nothing more serious mentioned than the axing of the Jeremy Kyle show. Amanda forgot about the note. She sat back in her seat and watched, over Pri's shoulder, the pedestrians streaming past the window outside, the constant movement almost hypnotic, her mind blissfully empty. She saw someone stop, but didn't really pay attention until they approached the window, cupping their hands about their face and pressing it against the pane, peering into the restaurant. She blinked. It was a man, tall, dressed in dark clothes, wearing a red hat, a red beanie hat. Her coffee cup clattered against the saucer as she put it down, and it toppled onto its side. She dropped her gaze to it, relieved to find she'd finished her drink and it was empty. She took a gulp of air.

'What's the matter, Amy?' Pri said. 'You look like you've seen a ghost.'

Amanda said nothing for a moment, glancing up to the window again, staring at it. But now there was no one there. She wondered: had there been anyone there at that window in the first place? Or had she just imagined it? She continued to stare, but couldn't be sure; she couldn't be sure of anything.

'One minute,' she said, rising. She walked quickly through the restaurant to the door and stepped out onto the busy street, looking up and down. She couldn't see the person.

She suddenly felt very foolish. The mind can play tricks, she knew, as if it, the mind, had a mind of its own.

She went back inside, catching the wary sidelong glances of some of the other diners.

'I thought I saw someone,' she said, back at the table again, but she didn't sit down. She needed to get back to work. 'The person who left the note on my car. I had to go and look.'

'That again,' Pri said. 'And was anybody there?'

Amanda shook her head. 'No,' she said sheepishly.

'Okay then,' Pri said, getting to her feet too, 'I think we need to talk so I can judge just how bad this secret is. In the meantime, can you let it go, please? This is doing you no good, no good at all.'

Amanda nodded, 'Yes,' determining that she would. 'Let me go and get the bill.'

'I've already looked after it,' Pri said.

'You didn't.'

'I did.'

'That's naughty, Pri; it was me who invited you, remember?'

Her friend adopted a deep, husky voice, batted her long eyelashes.

'Moi? Naughty? Well, heaven forbid.'

They laughed and left the restaurant.

ON THE DRIVE back to work, she looked in the rear-view mirror and imagined the envelope and note floating away behind her; she imagined that she was leaving both further and further back in her past until eventually there was nothing there, both had simply vanished. There hadn't been someone outside the restaurant window, she decided, well, not that person. What, in a red beanie hat and dark clothes just like the one on the CCTV? That would have been too much of a coincidence. How would they even know she was there, for God's sake? It wasn't possible. And then just disappear again like that? What was the point? Yes, it was all a result of that overactive, anxious imagination of hers. Had to be.

Back at the surgery, she spent five minutes going through her list for the remainder of the day. All thoughts of the freakish coincidence had gone. She placed the clipboard onto her desk and realised that she was humming a song. She smiled just as the intercom sounded.

'Dr Jackson,' Layla said, 'your three o'clock appointment is here. Shall I send Mrs Clooney in?'

'Of course, Layla,' she replied brightly. 'I'm waiting; send her in.'

AT THE END of the day, as she returned to her car parked in its usual spot in the car park, it returned – the dread, as her heart began to beat faster, fear tickling the back of her neck. But this time when she looked at the Mercedes, her gaze did not flinch; rather it was steely, almost defiant. She walked up and looked it over carefully. All was exactly as it should be, with nothing on it that shouldn't be there. No note. Nothing. She began to hum again, scarcely even aware of it, as she pointed the key fob and – squelch, blink, blink. She smiled and got into the car.

At home, she went into the drawing room and made herself a gin and tonic. A small one, mind. She decided there would be no topper-uppers slipped in before Edward got home, even if it was a Friday. And tonight, with a bit of luck, she would sleep until morning, when she would awaken refreshed. That was a plan.

She wasn't hungry, not after the hearty lunch she'd had. When Edward got home, she'd cook him something, she liked to do that, and she would be extra nice to him too, because she couldn't help but feel the tension between them was her fault. In the meantime, she had the house to herself, and she loved that. She noted fresh flowers in a vase on the bog oak coffee table she'd had specially commissioned from a craftsman down in Clare some years ago, and on the chest of drawers against the end wall was another set within a half circle of family photos. Of course, she'd forgotten. Today was one of the two days her part-time housekeeper came in. Bridie used to work Monday to Friday when the kids were young, but now two days a week were sufficient.

Yes, she thought, I need a good night's sleep. Tomorrow, everything will be back to the way it should be.

She must have dozed off. When she opened her eyes again, she was staring at a large dark patch on her skirt. She looked to her glass of gin and tonic and saw it was lying empty on its side on her lap.

'Shit,' she said, jumping to her feet.

The glass fell from her lap and shattered on the hardwood floor.

'Christ.'

There was a noise from the hallway.

She glanced to the antique grandfather clock. Yes, of course, it was that time, just gone six. A familiar voice sounded.

'Darling, I'm home.'

Amanda froze. She heard Edward's footsteps crossing the hall, and then he was standing in the doorway. He stopped, looking at her, noting the stain on her skirt, the shattered glass on the floor.

'I fell asleep,' she blurted. 'I woke up with a start. It just fell to the floor. I'll clean it up; it's no big deal.'

His eyes became hooded, and she could see his five o'clock shadow was deep and pronounced, like black polish on his skin. He always looked like that when in a foul mood.

'This,' he said, 'is what I come home to. Really? This?'

She stood there, her hands by her sides, feeling help-less, dejected, useless. I deserve this, she thought, I deserve everything that happens to me. She began to sob, and this sparked something in Edward, a look of pity crossing his face. But she didn't want pity, she wanted something other than pity. Why did he only feel either anger or pity for her? Why? She needed something, anything, to escape from this moment, one that would make Edward happy, make them both happy. In a flurry she ran to him and wrapped her arms around his neck, causing them both to lose balance and stumble against the wall. She didn't care; she pressed her lips hard against his. 'Please,' she said, 'please, take me to bed, make love to me. I want you. I need you, please.'

Edward stared at her. She couldn't work out the emotion, but one thing was certain, his blue eyes were twinkling.

Dr Amanda Jackson, she of the cool, professional, clinical, detached demeanour, made love frantically, desperately, escaping into that blissful world of sensual pleasure, a screaming, grunting rollercoaster escape that left her panting and exhausted when it was over. She had heard a term for it: survivor sex. Crazy or not, but that was how it felt.

As she lay there afterwards, her head resting against Edward's chest, floating on a sea of calm, her husband's gentle breathing signalling that he had fallen asleep, she was reassured that all was not lost with her marriage, that underneath everything, there was still something strong holding it together. She had never begged Edward to come to bed with her before, but she could tell that he had liked it. What she couldn't be certain of, however, was whether it was the offer of sex that had turned him on, or the control he felt from having her beg him for it. With a pang she realised that maybe she was fooling herself after all; maybe there was nothing strong about her marriage, but rather, something rotten to its very core. She closed her eyes against this thought, hoping that she was wrong, but knowing too that she was probably right. She desperately sought and needed her husband's approval, thus giving him the power to dictate how she felt. Tears began to gather in her eyes, and she squeezed them shut. All I want is love, she thought, both to give love and be loved in return. Nothing more. Nothing less. That's all. A pure love, untainted by cruel emotions. Did it even exist?

Her mobile phone on top of the bedside locker suddenly pinged an incoming text alert, the noise loud and sharp in the silence of the room. She stiffened, expecting it to wake Edward, but her husband didn't stir. She reached out, fumbling about until she located it, bringing it close to her face as she brought up the message and peered at it.

And then, it was as if a chasm had suddenly opened beneath her, and she and her world tumbled through it into a great black void; she read the words:

BITCH. WHORE. I KNOW YOUR SECRET.
DID YOU THINK I HAD GONE AWAY? NO
I HAVEN'T. YOU BITCH.

She dropped the phone onto the bed as if scalded by it. She began to cry silently, her body shaking as she tried desperately not to make a sound. It had not gone away, none of it; she had been fooling herself all along, all her life, in fact, about everything, and not only this.

Who, she wondered, could hate her so much to do this now, after all these years? Who?

That was the burning question.

Who?

8

1994

Four empty Pils bottles sat on the wall ledge next to them. There was no space on the table to put them down, it being taken up by too many elbows, other glasses and an overflowing black ashtray with the letters JPS written in gold lettering along the sides. The pub was packed, the band just about visible on a low stage above which neon lights flashed in sync to the beat of the bass guitar.

Amanda sat on the edge of her stool, sharing it with Fiona. They'd decided not to bother fighting their way to the bar again for another drink. The air pulsed with the sounds of music and laughter through a curtain of cigarette smoke.

The band started up another song, 'Living Next Door to Alice', with the addition of the unofficial extra chorus, 'Alice, who the fuck is Alice'. Amanda and Fiona scrambled to their feet like everybody else, laughing and belting out the extra chorus. Their glasses were half full, and they held them in their hands. Someone pushed into Amanda from behind, and she turned, but all she could see was a swaying sea of faces. She turned back to look at the stage, unaware that her flat beer was suddenly effervescent.

'Hi, Amy.'

The sound of the greeting was nothing more than an audio scratch against the mountain of noise. Amanda wasn't sure she'd even heard it. She looked to the side, recognised the person.

'Ah, Christopher,' shouting to be heard. At that moment the band fell silent as she added, still shouting, 'It's you.' She laughed. 'Sorry.'

He smiled. She wondered if he thought she was unable to contain her exuberance at seeing him rather than just shouting to be heard. Christopher fancied himself, but she considered he was one of those people who looked much better when they didn't smile. When he didn't smile, he looked broody and handsome, but when he smiled, it pulled down one side of his face, the lip drooping in a corner, making him, well, look odd. Amanda thought: if only he didn't smile, then maybe...

'I'm here with a couple of the boys.' He nodded. 'They're over there. And you?'

Amanda placed her free hand around Fiona and pulled her in close.

'I'm with Fiona, my amigo, my girl.' She laughed, the almost two bottles of Pils she'd had just enough to loosen her knots.

'Want to join us?' Christopher's eyes widened. She could see a little pulse beginning to throb on the side of his forehead.

She felt a discreet nudge into her side from Fiona.

'Um, sure, we'll follow,' she said.

Christopher pointed. 'We're over...' A screaming guitar riff drowned out his voice.

Amanda mimed the words, 'We'll find you,' and Christopher gave another of his lopsided smiles that he probably thought was his most irresistible feature. He pointed to her glass and brought his hand to his mouth, tilting it in a drinking motion, telling her he was going to get more drinks.

Amanda nodded, draining her glass before scrunching up her face and smacking her lips, poking her tongue out.

'Ugh, tastes a bit off.'

Fiona leaned in. 'What did you say?'

'Nothing. Let's go over to them.'

Fiona ran a hand through her hair and opened an extra button on her blouse.

'Christopher, really?' Amanda said. 'You fancy him?'

Fiona smiled. 'Maybe... and it's not Christopher? Everyone calls him Chris. I could say the same about Edward, you know.'

Amanda pursed her lips.

'Yeah,' she said, 'and you'd probably be right.'

They both laughed.

'Then why the hell are you with him?' Fiona asked.

Amanda looked around. 'I'm not with him, am I? I don't see Edward anywhere here, do you?'

'You know what I mean.'

'Yeah, I know what you mean. I'm not with Edward; it's strictly casual, okay? I'm not with anyone, okay? I'm just out to enjoy myself, nothing else. And I've told Edward the same. But he's persistent.'

Fiona nudged her again. 'Then get a move on, girl, before all the good ones are gone... I bet you like the attention though, don't you, just a little bit, go on, admit it, don't you?'

Amanda shook her head. 'Actually. No. I don't.' But she couldn't help give a slight smile. 'Well, okay, maybe just a teensy bit.'

Fiona laughed as Amanda suddenly stumbled backwards, bumping into the woman behind her, spilling some of her drink.

'Hey,' the woman called, 'look where you're going, for God's sake.'

'Amy, you alright?'

The sound of Fiona's voice was distant, muffled, fading, other sounds too, as the lights dimmed, like everything was being sucked out of the world, disappearing into a black hole, becoming smaller and smaller...

She suddenly felt like she was going to be sick.

'I don't feel so good.' Her voice sounded distant, feeble.

She lurched forward; then everything went black.

9

She wasn't sure how she got through that evening and the long night that followed. But somehow she had. They had got up after a couple of hours, and without consulting her, Edward had ordered in a takeaway meal for two from the new organic Thai restaurant everyone was raving about. They had sat in the kitchen, eating straight out of the cardboard takeaway containers – unusual for Edward – and sharing a bottle of wine, because Edward had decided that that was okay too. He had mellowed, cracking terrible jokes to his usual standard, and she had laughed uproariously at each, masking the torture she was going through – because that was what it was, torture. At the first opportunity she yawned, feigning tiredness, adding with a cheeky grin that a certain workout had left her feeling exhausted. But the truth was she craved the darkness of the night so she could hide within it, so she wouldn't have to pretend, where no one could see her, where no one could find her. It was taking every ounce of her energy just to pretend, and she couldn't continue. It was then she had decided she needed to get away. If only for this weekend. Because it would be impossible to stay here. She would literally fall apart if she had to keep this pretence up, and she knew, with a new day and a slight hangover, Edward would be impossible to be around. He would notice; he would ask questions; he would keep scratching, scratch, scratch, to get to the bottom of what was wrong with her. No, she had to leave. There was no alternative. None. A couple of days away would buy her time... but for what, exactly? To help her decide how to deal with this, surely? Because to stay was to live inside a pressure cooker, the pressure building and building, requiring more and more lies in order to release enough steam so that it didn't explode. But what if it did explode, what then? She had shuddered at the thought, and the bile had begun to build at the back of her throat again. She had kissed Edward goodnight and gone to bed and, as before, made it to the en suite just in time before getting sick.

The next morning, she knew Edward would be playing golf just as he did every Saturday morning. She waited in bed until she heard him leaving for the club, then got up. She had a tentative, sketchy plan in mind, but nothing more. She had turned her mobile phone off after receiving the text message the evening before, and would not turn it on again until she had left the house. She used the landline instead to ring the hotel she usually stayed at in Dublin. They had a room available for that night. She booked it and paid in advance.

As she packed her bag, she felt a little better. But what would she tell Edward? Should she ring Pri, discuss it with her? She decided against that. Because there was a fine line between discussing something and procrastinating over it. Ultimately, this was her problem, not Pri's, and this was something she needed to do herself.

When she was ready to leave, she sat at the kitchen table, a pen poised over a blank sheet of paper. She still didn't know what to say, but began to write anyway:

Darling, I feel dreadful, so have decided to take myself off to Dublin and have booked myself into a wellness centre, you know the one, on Dawson street. I went there before...

No, that wouldn't do. What if Edward were to ring the place and ask for her? So she took another piece of paper and started again:

Darling, I feel dreadful, so have decided to go to Dublin and take a couple of sessions in a new holistic centre I heard about. They had a last-minute cancellation and can fit me in. Sorry about doing this without any notice, but I'm sure you understand. It's only for one night. I'll be back tomorrow. Please don't be mad. I didn't ring to tell you because I know you're playing golf. Will talk later. Love you. Hope to be back Sunday afternoon... oh, I'm going to call in on Danny and see how he's doing, and no, he doesn't know I'm coming. I'll tell him on the way.
Amanda, XXX.

She knew he would blow a gasket, but there was no alternative. Anyway, she wouldn't be around to see it, and by the time they spoke again, hopefully he would have calmed down.

Now, as she drove along the motorway to Dublin, she

rang Danny on the Bluetooth via the steering wheel controller. No surprise when there was no reply, which suited her just fine, so she left a message instead.

And then, now that she was actually driving in silence to Dublin, with all the frantic activity over, which had served to act as a huge diversion, it returned. She could not ignore it. Could not keep it at bay. The fear. The numbing fear. As images from the past flashed across her mind, bringing her back there, to everything that had happened...

There was a sound, a piercing screech that wrenched her back into the present, with it an explosion of white, intense light. It came again and again. The motorway lane stretched ahead of her, strangely empty. She realised she was in the fast lane, but her speed was so slow she was crawling along. The sounds and the explosions of light were the flashing of headlamps and the honking of horns of the vehicles behind her. She checked her mirror and moved into the far lane, staring ahead, avoiding the glares and gestures she was certain she was receiving from those passing her by.

In the rear-view mirror a flashing blue strobe light appeared suddenly and with it the alternating wailing of a siren. She took a deep breath, gripped the steering wheel tighter, glanced in the mirror again. The police car was much closer now, barrelling along the fast lane, the vehicles before it scampering out of its way – heading straight for her.

10

1994

She felt something, like a brush stroke against her naked flesh, and realised it was a draught of cold air. She swung her head to the side towards it, her eyes discerning shapes in the murky light, of furniture and a door, slightly ajar, that same grey light that seeped around the edges of the curtains seeping through here too.

She took a breath and held it, realised that someone had to have opened that door. She peered ahead, taking in a contoured shape in the gloom, like a cardboard cut-out.

And knew.

Someone was standing here, in the room.

She watched and waited, could hear the sound of her own breathing, like the winds of a hurricane, filling her ears, filling the room, filling everything. She watched, not daring to blink, every image in the room scorching onto her memory, objects identifiable only by their shapes: the outline of a TV fixed high up on the wall, that of a long low dresser, and beside it a wardrobe, in a corner a curved-back chair and a small circular table before it. Her eyes took them all in.

And the contoured shape, which began to move now, her body juddering in response, an involuntary movement. Amanda began to shake with fear. The shape had a strange fluidity about it as it moved, like a shadow within a shadow, a shapeshifter. It approached the window and stopped, the edges rimmed in that grey syrupy light. But it was enough to discern it as a male, the hairy thigh and lower leg like an animal that was standing on its hind legs, the edge of a belly, a milky white arm, the corner of a neck...

She stopped herself from looking up. To the face. Because she knew to see it, or part of it, would carry grave risk. From somewhere her mind flung out a headline for her to ponder, a warning: Accused said he killed the victim because she had seen his face and could later identify him.

No, she could not look at his face.

As if he had read her mind, he reassured her: 'It's alright. You can look.'

She knew she shouldn't, and everything screamed for her not to, but her head raised itself anyway, and she stared with fatalistic resignation.

And screamed.

11

'No parking on campus, ma'am.'

'What?' Amanda said. She had turned off the busy city street into a Trinity College entranceway. She hadn't expected to meet a security guard and a closed barrier gate. 'You mean there's no parking on the college campus?' she added.

'Staff and designated visitors only, ma'am,' he said, glancing behind her to a van that had pulled up. 'Now, I'll have to ask you to move. You're holding up deliveries.'

Last time she had been able to park here. Her hotel was a city centre townhouse and didn't have parking.

'Where can I park, then?'

The security man gestured to the van driver, indicating with hand motions for him to reverse.

'There's a parking area further along Pearse Street,' he said with a gruff, distracted air, 'turn left, right again at the lights, you'll see it.'

'You mean left after I reverse out of the...'

'Please, Mrs, will you reverse? Now. I've been polite.

You'll have the whole area clogged if you don't get a move on sharpish. Come on now, reverse, please.'

She began to do so. The van behind her was holding up traffic on the roadway outside, so she was able to swing out without difficulty. A police car travelling in the other direction passed by without showing any interest. She thought of earlier, on the motorway, the police car that had been barrelling along behind her. She'd felt certain it was coming for her. It wasn't. It had simply zoomed by, on its way to some emergency or other. Fear wrapped its cloak tightly about her as she thought of it, as she thought of all that had been happening to her lately. She shook her head, clearing her mind, for a short time at least.

She found the parking area; it was little more than a strip of derelict waste ground with a billboard above it announcing that construction of a new office block would commence early the following year. In the meantime, a stooped man with a money bag slung from his shoulder was collecting €20 for twenty-four-hour parking. Amanda was grateful to pay it and be free of her car.

A blast of warm air suddenly pushed against her, and the ground vibrated, with it a loud rumbling noise. She found she was standing at the intersection of the busy street without having any recollection of having walked there. The tips of her shoes were over the edge, her body dangerously close to the passing traffic. The warm air and the rumbling noise she had heard had come from a passing box truck. She stepped back, catching the looks of those around her. When the lights changed, she hurried across the road and went through the gates onto the Trinity College campus.

A strong gust of wind suddenly stirred, pushing before it an empty Coke can that tinkled over the ground as it was swept along. Why couldn't the lazy so-and-so who had thrown it there have placed it into a rubbish bin instead? Was that so difficult? Maybe it was her own son who was responsible? Would he do such a thing? She forced herself to consider the matter, seeking any diversion from her thoughts she could find.

But then she heard a sound, something other than the clumping of footsteps all around her, because Trinity College was also a busy pedestrian thoroughfare too. She turned her head as she walked, cocking an ear. She listened, filtering out all other sounds, waiting for whatever it was to come again. But it didn't, so she continued, dismissing it once more as the work of her imagination. But just as she did, there it was, unmistakable this time, drifting on the air...

'I know your secret.'

She froze, stopping in her tracks. As she spun around, the person walking behind crashed into her with a loud ooomph. It was a young woman dressed in a red floral-pattern dress. The woman glared at Amanda before she patted herself down and walked around her, giving Amanda a wide berth, no longer staring, as if having decided that she was simply a crazy person and so best avoided. The young woman hurried away, glancing over her shoulder a couple of times, probably to make sure Amanda was not following her.

Amanda wondered: is this the person who left me that note and text message, who's begun to make my life a misery? And who just whispered those words? She was tempted to follow, but instead simply stood and watched, the distinctive red dress fading until it disappeared.

. . .

TO SECURE student accommodation on campus required luck and perseverance. In her son's case, it was mainly luck. Amanda always considered that if only he had to actually work for something, then Danny might appreciate it, but he never had.

She pressed the button labelled 15A in the panel by the door of the student hall. The building was a long three-storey red-brick affair with limestone columns, in keeping with the general architectural style of the college.

There was no reply, so she pressed the button again, longer this time, more insistent.

An electronic crackling sound followed; then a disjointed voice came through the intercom, unmistakably her son's: 'Yeah.'

'Danny, it's your mother. Let me in.'

'One sec.' He sounded sleepy. There was a buzzing sound and a loud click as the door unlocked. She pushed it open and stepped into the foyer.

The apartment was on the second floor. When she went in, she saw that it was surprisingly clean. Not spotless, and not exactly clean, but surprisingly clean. Danny was dressed in flip-flops, grey sweat shorts and a green T-shirt that had a prominent stain on its front below the collar. He needed a haircut, too, and was unshaven, his blue eyes bleary. She got the distinct impression he had hurriedly tidied the place up just before she'd arrived. For a moment, as she observed her son, she completely forgot the reason she had come here, her mind blank, as if she had passed through into the eye of a storm. But just as quickly it was gone, and the great weight pressed down again on her shoulders, threatening to crush her beneath it, and as it did, she felt her knees begin to buckle. She reached out, but there was nothing to hold on to. Then, just in time, Danny rushed over and scooped her in his arms as she began to fall.

'Mum... What's wrong? Are you okay?'

He led her to a sofa and sat her down.

'Mum?' he said.

She forced a smile.

'It's nothing. I just felt a bit light-headed. I'm fine.'

'No, you're not. You almost fainted, for God's sake. And where's Dad? Why are you here anyway? On your own? You look terrible. Have you and Dad had a row? Is that it?'

She laughed aloud. She and Edward hardly ever rowed. She could count on two hands the number of times they had, and that was with a couple of fingers surplus. Edward didn't need to have a row to get his point across, and she knew better than to provoke him.

'No,' she said, 'of course not.'

'Why then? Tell me.'

She stared at her son, her beautiful, young, impetuous, gregarious, and in many ways still innocent as a child son. As she thought this, she caught a movement in the corner of her eye. She turned. Standing in the doorway of her son's bedroom was a girl dressed in nothing but a bra and knickers.

Maybe her son wasn't so innocent after all.

12

'D anny,' the girl said, 'have you seen my clothes anywhere?' and looking at Amanda, raised a hand, wriggling the fingers in greeting. 'Hi.'

'This is my mother, Sally,' Danny said.

'Hi,' Sally answered, displaying not the slightest hint of embarrassment. 'Oh, I see them, it's okay.'

She crossed the room and stepped behind the kitchen counter. Amanda didn't want to think of how her clothes had ended up there. She pulled on jeans and a sweatshirt and caught Amanda's look again.

'Oh, don't ask,' she said, stepping out from behind the counter, pulling on a pair of Ugg boots. She went and kissed Danny and walked to the door. 'Dan, catch you later, yeah? Nine o'clock, yeah?'

'Yeah,' Danny said, 'see you there.'

She raised her hand and wriggled her fingers again. Amanda was beginning to find this irritating.

'Bye,' she said and left the apartment, the door closing gently behind her.

Danny ran a hand through his thick hair and looked

to the floor, seemingly waiting for his mother to say something about Sally.

'I'm staying overnight,' she said instead, quickly forgetting all about the girl.

He looked like someone who'd just been asked for a fifty-euro loan.

'It's okay, Danny, don't look so alarmed. I don't mean here...' She looked around. 'Although I could; it's actually tidy for once. I'm staying at my usual, the W Hotel. But if you really wanted me to...'

'Mum, please, no...'

She laughed. Oh God, it was good to laugh, so good. 'I've only stopped by to see how you are, that's all. I'll be on my way again, Danny, don't worry. But maybe tomorrow we could meet up, a spot of lunch or something, you can take... Sally, isn't it?'

'It is.'

'You can take Sally along?'

'Yeah, sounds great, Mum. Maybe a late breakfast.'

'It's called brunch, Danny.' She raised her eyebrows. 'For your hangover, I know.' She turned towards the door, suddenly remembering she had not turned her phone back on. She fished it out of her bag and pressed it to life, stepping forward. The phone pinged once, then twice... then again.

She glanced down, seven missed calls. All from Edward. Nothing was funny or amusing anymore. Her belly heaved. Suddenly it rang again, giving her a start, Edward's name flashing across the screen. She took a deep breath, answered it, pressing it to her ear. 'Edward, I'm—'

'Amanda, what the hell? Where are you? You're not answering your phone. And you just took off li—'

'Please, Edward, I'm not feeling very well; not now, I don't need it.'

'You never told me,' he exploded, ignoring her plea. 'You never mentioned. Not one word. And for what? A holistic centre? You don't need a bloody holistic centre, you're a doctor, for God's sake; we both are.' His breathing sounded like small explosions in her ear.

'Sorry,' she said softly, knowing to do anything else was useless. You can tell him the truth, can't you? Because, whatever else, he's your husband, after all.

'Is there something you want to tell me?' he demanded, as if reading her mind.

'No,' she said, alarmed, shocked that she could even contemplate telling him. She would tell, could tell, Edward nothing.

'Are you having an affair?' he asked, his tone low, blunt.

'What?' she spluttered. 'Is that what you think?'

'It crossed my mind, but then I thought that if you were, you wouldn't draw attention to yourself the way you're doing now. I don't want to be made a fool of, Amanda. I don't want to be cuckolded... God, what a word.'

'I... I...' she began, and fell silent. Then: 'I have never been unfaithful to you. How could you even think such a thing? Especially after...' She glanced at Daniel, who had moved to stand by the breakfast counter out of earshot. 'After last night. Can't you tell?'

'What, of how desperate you are, is that it?'

His words hit her like a punch to the stomach.

'I'm sorry,' he said, but he didn't sound it, 'that was uncalled for.'

'Yes, it was. But what's new? You know how to hurt,

don't you, really hurt, I mean? Those little comments of yours, sharp and pointed, you know how to twist them in, right in.'

'What?'

'You know what I mean. An affair, you say. Maybe you're the one having the affair? Why mention it? You think I feel good enough about myself to have an affair with anybody? Do you?'

'So, you've thought of it, have you? Amanda, don't turn this onto me now?'

'Just answer, Edward.'

'No. Of course not.'

'But you would say that, wouldn't you?'

Again, he fell silent. There was only the sound of those little explosions in her ear. Then he spoke slowly.

'I'm worried about you. I'm beginning to think you need—'

'You're beginning to think I need what?' she snapped, cutting him off. She rarely, if ever, snapped at Edward.

'To talk to someone, for God's sake, a counsellor maybe.'

'A shrink, that what you mean?'

'Yes, if that's what you want to call it. A counsellor. Why not?'

'I told you, Edward. I don't feel so well. A session at the holistic centre should help. Please, can't you just understand that?'

'I'm trying. But you're not making it easy. In fact, you don't make anything easy, you know that, don't you?'

Yes, I do, she thought.

Edward laughed softly, the sound almost bordering on a sneer. 'You come home when you want to, Amanda, okay. You do whatever you want.'

'I'll be home tomorrow afternoon. I've work Monday.'

'Fine. Whenever. We'll talk then. See if we can work this out. But I'm tired of it all. Very tired. In fact, I think I might have had enough.'

He hung up. She took the phone from her ear and looked at it, at the same time noticed that Daniel was standing much closer to her than she had thought.

'An affair,' he said. 'Mum...?'

Amanda couldn't help it; she burst out laughing, opening her arms wide.

'Come here and give your mother a hug. What do you think? An affair?'

She was surprised when Daniel came to her without hesitation and squeezed her in a tight embrace.

'I know what Dad's like, Mum. It's not your fault. I know you're not having an affair.'

'Not my fault?' she repeated, as if she had never considered that before. 'You mean that?'

'Yes, Mum, I do. Dad's a pain in the arse, everyone knows it. And he's said before he was going to leave, but he never does. Truth is, I don't know how you put up with him. I don't know why you don't just leave.'

'You don't?' she said.

'I love Dad an' all, but no, I don't. I told you this before.'

'You did, Daniel, yes, you did.'

'But you need to be reminded of that, don't you? You're the best, Mum, you really are.'

And with that comment it all returned. Her secret. The calamity. You're the best, Mum.

Oh no. I'm not the best. I'm the worst. I'm evil.

13

Her hotel was within walking distance. She dropped off her bag and went for a stroll along Grafton Street, mingling with the bustling crowds on one of Dublin's most prestigious and busiest thoroughfares. She had something to eat and browsed in a couple of shops. But it was no use; she was only attempting to fool herself. Amanda scarcely noticed anything except, that is, the tight knot of anxiety in her belly, the heaviness pressing down on her shoulders. She caught her reflection in a jeweller's shop window, looking at the pinched, worn expression of the woman staring back at her, the tired, frightened eyes. She felt alone among the throngs of people, all talking loudly, laughing, carrying their bags of shopping. She felt she was trapped in a cage, but one made of glass, where no one could see the bars that kept her locked away.

The heaviness pressed down on her further. Amanda felt utterly exhausted: she just wanted to go to bed. Coming to Dublin had been a mistake. It had offered her no relief.

When she got back to her room, it was still bright outside. She undressed and got beneath the covers, pulling the duvet about her. There was a narrow balcony, and she'd left the door to it ajar because the room, like many hotel rooms, was stifling hot.

Still, she fell asleep, a merciful dreamless void.

SHE AWOKE ABRUPTLY, her eyes snapping open. The room was in darkness. For a moment she lay there confused, reaching out to the other side of the bed for Edward, but he wasn't there; instead it was cold and empty. She sat bolt upright, looked at the ribbon of light around the curtained door to the balcony. An eruption of sound followed: boom, boom, boom, which she recognised as the pulsating bass line of some song or other being played at a very loud volume, and then the sound of a girl giggling, then a male voice shouting, 'Knock it back. Knock it back. Knock it back,' each shout accompanied by a chorus of grunting noises, getting louder and louder each time.

Amanda jumped out of bed, threw on her dressing gown, crossed to the balcony and yanked the door open. She stood looking down at a crowd of youngsters gathered round a street-side bench on the opposite side of the road before the high, wrought-iron railings of St Stephen's Green. Someone was standing precariously on the armrest, pouring the contents of a bottle of wine from a height down, she guessed, into the mouth of someone else lying there unseen.

She closed the balcony window with a bang, shutting out the noise. They were just – what looked to be, anyway, boisterous students doing what students seemed to do best – being drunk and boisterous. All that mattered was her son wasn't one of them.

An image flashed across her mind, effervescent, not making any sense, but she knew it was from that night... a boisterous night, the sounds all around her, music, voices, an arm coiling itself around her waist, beginning to lead her away. The night it had all started...

That night.

Amanda's breath caught at the back of her throat. She took a step and wobbled, reached out to hold on to the small table next to the balcony door, grabbing it, knocking it over, her phone falling off it to the floor. She turned, slumping against the wall, and slid down to the floor, her breath coming in short, hollow gulps. What was happening to her? She could feel her heart galloping inside her chest. Was this a heart attack? She was a doctor and should know. But she didn't. Oh Christ, am I about to die? She needed help. Danny. She'd ring her son. Amanda felt she had no choice, fumbling about for her telephone, finding it, bringing up Danny's number and pressing call. She listened as it rang out. He was never going to answer it, not at this hour... but then:

'Mum, what's up?'

'Oh, Danny, please, can you get over here. I need you. Now!'

He didn't hesitate. 'I'm on my way.'

She sat slumped against the wall until she heard the door buzzer sounding a little later. Then slowly, uncertainly, she got to her feet and made her way along the wall to the door. She opened it, and her son rushed in. Amanda was grateful he was alone: she didn't want Sally seeing her like this.

'Come on, Mum.' He helped her back towards the bed, laying her down, then pulling a chair over, sitting.

'What happened, Mother? I'm worried about you. I really am.'

'I'm sorry, Danny, for ringing... I just panicked, that's all, I thought... I don't know what I thought... I'm sorry, I shouldn't have bothered you.'

'You didn't bother me, Mum. I'm worried about you. What happened?'

'I don't know. I felt faint... just a little dehydrated, I think. Yes, that's probably all it is. I haven't drunk much water. I'll be fine.'

Danny got up and went over to the mini fridge, took from it a bottle of still water, came back, opened it and held it out. Amanda took a few sips, but she wasn't really thirsty at all. She handed the bottle back, and Danny placed it on her bedside locker.

'You don't look good, Mum. You're as pale as a ghost.'

'I'll be fine, Danny.'

'Should I call an ambulance?'

'Good God, no.'

'Well, what then? I can't leave you like this. I'm going to have to ring Dad.'

'No. Please.' Her voice rose an octave. 'Don't do that either. Please.'

Danny said nothing.

Amanda felt stupid for having implicated her son in this. It wasn't fair. I'm his mother. I look after him, not the other way round. She could feel tears begin to well in her eyes. I'm pathetic, I really am... She squeezed them shut, but it was no good, the nightmare memories came flooding in. She could feel the ropes that tethered her to the bed, chafing against her skin, drawing blood. She could feel the dark cloak of fear pressing in on her. Her eyes opened, and she stared at her wrists, as if seeing them for the first time. There was nothing there, no rope, nothing. She looked about, in a daze, began moving, pulling back the duvet, getting out of the bed, half staggering, half stumbling across the room towards the door. She had to escape. Had to. Before she reached it, she felt her legs give way, and she fell to the floor, on her knees, sobbing, drowning beneath the memories.

In the background, Danny was speaking frantically into the phone with his father.

14

1994

I t was grotesque. His face. Or rather the mask that covered it, of rubber it seemed, black, with slits for his mouth and his eyes, the whites stark against the black, like two portals to a pool of endless evil. She stopped screaming, found she was no longer shivering; the room had become suddenly hot, so very hot, the air thick and clammy. Her mind felt limp and heavy, but her body seemed to have detached itself and floated off, was separate; she could no longer even feel her arms. He took a step towards the bed, and she registered it with little more than a twitch of her eyes. She felt like an observer, watching from somewhere far off, and she felt strangely unafraid; rather, she felt resigned. Still, the mask fascinated her. The light had softened, not only was it visible along the edges of the curtains, but through them too, like they had been dipped into a pool of light and taken out again, leaving them soggy and dripping with it. Without taking her eyes from him, she could see in the periphery of her vision the shapes taking on colour, as if being painted by an unseen hand, all bland beiges and browns except for the curved-back chair, which was a series of bright swirls and hexagonals, like it was demanding, shouting out to her for attention. Instead, now that she could see it, she completely ignored it. Her complete focus centred on him, totally on him.

He reached the foot of the bed and stood there. She wondered at her calmness. Why was she not as frightened now? Was it because the mask was not so much scary as odd? It stretched over his face, cling-wrapping his ears and nose, buttressing his lips, cobwebbing his eyes behind a fine mesh.

She shook her head, trying to shake away the heaviness there, the movement as if in slow motion and seeming to continue even when she'd stopped. He was standing just a little down from her when she peered again. There was a creaking noise, and she saw that he was sitting on the bed. She felt something on her leg, soft and warm, and she shifted, trying to push whatever it was away, the same slow-motion sluggishness as before, the movement seeming to flicker and continue even after her leg had stopped moving. It started to crawl up her, and she narrowed her eyes and looked at it, saw it was a hand, his hand, as it turned and went over the crest of her thigh, disappearing into the crevice between her legs.

She spoke, a slow, slurred, rasping sound.

'You bastard. Fuck off. Bastard. Fuck off.'

15

W hen she opened her eyes again, she felt like she had a filthy hangover, her head hurt, she was nauseous, but more than anything, she had absolutely no recollection of how she had got... well, where, exactly?

She looked about the room. A mirror on the lilac-coloured wallpapered wall reflected the sunlight through the window, as did the mini chandelier that sent dancing orbs around the ceiling.

She recognised it now. It was one of the spare bedrooms in her house.

'You're awake.'

Her head spun round, sending a bolt of pain through it. She winced, then blinked twice.

'Lauren,' she said.

Her daughter rose from the chair by the bed and smiled, then leaned down and hugged her mother.

'It's okay,' she said sweetly, 'just let me do this first, Mum.' She reached for Amanda's wrist with one hand to check her pulse. 'Much better,' she said as she rested her hand back onto the bed.

'Lauren, darling, I'm so sorry...'

'Please, Mum,' Lauren said, resting her hand gently against her mother's cheek. 'Scchhh. It's okay, we all need a little help sometimes. You were always there for me, remember. Now it's my turn.'

'I'm your mother, Lauren. I'm supposed to be there for you.'

'And I'm your daughter. I'm supposed to be there for you too. Okay?'

Amanda forced a smile. 'You've turned out to be a fine young woman. I'm proud of you. And Danny... God, Danny, I have some explaining...'

'Scchhh,' her daughter said again, 'don't agitate yourself, Mother, everything is fine with Danny.'

'Really?'

'Really.'

'What day is it?'

'Sunday evening, Mother.'

Amanda processed this information. The pain in her head had subsided. She felt unusually calm. She glanced to the bedside locker, saw a container of pills.

'Dad prescribed you something, Mum; it's really helped.'

'It's given me a hangover,' Amanda answered. 'Sunday. I've lost a whole day. My God. Tomorrow. My patients...'

'I've told Layla that you've come down with something. I rang her at home; there's no problem; she's contacted all the patients on your list. I told her to do it for Tuesday too. Yes, Mother, you're going to need a couple of days' rest. You haven't been a day off sick in years. So no work until Wednesday, okay?'

Amanda smiled. 'Thank you, and, Lauren?'

'Yes, Mum?'

'Am I losing it? I mean, really.'

Lauren was silent. Then, 'I think you need a little rest, Mum, that's all; afterwards you'll be fine, really.'

Amanda tried to sit up, but slumped back against the pillows as a stab of pain cut through her head again.

'Mum, take it easy, please; come on, don't move now.'

'Okay,' Amanda whispered, 'but for God's sake, tell me what happened, please. Sunday evening, I can't believe it.'

Lauren took a breath. 'Dad went up to Dublin to get you. He left here straight after Danny rang, got there about five o'clock in the morning.'

'Edward,' Amanda muttered.

'You were...'

'I was what, Lauren?' she asked when her daughter didn't finish. 'Tell me.'

'You were crying when he got there, rambling stuff... you don't remember anything?'

'No, sweetheart, I don't... and, Lauren?'

'Yes, Mum?'

'I'm sorry, from the bottom of my heart, for all this. You understand that, don't you?'

'Of course I do. You're my mother, and we're family. This is what it means to be family. This is what we do. Dad put you in the car and brought you home. He's been thinking about contacting Andrew.'

Andrew O'Shaughnessy, consultant psychiatrist at Galway University Hospital and a golfing buddy of Edward's. His wife, Emily, moved in the same circles as Amanda. She felt a ripple of anxiety run through her. She didn't want that woman knowing anything about this.

'He didn't, did he? Ring Andrew? Tell me he didn't.'

'No, Mum, he thought you wouldn't like that. He prescribed something himself instead, hoping that would help.'

Amanda sighed. Thank God.

'I think he called it right,' Lauren said. 'By the way, Pri rang. I told her what happened. I hope that's alright, Mum. It's Pri, after all.'

Amanda smiled. 'That's alright. Pri, I don't mind; you know I don't mind. I was going to tell her myself.'

They were silent then.

'Is that it?' Amanda asked her daughter. She had the feeling Lauren wasn't telling her the whole story. 'What about Danny? How is he?'

'He's been surprisingly mature about all this. Danny was concerned solely with looking after you. I'm quite proud of him, actually.'

'And me too,' Amanda said.

'But, Mum, now you have to tell me. Are you going through something? Do you need to talk about it? I need to know. We need to know. You understand that, don't you? We're all worried about you.'

Amanda nodded. 'Of course I understand, sweetheart.' She paused, because she hated having to lie to her daughter, to her family. 'I'm not going through anything. I was a little unwell, probably had a temperature, that's all, but I'm feeling much better now. It's the tail end, that's all. You know, I had a patient one time who had a temperature of a hundred and three degrees, thought he was Superman, absolutely off his rocker. That's what it can do. I'm sorry, but I'm fine now.'

Lauren looked at her gravely.

'Are you sure, Mum, there's nothing else? You would tell me, wouldn't you?'

'Of course, Lauren, sweetheart, and I'm sure there's nothing else.'

But how much longer can I keep pretending? How much longer before my secret is out?

Lauren bit her lip. 'You were sobbing, saying you were sorry. What were you sorry for?'

'I don't know, Lauren. Like I say, I was raving. Now, darling... shouldn't you be at the hospital, your internship? I really don't want to interfere.'

'Don't worry, Mum, the first module is genomics and stuff like that. That thesis I did last summer. DNA, you know. No big deal. It can wait.'

Amanda felt an invisible kick to her belly, did her best to disguise it. 'DNA?' She forced her voice to remain calm. 'I didn't know it was on DNA.'

'Yes, Mum, DNA.'

'I don't think I ever studied DNA at college,' she said, trying to appear casual. 'What's it about?'

Lauren laughed; she seemed relieved her mother was interested in something other than her present predicament. 'Things have moved on, Mum. Yes, DNA. DNA strands, what they call the DNA tree.'

'The DNA tree?'

'Yes. But we can talk about that again... Mum, what's wrong? You've gone pale.'

'Y-your dad, does he know about this?'

'Of course. I took a swab.'

'A swab?'

'Yes, the strangest thing, he wanted it back once I told him what it was for.' She smiled. 'He thought it was for a DNA profile on him, you know, ninety per cent Irish, five per cent English, propensity for gout and all that.'

'Did you give it back?'

'No, I did not. I told him not to be so odd. Look, I shouldn't have mentioned this at all? Your reaction...'

'It's nothing, Lauren. I just don't feel well again...' She took a deep breath, held it, imagined those potatoes tumbling from a sack. You have to hold it together, she told herself. Do what it takes. Pretend. Fake it till you make it. You must. DNA. A family tree. Oh my God. She felt she was on a train, one she couldn't get off, hurtling ahead, gaining in speed, faster and faster, with no way of stopping, heading directly for the buffers...

She closed her eyes. 'I don't feel so good, darling; can we talk about this later?'

She could feel her daughter's eyes on her, her uncertainty, could sense her debating what to do. Despite the medication, Amanda's heart began to race again as the dark cloak of fear tightened about her once more.

'Now, I'd like to rest a little while, darling, okay?'

'Of course, Mother.'

'You can go if you want.'

'No. I like sitting with you, if that's alright?'

'Of course... and, Lauren?'

'Yes, Mother?'

'Your dad. I don't want to, I mean, I couldn't face... Just, don't tell him I was awake. I'll talk with him in the morning; can you do that?'

Lauren did not reply for a moment. 'I understand, Mother,' she said. 'Have some rest. Don't worry about Dad.'

Amanda closed her eyes and lay still, hearing the sound of Lauren sitting back in her chair by the bed, and thought, What am I going to do?

16

1994

The shower had been running for ages, the grinding noise of the motor piercing her brain, a pounding pain beginning to build behind her eyes. The silence that followed amplified her confusion and so too her hopelessness. She stared through an open door to the right of the bed, a vista of a toilet bowl, empty shelves above it, the corner of a window high up on the wall, all shrouded in steam. There was a raw wetness to her crotch. She knew without remembering, she knew, and felt disgust, but more than anything: fear.

She listened. There was the soft padding sound of feet from behind the door, then a buzzing, like a swarm of bees. She recognised it as that of an electric razor. The normal sounds of a morning, but there was nothing normal about this. It was morning, after all, well, wasn't it? The light through the windows told her so. A bright, hard, cold light, not the waning glow of evening.

There was another sound, like a brush across a floor, as she saw the door move, opening wider. She took a breath, held it, forgetting all about the growing pain in her wrists and arms, waiting...

A hand appeared around the corner of the door, and a man stepped out from behind it, shrouded in the swirling mist from the shower, a malevolent apparition, transfixing her with fear, the mask that cling-wrapped his head glistening. And she wondered: is this the end?

His feet made a squelching sound as he walked across the room towards her. Her sense of vulnerability was acute, and she crossed her legs, pressing her thighs tightly together. The rawness in her crotch became a burning sensation, but she ignored it, squeezed even tighter.

He reached the bed, and his hands hovered over her face. She felt a pressure on her nose, knew it was his fingers squeezing her nostrils closed, forcing her to open her mouth, dropping a pill into it when she did, sealing it shut again with his hand and, still pinching her nostrils, forcing her to swallow. Then he released her, and she gagged, listening to the sounds of his footsteps retreat from the room. She didn't know how long it was – could have been an hour, could have been a day – before she heard footsteps returning, and the side of the mattress sagged. She turned to see him climbing onto the bed beside her.

'No.' Her voice was a garbled muffle. Squeezing her thighs, she ignored the pain, but her strength was ebbing, and she was beginning to feel numb and sleepy. She looked on, a mere observer again, as he nudged her legs apart with one hand, rising momentarily before her, then coming down and settling.

She tried to turn her body away, to shift him off her, but it was no use; he was much too strong and heavy. Everything started to dim again, fading, fading, then gone.

17

I t was late afternoon. Amanda and Lauren were sitting in the conservatory, the sun streaming through the glass panels making it very warm.

'You're not cold, Mother, are you?'

'No, sweetheart.'

'I just saw you shiver,' Lauren said. 'I hope you're not getting another fever.'

'No, I'm sure I'm not, a bodily reflex, nothing more, as it returns to normal. My headache is gone, and I don't feel groggy. Yes, I'm much better.'

'If you're sure.'

'I'm sure.'

Amanda stood, rearranged her dressing gown, securing the cord tightly around herself. 'I'm going into the garden for a breath of fresh air.'

Lauren was about to get up.

'No,' Amanda said, 'on my own, if you don't mind. I want to get my head in order.' At least that part was true.

'Of course, Mum, whatever.'

'Good. Then let me get some fresh air. We'll talk later. Have you seen your father?'

'This morning, at breakfast, before he went to work.'

Amanda said nothing. It was obvious Edward was avoiding her, which suited her just fine.

'I told him you were doing well,' Lauren said. 'He asked.'

Amanda nodded. 'It's okay,' she said, noting Lauren's look of concern. 'I can manage.'

She went outside. The air was fresh and bracing, holding, she detected, the first chill of the approaching autumn. At the end of the garden was a shaded nook between two old spruce trees. From a branch of one hung a wicker egg chair. It was one of Amanda's favourite spots. The house was not visible from here; it was her own little corner of the world. But what she had said was true; she did feel much better. Because she'd had a realisation, like the first time as a junior doctor when she had encountered an emergency and had looked around to find nobody was there to help. That she was on her own, the life of someone depended on her and her alone, no one else. So she had learned to cope, to deal with whatever was thrown her way. And now she had to deal with this too. She took a breath, for the first time rationally considering her options.

WHEN SHE WENT BACK into the house, she was taken by surprise. She could hear voices from the drawing room, one of which was Edward's, but he was supposed to be at work. The other was the unmistakable booming tones of Andrew O'Shaughnessy. She didn't want to speak with either of them because she knew Edward sought to test her mental stability. She wanted nothing to do with it, as she wasn't certain of what the answer would be. As a doctor, she knew all it sometimes took was a signature on a piece of paper to have someone locked away for their own good. Perhaps she was a little paranoid, but much had happened – was happening – to give her cause to be this way. She crossed the hallway quickly, heading for the staircase, planning to go back to bed, lock the door, stay there until...

'Amanda.' Edward's voice was sharp as it echoed across the hallway.

She turned. He was standing in the doorway to the drawing room. She considered he had been standing there all along, out of sight, waiting for her. 'Andrew is here. Come on in and have a word, won't you?'

She hesitated.

'Well, won't you? You don't mind, surely?'

His voice was pleasant, which it wouldn't have been if his eminent friend hadn't been there. However, there was a hardness in his eyes as he stared at her. For a fleeting moment she considered feigning a headache and going to her bedroom anyway.

'No, of course not,' she said meekly instead, walking towards him.

Andrew O'Shaughnessy was standing in the centre of the drawing room, hands casually in his pockets. He was wearing a crumpled linen suit, and she guessed he had come directly from his practice. She felt guilty at the inconvenience she was causing both the psychiatrist and her husband, who would have had to juggle his own work schedule too to be home this early. She picked up immediately on a sense of forced relaxation about both men, especially her husband.

'Amanda, how are you?' Andrew said casually.

She was aware that she looked dreadful, without any make-up, her hair a mess. She ran a hand through it self-consciously.

'How's Emily?' she said, because it was all she could think of. She heard the door close and looked around, saw that Edward had left the room. It was just her and Andrew now.

'I'd like to talk to you, Amanda, if I could. And don't you worry about Emily. I promise this will be strictly between ourselves. I won't say anything to her, nothing; you have my professional word on that. Shall we sit down?'

His tone was sombre. She stood silent, staring, as a fleeting thought crossed her mind. Could she tell him, could she tell him everything? Because this was her chance, perhaps her only one. And then it was gone just as quickly again.

No. She couldn't tell him. Of course not. She couldn't tell anyone. The thought of what would happen if she did chilled her to the bone. No, she could not take that chance. Ever.

'Yes, let's sit,' she said, walking to an armchair and sitting, indicating to the one opposite, smiling, determined, desperate even, to convince this man, and everyone else, that there was nothing wrong with Amanda Jackson.

They spoke for almost an hour. In fact, Amanda enjoyed the experience. She spoke about the stresses of her job, because she knew it was a common topic for them both to agree on. She even coaxed the consultant psychiatrist to talk about himself a little. 'Yes,' he'd agreed, 'job-related stress, particularly in our disciplines, is a challenge for all healthcare professionals.' He seemed to realise he had gone off topic and brought the conversation back onto her. So she spoke about herself truthfully because she knew he could spot a lie a mile off. She just didn't talk about that. She was surprised at how easy it was, to act like everything was alright, like nothing had happened. And it was a relief of sorts to just pretend that all was fine. Because as she talked, she began to believe that everything was alright herself.

Andrew concluded their conversation with a conspiratorial whisper, 'I can safely say, Amanda, you are in a condition of most robust mental health, with a refreshing lack of reserve in talking candidly about yourself. I'll tell Edward if I may; he will be greatly reassured.'

Amanda smiled. 'Yes, of course.' Wow, that was easy. 'And while you do, let me go and get changed.'

'However...' he added, like a mere afterthought, 'I would like you to drop into my office sometime for a chat.'

'A chat? You would? Why?'

'Because...' His voice trailed off.

'Yes, Andrew, because?'

'Well, Amanda, what I'm trying to say is that things are not always as they seem, are they? There has to be a reason for your... well, your recent, shall we call it little upset? Yes, let's call it that.'

'My upset? I had a turn, Andrew, that's all. It happens. I was dehydrated.'

He smiled, his psychiatrist's best reassuring smile. 'Yes, of course, Amanda. Anyway, just drop in sometime. Yes? Will you do that for me?'

Amanda wasn't going to commit. Instead, she lowered

her head and brushed past him. 'Goodbye, Andrew,' she said, and quickly left the drawing room. She went up the stairs, but not to get changed. There was something else much more pressing she had to do instead.

18

At the top of the house was a small cluttered room they called the office. Amanda went in and closed the door, sat at the desk and turned on the computer. Despite being up to date technically on medical matters, she was a novice when it came to social media. Which was the way she liked it, although a couple of friends, including Emily O'Shaughnessy, had urged her to update her Facebook profile, to at the very least add a photograph of herself and generally become more active, just as they were. But she never had, limiting her activity to messaging her children and extended family. It was very effective for that, no more trips to the post office to send letters. But she had no interest in posting pictures of herself or her latest purchase of shoes or a half-eaten carrot cake in some city centre café or other, and couldn't understand people who did.

Now, however, she wished she had been more active, wished that she knew more about it. Because now she needed Facebook.

She stared at the computer screen. Where to start?

She rested her right hand on the mouse and moved the cursor across the screen, dropped it into the Facebook search box, typed in the name, pressed return. She went through a list of people, narrowed the search by location – Fiona had been from Limerick – tried again. No luck. Perhaps she wasn't on Facebook? It was a fact, not everybody was. She closed her eyes and folded her arms, thinking. It had been a long time ago, such a long time. They'd met as final-year medical students at University College Dublin.

She opened her eyes and stared at the screen. She noticed the cursor was no longer in the search box. Perhaps she had inadvertently nudged the mouse, and it had moved. Yes, she decided, that must be what had happened. As she reached for the mouse, and before she touched it, the cursor started moving of its own accord, across the screen in a series of looping motions.

What the...?

She grabbed the mouse, pulling it towards her. The cursor moved downward across the screen, just as it was supposed to. She sighed. Just a glitch, that's all. But a second later it suddenly veered up again, as if it had a mind of its own once more.

As if it had a mind of its own.

She considered that.

An icy coldness spread through her as a thought formulated in her mind. Her eyes drifted upward, settling on the tiny webcam in the centre of the black casing surrounding the screen.

Her dressing gown had fallen open, the top of her nightdress sagging, revealing her cleavage. She pulled it tightly about her.

She stood abruptly, her heart thumping, her panic

beginning to rise. Amanda opened her mouth, gulping for air, staring at the webcam. She was certain someone was at the other end, staring right back; she could almost feel their malevolent eyes upon her.

She was aware of a sound, two dull thuds, and realised someone was knocking at the door. 'Are you in there?' She looked towards it, saw the handle begin to turn, as an inner voice screamed, Don't let him see you like this. She snapped her head back to the computer again, saw the cursor had jumped back to the search box, letters appearing in it unaided. She felt like she was watching a scene from a horror movie, except this wasn't a movie, this was real, and she was in it.

The letters formed into words. They read:

BITCH. WHORE. DID YOU REALLY THINK YOU'D GET AWAY WITH IT? YOU STUPID FOOL. I KNOW. I KNOW EVERYTHING. I KNOW YOUR SECRET.

19

BEFORE...

Had she been sleeping? Her head was heavy, her throat dry. She didn't know what time it was, whether it was night or day. Nothing. She stared about the room, in darkness now save for beams of anaemic light filtering through mostly unseen windows.

Windows? She remembered the sounds of a shower, so long ago it seemed, and a window high in a wall, a bathroom wall. She looked, and there it was, a small rectangle of light as the images tumbled into her mind, of the swirling mist, the door opening and... Him, standing there, the apparition. But just as quickly the images trailed off, and there was nothing left in her memory. She knew that was when she had blacked out.

On reflex she raised her hands and began kneading each of her tender wrists in turn, feeling the sharp ache of her arms and shoulders.

It took her a moment to register the reality, that she was no longer tied to the bed, that her arms were free. She turned onto her side, the bed sheet sticking to her back, but falling away as she continued to turn, her flesh feeling puckered and tender. She lay back again, raised one leg, then the other, scarcely believing it. Nothing was constraining her. She gave an involuntary shiver, suddenly aware of the bitter cold carried on the dark air. She took a breath, held it, a temporary heat rising in her as she withheld oxygen from her body, straining to hear any sound, any sound at all. There was none. She knew she was alone, that he had gone, just knew. She rolled off the bed and fumbled along the wall for a light switch, her legs weak and unsteady, found the switch and pressed the light to life. She felt dizzy as a pain pressed in against her chest, and her mind seemed to cloud over, pushing out all thought. She felt herself growing warm, could feel sweat forming along the base of her neck, the dizziness getting worse. She realised she was still holding her breath. She exhaled in a loud whoosh and began to run.

20

She tore her eyes away from the computer and those words on the screen. Just as the door opened, she rushed over to a stack of papers on the floor and rifled through them, like she was looking for something, her back to the door.

'There you are,' she heard her husband say from behind, his voice surprisingly affable and relaxed.

She stiffened, picked up an old bank statement, turning it over, pretending to read it.

'Wh-what? Oh yes,' she stuttered. 'I was looking for this.' She turned to him now and beamed a smile. 'Did you want me?'

He seemed to appraise her for a moment; then he smiled too and crossed to her. He rested a hand gently on her elbow and kissed her cheek, the nice, caring Edward. She glanced to the computer. With a sickening feeling she realised she had not turned it off; the words were still there, goading her:

BITCH. WHORE. DID YOU REALLY THINK
YOU'D GET AWAY WITH IT? YOU STUPID FOOL.
I KNOW. I KNOW EVERYTHING. I KNOW YOUR
SECRET.

'You had me worried for a while,' he said.

'I was only looking for this, that's all.' A tremor in her voice.

He shook his head. 'No. Not that. The way you're... well, behaving, the way you haven't been yourself lately, let me put it like that. I was worried sick. We all were. Andrew has greatly reassured me.'

Amanda was a little unsettled by her husband's soothing concern. She had expected the opposite, had been prepared for it. But not this. She went quickly to the computer, standing in front of it to block his view, and clicked out of the page. She turned to face him again, saw the questioning expression.

'I'm sorry.' And she genuinely was. 'I really must have caught a virus. I'm certain I had a high temperature. It made me act all weird.'

He stared off into the distance. Did he believe her?

'Well, we can deal with that.'

'Yes,' she answered, glad for the change of subject, 'we certainly can.'

He nodded and came to her again, embraced her tightly, then quickly dropped his hands, took a step back, his nose crinkling.

'Yes, I know, I need a shower,' she said.

'Phew. You certainly do.'

Her eyes wandered to the computer, a glint of light reflecting on the small black circle that was the computer webcam. They were being watched, she felt certain of it, by an enemy, an intruder, one she did not know yet was mere inches away. She forced herself to pull her eyes from it before Edward became suspicious.

He began to walk towards the door.

'Have a shower,' he said. 'I really can't stand that smell any longer.'

'Of course,' she said meekly, 'of course. Sorry.'

LATER THAT EVENING, after a lovely dinner cooked by Lauren, she took her chance and left daughter and dad chatting in the living room while she went into the conservatory. She did not trust the desktop computer in the office and would have to think of an excuse to get rid of it, even if it was less than a year old. She sat in a chair and instead used her phone to search the web. As she typed the name Dr Fiona McBride into the Google search box, she wondered if her phone was safe. She imagined it would be much more difficult to hack into a networked mobile phone than a computer. But she might be wrong about that. In any case, she had little choice. She scanned the first page of returns on the small screen. None were what she was looking for. Her one-time colleague and friend had probably married, so her surname had likely changed. She didn't know anything about Fiona now. Nothing. After that night they'd drifted apart, and a few months later had gone their separate ways, never to see each other again, never to hear from one another again either. Amanda closed her eyes, the coldness spreading through her again, trying not to think back to those times, but knowing she had to. She opened her eyes and typed, 'Dr Fiona, Limerick'. There was a photograph among the returns, of a group of people, a formal occasion, black ties

and elegant dresses. She clicked on it, and a sidebar
popped up, an enlarged copy of the photo with the
heading:

Munster Sports Psychiatry Association Annual Dinner Dance.

Which would make sense, because Fiona McBride
had been studying to be a psychiatrist. Her eyes scanned
the faces and returned to one in particular, a female third
from the end on the left, dressed in a sombre black dress,
long sleeves, high neck. She scanned the names in the
caption beneath, felt something fizzle through her as she
read the female's name, Dr Fiona Crowley. This was her...
Or was it? She brought the smartphone to within inches
of her face, peering at it intently. She couldn't be certain.
Just like a question in a pub quiz, where the initial
certainty of the answer fades to doubt. Fiona, she remembered, conjuring up her image, was of medium build, with
black cropped hair, wide brown eyes holding a hint of
something – pain perhaps? The woman in the photo
looked similar, a little heavier certainly, but the hairstyle
was the same. As for anything else, the photo was too
indistinct and her memory too vague to be completely
sure. She noted the date, December 12, 2016. Four
years ago.

Amanda closed out and returned to the search results
page, noting a line of text above the photograph that she
had initially missed because her attention had been taken
by the photograph. She read it now, scarcely believing
what it said:

Psychiatrist struck off for failings in care of vulnerable patient,

*repeatedly ignored threats of suicide, eighteen-year-old youth
subsequently drowned in river.*

She clicked on the link, and the story appeared, from a
national newspaper dated March 2017:

Limerick Doctor Fiona McBride Crowley –

So it was her, had to be.

*– was struck off by the General Medical Council
following a hearing in Dublin today (Tuesday) for failings in the care of a vulnerable patient, who died by
drowning after repeated threats to end his own life. No
further details were given, but the council president,
Professor Anthony Brady, said such behaviour was
inexcusable and broke every bond of trust between
patient and doctor. Fiona McBride Crowley apologised
for her failings and said her actions were unacceptable.
She remarked that she will have to live with the consequences of what she had done for the rest of her life.*

Amanda considered what she'd read, staring at her
phone. She closed out of it and dialled Pri. The phone was
answered on the second ring.

'Amanda, I've been waiting to hear from you.' There
was urgency in Pri's tone. In the background was the
sound of a door sliding open and closing again.

'I'm sorry it's taken so long,' Amanda said, her voice
low. The light outside was dim, casting reflections on the
panes of glass. She looked ahead to the house at the top of
the garden, watching for anyone's approach. There was

the sound of footsteps on gravel in the background on the phone now, and another door opening.

'Something must have happened,' Pri said, the door closing with a metallic clunking sound. Amanda knew she was sitting in her car, where she often went for a quiet moment on the phone. 'I mean, to have you go to Dublin like that – Lauren told me about it, by the way; she said you had a... well, a...'

'Meltdown?'

'Crisis was the word she used. But what I want to know is, how are you now?'

'I'm fine,' Amanda lied, because she didn't want to get into it, not fully, not now. 'I panicked. I know that now. Everything just overwhelmed me. I couldn't cope, and I needed to get away. That's what happened. I feel better now, stronger, you know.'

'Good.'

'Look, I have to deal with this, Pri. Just have to. Because it's not going to just go away.' She quickly recounted the messages she'd received on her phone and computer, but not what Lauren had said about her DNA thesis.

'Jesus Christ,' Pri spluttered. She only ever said those words when completely taken aback. Amanda imagined her quickly blessing herself, as she always did immediately after she'd said them. Not that she was religious, she wasn't, rather it was an inherent sense of Catholic guilt shared by most Irish people that made her do it. 'You know you have to go to the police with this, don't you? You just have to.'

Amanda was silent for a moment, then: 'I can't, that's out of the question.'

'Why is it out of the question? This is getting serious, Amanda. Come on.'

'Because. I told you...'

'This bloody secret. Come on, Amanda, get things into perspective here. Nothing is worth...'

'Pri, don't tell me what to get into perspective. This is serious, and I don't want anyone to know about it. Can't you just accept that?'

Like you did when it was your secret. It was on the tip of her tongue to say it, but she didn't.

'I shouldn't have told you about it,' Amanda said instead. 'It wasn't fair. I should have kept it to myself.'

'I apologise. I just want to help, that's all. Amanda, I'd be hurt if you'd kept this to yourself, what you're going through. This is what friends are for, Amanda... so won't you tell me, please, of how I can help? If you at least told me what this was all about, I might be able to.'

'Answer me a question,' Amanda said. 'That will help.'

'Of course.'

'And I will tell you, I promise, I'll tell you everything, but not just yet. Okay?'

'Okay.'

'Suppose you were me. And something came back, from your past, out of the blue, like it has. And there was one person, from way back then, whom you were friendly with. Who knows a little about what went on, but not everything. My question: what would you do? Would you contact them? Even though you haven't seen or spoken to them since that time, which was almost twenty-two years ago now. You didn't stay in touch because you're ashamed and you want to forget, although you never can, that's impossible. What would you do?'

Amanda could hear Pri take a breath, hold it, and release it again slowly.

'I have to say, Amy, this would be intriguing if it weren't so bloody scary. I wish you would tell me... yes, I know, I know you will, but not just yet. Anyway. A thought. You say you're ashamed, of what they, this person, might know, indeed, of the little they actually do know. But what do they know? I'd like to ask. Maybe they know nothing at all. Have you ever thought of that?'

Again, Amanda fell silent. 'In a way, you've just answered my question,' she said.

'I have?'

'Yes. I realise now I do need to contact them. I should have done it a long time ago, should never have carried this for as long as I have, like a festering sore. Now it's forcing me to face up to it... Still, on the bright side, maybe something good will come out of this in the end; every cloud has a silver lining and all that. But it's hard to imagine that at this particular moment. I don't know how to find them. In fact, I've already been trying. I've been trying Facebook, Google, no luck.'

The only sound on the line was that of static, and it stayed like this for a long time.

Finally, Pri spoke, an excitement in her tone.

'I just thought of something.'

Amanda waited for her to continue.

'You'd never think of it.'

She fell silent.

'For God's sake,' Amanda said, 'will you just tell me? What is it?'

'A phone book. That's what. Remember those? This one is big, says "National" along the side, the year nineteen ninety-eight. On a shelf in my living room. Bit old. Still, worth a look. What'd you think? She might be in it.'

'Of course. Go on, have a look.'

'Give me a name and the details? I'll go and do it. Right now. Ring you back, okay?'

'Okay. Great. Thank you,' Amanda said, 'you're a good friend, you know that. I'm sorry if I'm a little short with you. Give me a margin, yes?'

'Of course, darling. Just as you've given me plenty of margins. We're here for each other. Thick as thieves, that's what. Now, that name and details.'

A FEW MOMENTS later Pri rang Amanda back. It was that simple. It was there, in a good old-fashioned phone book. The entry read:

> *Dr Fiona McBride Crowley, Castle House, Raheen, Limerick*

The actual telephone number didn't seem correct, though; it didn't look like it had enough digits. A quick Google search by Amanda revealed an extra prefix, zero, had been added some years before. That was all that was missing. As they said their goodbyes, Pri added: 'This could be the person who's doing this to you. Be careful. Talk to me before you do anything about it, okay?'

Amanda assured her that she would, and hung up.

She sat silently staring at her phone, thinking things over. It was dark outside, but the lights were on in the house, so she kept the lights off in the conservatory. This way the house remained clearly visible and allowed her to see if anyone approached without been seen herself. She checked the time on her phone: 9:15. It was a little late, so it would be best to leave this until morning. In any case, Lauren or Edward, she felt sure, would come looking for her soon.

Still... she found herself bringing up the keypad on her phone, entering the number, hovering her index finger over the call button, forcing any internal objections from her mind, and pressing...

Her heart jumped as it began to ring. She wasn't certain, of course, that this number was still Fiona's, and she imagined someone answering, telling her it wasn't, apologising and having to hang up.

This tempered her excited anxiety. But instead of someone answering, there came a high-pitched piping noise, and she knew she was being connected to an answering machine. No message was on it telling her when to speak, just a click followed by a low static sound. 'Um,' she spluttered. 'Hello, my name is Amanda Jackson, Dr Amanda Jackson... Is this...? Look, I don't like talking into an answering machine. I'll ring back another time. Goodbye.'

She dropped the phone onto her lap, annoyed, frustrated, and feeling a little sorry for herself. Why couldn't she just be left in peace? Was that too much to ask? Hadn't she been through enough already? Why did she have to deal with this now? A voice inside her head answered, Boohoo, you mightn't like it, but this is just the way it is, Amanda. Feeling sorry for yourself won't help. Get on with it; you have no other choice.

She knew the voice was right; she didn't.

Then her heart jumped again as the telephone screen illuminated the way it always did just before it rang. She snatched it up, cutting off the first ringtone.

'Hello.'

'Dr Amanda Jackson?'

'Yes.'

'You just rang my number.'

The voice was deep, a smoker's perhaps, or this person had just woken up and was groggy, but it was female, with the sing-song drawl of the southern counties. The same accent, she remembered, as Fiona McBride.

'It's you, isn't it?' she said.

'Who?'

'Fiona... Fiona McBride?'

'That Dr Amanda Jackson. I was wondering. What do you want? You do want something, don't you? Otherwise you wouldn't be ringing me after all these years?'

Amanda was taken aback by the confrontational tone.

'Well, yes, you're right. I do want something. I want to talk to you, that's what.'

'You took your time.'

'W-what does that mean?'

'You know what it means. That night. It's that night, isn't it? You took your time.'

'That night,' she repeated, the now familiar icy chill coursing through her.

'Yes. That night. How many times must you say it? And you want to talk to me?'

'I do.'

'Not on the phone. If you want to talk to me, you'll have to come and meet me. Face to face.'

That icy chill ran colder.

'Why?' she asked. 'Why must I come meet you? Can't we just talk... now?'

There was a chuckling sound, and Amanda realised that Fiona was laughing.

'What's so funny?' she asked, her voice rising slightly.

'Well, you wanted to meet people that night, didn't you? It's why we went out, remember?'

Amanda spoke before she realised what she'd said. 'Did I?' Because much of that night was a blur, much of it she could not remember, but all of it she would never forget.

'I've been getting notes,' Amanda continued, 'messages on my computer and phone about what happened. Someone...'

'Someone what?' she said when Amanda didn't finish. 'You mean someone... you mean me, don't you?'

'I didn't say that.'

'No, but you meant it, didn't you. I can tell by your voice. I can tell a lot just by that. I spent my life, you know, scraping through the layers, down and down, to find out what lies beneath in people, to release the bile and pus, the rot, to help people heal, to set them free... and what thanks did I get?'

You still haven't said if it was you, Amanda thought, who left that note on my car? And all the rest of it?

'I don't want to talk anymore,' Fiona snapped. 'I told you. And I don't trust phones. Someone could be listening. They do that, you know?'

Oh, I know, Amanda thought, I know.

'The King John Hotel, you familiar with it?'

Amanda was. On the outskirts of Limerick City, she'd been there once.

'Yes, but...'

'No buts. Tomorrow morning at ten. I'll be there, sitting in the foyer, watching the door. If you want to talk, be there. If not, don't bother me again.' And with that she hung up.

The Fiona Amanda remembered had been soft spoken, kind and reserved. Not any longer, that much was apparent. She noticed the back door to the house open, the familiar silhouette of Lauren appear and step out into the night, walking through the hollow of light towards her. She suddenly felt an overpowering sense of love for her children. She had to protect them. She had to protect herself. She knew what she had to do.

Go to Limerick, and meet Fiona. That's what.

21

L auren went back to Dublin on the early train, having reached her decision after talking with her dad the night before. It was just gone nine o'clock now, and Edward had left for work, while Amanda was about to leave on the forty-or-so-minute drive to Limerick to meet Fiona. More lies, because she had assured Edward she would not leave the house. She felt she had no other choice.

No other choice. She could almost hear the clock ticking. If Lauren completed her work on her and Edward's DNA strands, then her daughter would know. The truth. Amanda couldn't risk that. Certainly not. And something else. Because once that secret was out, others would follow.

The thought of it was almost too much to bear. Earlier, as Edward had showered, she had checked her car. There was no note. Maybe whoever had placed it there did not know her address, but she doubted that was the case. As she drove through the automatic gates and swung onto the road, she felt she was at least taking action now, perhaps embarking on the first leg of a journey that would take her to the heart of all this – this nightmare. And if that were the case, what would she find? The thought of it petrified her as much as anything else. But she drove on.

She had just turned onto the dual carriageway for Limerick when her telephone rang; it seemed shriller, louder than normal, Edward's name flashing across the Bluetooth-connected dash console. She clicked the button on the steering wheel and answered it. Edward's voice boomed through the speakers, so loud it caused her to wince: 'Amanda, where are you?' What he said next hit her like a gut punch. 'I'm here, at home, and you're not. You're not allowed to leave this house. Where the hell are you? Come on, tell me.'

'You're at the house?' she said, scarcely believing it.

'Surprised, aren't you?' he bellowed. 'Yes, I came back for something, and you're not here. Where the hell are you?'

'Please, Edward, can we talk about this when I get back? I'll be home later. I had to go out. We'll talk then. I can't talk now.'

'No. We won't talk then. We'll talk about this bloody well now. Where are you? I demand to know. How dare you not tell me.'

'I can't talk, Edward. I just can't. We'll talk when I get home. I'm sorry. I have to go.'

'Don't you bloody well hang up on me. Don't you dare—'

Amanda pressed the red telephone icon, terminating the call, and immediately switched the phone off.

'Oh God,' she said aloud, 'that's all I need.'

As she thought about it, she wondered if, when she returned home, he would be livid enough to... no, no, he wouldn't, he couldn't. That was years ago; it had happened just once. But it had happened, she reminded herself. Yes, it had, one time or not, it had happened. When Edward had hit her. God knows she'd had enough warning beforehand, when he'd thrown cushions, punched the settee... she really should have known better, shouldn't have antagonised him like she had, should have realised he was in a foul mood, should have just left him alone, walked out of the room, left him to himself. But after he'd thrown the cushions, after he'd punched the settee, well, then he'd punched her. She remembered it clearly, that blow to her stomach, powerful, solid, the pain excruciating, leaving her gasping for breath.

He'd regretted it immediately, of course, his mood instantly switching, contrite, promising he'd never do it again, saying how sorry he was, how much he loved her... but adding at the end, what she thought was, 'You bloody well drove me to it, you know, you pushed me too far. This is your fault.' His voice had been so low she could hardly hear, so she was never completely certain of what he'd said.

And he had never done it again. So she forgot about those words. But he had done it.

He had done it.

The question was: would he do it again? She felt that he might.

She drove on, thinking this day couldn't get much worse.

She was wrong about that.

It could.

And it soon would.

22

She turned from the dual carriageway onto a road with a sign next to it that announced, This way to Raheen. A little later the King John Hotel appeared at the end of a tree-lined avenue. She was looking ahead so intently that she failed to check her rear-view mirror, didn't see the flashing blue lights on this occasion, even though she was aware of the wailing of sirens, loud and piercing, like something from another world, unconnected to hers. Because unlike on the motorway to Dublin the other day, it never entered her mind that those sirens and lights might be coming for her. Even when she eventually noticed the row of flashing blue lights behind her, she still thought this.

But she was wrong.

Because they were.

They were coming for her.

They appeared all around her as she reached the hotel entrance, like an angry swarm, a police car swooping in front, another behind, and yet another alongside. She realised she was being boxed in, which she thought

absurd. Whatever this mix-up was, all they had to do was
ask, she thought with incredulity. She jammed on the
brakes and came to an abrupt stop, stared ahead,
completely frozen, as the door was yanked open, and
voices sounded, aggressive and loud, and a hand, a big
hairy hand, clamped onto her wrist and began to pull her
from the car, with something unseen tugging her backward, sharp and painful, tearing into her shoulder.

'The seat belt,' a female voice shouted, 'the bloody
seat belt's holding her in.' A body leaned across her, gone
again just as quickly. The seat belt had been released, and
she was being dragged out through the open door,
oomph, landing on her arse on the road, pain juddering
up her back, staring at the bodies gathered round. She felt
hands on her, searching, a female voice, stressed, a little
fearful. 'Any sharp objects? Tell me!'

'No,' Amanda spluttered, 'of course not. What is this?'

Another voice, male. 'You and your vehicle are being
searched under Section 23 of the Misuse of Drugs Act.
Information has been received that you are in possession
of Class A drugs for sale and supply. Now, where are the
fucking drugs?'

Amanda couldn't believe this and froze, unable to
move. As she was being pulled to her feet and led away,
she could see that someone was standing on the pavement, staring at her, a tense, angry expression on their
face. A woman. The woman in the newspaper: Fiona
McBride Crowley.

DRIP, drip, drip. The tap in the steel sink in a corner of the
cell at the police station was faulty. The sound of the dripping water seemed to drown out all else – the voices

outside, the banging of doors, the ringing of telephones – echoing around her head, becoming louder, louder... LOUDER. She was sitting on the side of the fold-out steel bed on top of the hard, thin mattress, bent double, hands pressed against her ears. The horror movie continued, becoming scarier and more desperate at every turn, with no end in sight. She had been taken here in the back of a police car between two burly officers. They would not speak with her, even when she had tried to tell them that they had made a terrible mistake, that she was the victim of malicious false information, a hoax. She had been further humiliated at the station, forced to undergo a strip search – a strip search – so a stranger could inspect her most intimate places. They were treating her like a criminal, an animal. She was neither; she was a respected medical doctor.

Drip, drip, drip.

'Amanda.'

She looked up. She hadn't heard the cell door open. The officer was looking at her without expression, her eyes cold.

'Come with me,' the officer said.

'Where?'

'Detectives want to talk to you. Come on, they're waiting.'

'No. You can't treat me like this. I have rights. I want a solicitor.'

'Fine.' The officer began closing the door again. 'I'll tell them you said that.'

'Wait. What about...? Why do they want to talk to me?'

The officer had almost closed the door. She pushed it open again. 'Why do you think?'

'Me? What do I think?'

The officer threw her eyes to heaven. 'Yes. There's no one else here, in this cell. Why would they want to speak with you? Tell me.'

'Do you speak to everyone in this way?' Amanda asked softly. 'No, I don't think so. I've done nothing wrong. I'm a completely innocent person. How would you like it if someone spoke to your mother or your sister the way you're speaking to me?'

The officer blinked, apparently stung by the comment.

'You don't sound very convinced of that,' the officer shot back, 'if I'm honest.'

'I want a solicitor.'

'I know. You just said. I'll go and tell them. Look, they only wanted a friendly chat. You haven't been charged with anything, not yet; you're simply being held while we search your car, that's all... course, if you want to make it into something a lot bigger than it is, then that's up to you.'

Amanda dropped her head. She didn't want to stay here a moment longer than was necessary.

She got to her feet.

'I'm coming.'

THERE WAS a smell of sweat and bleach in the small, windowless, clammy interview room. She sat down on a metal chair, realised it was angled lower at the front than the back, which meant she had to constantly push herself into it to stop herself from sliding off. Two detectives sat behind an unusually high table, high enough that she had to look up at them. A male and a female, neither looked older than her own kids. They peered down at her, and she felt utterly alone, desperate, and scared.

The male detective, he had gelled-back black hair and bad skin, turned on a recording machine, having told her she was being questioned in connection with the sale and supply of Class A drugs. He gave his name as Broderick, his partner as Kinsella. Kinsella was attractive with big blue eyes that Amanda imagined were normally friendly, but not now.

'Where were you travelling to when you were stopped?' Broderick asked.

Amanda said nothing.

'All the way from Galway,' Kinsella added. 'Where were you going?'

Now Amanda did speak.

'I was visiting someone, that's all. As for anything else, drugs, I've no idea what you're talking about.'

'Who're you visiting?' It was Broderick.

'Does it matter?'

'Actually,' Kinsella said, 'it does.'

'Fiona McBride, if you must know,' Amanda said. 'Fiona McBride Crowley. I went to college with her. She… well, she was a doctor.'

Broderick sat back in his chair, raised an eyebrow.

'Until she was struck off the medical register, you mean,' he said. 'I've heard all about her, worked with a colleague involved in that case, as it happens. Why would you be seeing her? Can you tell me that? Do you two often get together for a chin wag?'

Amanda shook her head. 'No.'

'Then why now? Why were you going to see her?'

'I can't say; it's a private matter.'

'Hhmm,' Broderick said, leaning forward again, placing both hands palm down onto the table. 'We don't receive information about people like yourself, a respectable doctor, every day of the week, carrying thousands of euros' worth of drugs. You're not our usual type of client, I'll grant you that. And I can tell you this, Fiona Crowley, despite everything, isn't either.'

'I'm glad you're beginning to see it,' Amanda said, 'because do you seriously think I would do such a thing? I mean, why would I? I'm a physician, as is my husband. I don't like to have to say this, but we're well off, very well off. I mean, why would I even dream of doing such a thing? Tell me that, please? And by the way, I abhor the use of illegal drugs. I've seen the terrible consequences they can have. I'm totally against it.'

Both young detectives exchanged glances. They didn't seem so certain of anything anymore.

'I dealt with a barrister once,' Broderick countered, puffing out his chest, 'who liked to shoplift clothes. We gave her the benefit of the doubt the first time. But she kept doing it. I wouldn't mind; the clothes weren't anything special, general department-store stuff, often out of the bargain bin. She could offer no explanation for her actions. It destroyed her career. People can be peculiar, wouldn't you say?'

He smiled, self-satisfied, but still, he looked uncertain. Then he appeared to think of something. 'If this is a hoax, as you say, I suppose you'll be making a complaint to that effect. It'd come under malicious intent or something similar, I'd imagine; I'm not quite certain. Anyway, I'll have to check when you make your complaint, that is, yes?'

His eyes narrowed as he looked at her. Amanda looked away, said nothing.

'I thought so,' Broderick said.

There was a knock on the interview room door.

Broderick got up, crossed and opened it, mumbled something to the person standing there, then stepped out, closing the door behind him. Kinsella said nothing, her eyes boring into Amanda, the silence becoming insufferable, suffocating, the warm thick air becoming even warmer and thicker. Amanda started to sweat, her hands moist, her blouse sticking to her flesh. If this went on much longer, she'd faint.

After what seemed like forever, the interview room door opened again, and Broderick came in. A cool breeze momentarily followed, floating around Amanda like a welcome, gentle embrace. Broderick stood inside the door and glared at her, his face like thunder, before using the back of his foot to kick the door closed. And the cool embrace was gone; in its place the clawed hands of fear pulled at her again.

'Well, well,' he said, his tone smug as he resumed his seat behind the table.

Amanda grabbed the legs of her chair with both hands, pressing her body back into it, realising almost too late that she'd been sliding off it again. She felt weak, so weak, needing all her strength to do it.

Broderick leaned towards his colleague and whispered in her ear. Then they both looked at her. A smile crossed Broderick's face.

'Now, Dr Jackson, is there anything you'd like to tell us?'

She looked at Kinsella. Whose big blue eyes gave nothing away, the same cold, hard expression on her face. Broderick's smile had broadened, delighted with himself.

'I can't take much more of this,' she said, almost in a whisper.

'What?' Broderick demanded. 'I didn't quite catch that. Can you speak up?'

'I said,' louder this time, 'I can't take much more of this.'

'No...' Kinsella said, her voice low and husky, 'I suppose you can't. Then why not just tell us? Get it over with.'

'What? What did you say?' Amanda asked. 'Tell you? Tell you what?'

'Suddenly hard of hearing, are you, Dr Jackson?' It was Broderick.

'I want to go home,' Amanda said. 'Why this? This change of attitude? What is it? What's happened?'

'One last chance,' Broderick said, 'is there anything you'd like to tell us?'

Amanda paused, staring at them both. What was this about?

'You've gone very quiet,' Kinsella said, and in that moment Amanda knew how it must look, how guilty she must appear.

She dropped her head into her hands.

'There's nothing in my car,' she said. 'There's nothing on me either.'

Because she was certain of both.

Or so she had thought.

When Broderick spoke, her hands fell away, and her head snapped up to look at him.

'That's where you're wrong,' he said. 'We found plenty in your car.'

He tossed something onto the desk. He must have concealed it when he'd re-entered the room, keeping it for the right moment. It was an A4 plastic bag, written across the front: 'Evidence', inside it another, smaller zip bag, and inside that a white, fine powdery substance.

Amanda stared at it.

'W-what is it?' she stuttered, her voice childlike.

'We thought you could tell us,' Broderick said.

'What? Are you saying that was in my car? That that's where you found it?'

Again, that half smile from Broderick.

'Nice one, Dr Jackson. You could convince me if I didn't know the truth. Yes. Of course. We found that in your car. Look, you're not helping yourself. So I'll ask again, what is that substance?'

'I don't know. I have no recollection. Maybe it dropped from someone's...' She fell silent. Maybe it had dropped from Danny's pocket. Her mind swirled. When was the last time he'd been in the car? She couldn't remember. Maybe it had happened when she'd been in Dublin? Who had driven the Mercedes home? She'd never enquired. Was it Lauren? Had to be, because she was the one at home; Danny had remained in Dublin; and Edward had driven his own car. So Lauren had to have been driving hers. But she couldn't implicate either of her children. No way.

'Pocket? Is that what you're trying to say,' Kinsella asked.

'Maybe,' Amanda replied, 'because I have no idea. Honestly.' She looked from one detective to the other slowly. 'You've got to believe me. I know nothing about this. Please, you've got to believe me.'

'Hhmm,' Broderick said, like he was contemplating, 'we're going round in circles here. You're not going to tell us, are you, Dr Jackson?'

'There's nothing to tell. I know nothing about it.'

'Fine. It's going for analysis; then we'll know for definite. But what I failed to say is that if it dropped from someone's pocket, how did it end up taped to the underside of the car jack in your boot? You don't even look surprised, Dr Jackson, I have to say.'

'I'm overwhelmed with it all, that's why. I have no answers. None.'

'Oh,' Kinsella said, 'I think you do – rephrase, I'm certain you do.'

No one spoke, the thick air suddenly thicker and the silence heavier.

'There is nothing else we can do today,' Broderick said, his tone one of resignation. 'When the results of the analysis come back, I have no doubt we'll be talking to you again, Dr Jackson.'

He then whispered into Kinsella's ear. She nodded and stood, left the room. He turned off the tape recorder.

'Right, come with me,' he said, standing and walking to the door without waiting for a reply. She followed him quickly out of the room, along the corridor, up a short flight of stairs at the end, along another corridor to a door. He stopped, punched in a number on a security pad, pushed it open. He indicated for her to go through. She passed into the foyer of the station, a counter running along the length of one wall, a glass hatch open in the centre. He went to the hatch, took something from the officer standing behind it. As he returned, she saw it was her handbag.

'Your car's out front,' he said, giving it to her. 'We'll be in touch.' She inspected her bag, and when she looked up again, Broderick had gone. She was standing in the foyer of the police station, feeling utterly alone and abandoned.

She walked across to the main door and out into the

bright, cold sunshine, stood on top of the station steps. A man in a bright, fluorescent tracksuit bounded up and gave her a toothless smile as he passed through. 'Alright, love?' he said. She went down the steps quickly and squinted, looking up and down the street. She spotted the Mercedes a short distance away, parked front end against the kerb. She hurried to it and tried the door. It was not locked. The key was in the ignition too. She got in and noticed the floor rugs had been haphazardly replaced, the glove compartment door was open, the contents topsy-turvy, and the front passenger door panel had not been properly screwed back in. She used to love this car, but now she felt she hated it, because it, like her, had been violated.

Amanda became aware of a person sitting on a wooden bench further along the street, in the shade of a tree. The person stood. It was a woman. She began to walk towards the car, her gait angled slightly forward, like she was walking on the tips of her feet. It was the same woman who had watched while she was being dragged from her car earlier. It was Fiona McBride. Amanda stared through the windscreen at her, undecided of what to do. But as the woman drew closer, she could not help but shudder. Now she could see those eyes, those wide eyes that had once held something – pain perhaps? – but now held a craziness, mixed in with a malevolent anger, and it scared her. She turned the key, and the engine came to life. Fiona McBride broke into a run, and Amanda could see she was holding something in her hand. She didn't know what it was, but it glinted in the sunlight. She turned the steering wheel, stomped on the accelerator and reversed from the kerb, crossing into the path of an oncoming articulated truck, the driver blasting his air horns in response. She rammed the car into forward gear and darted away with a screech of tyres, glancing in her door mirror to see Fiona standing in the middle of the road, staring after her, raising an arm into the air, gesturing for her to come back, it seemed.

Amanda wasn't going to do that. No way. She kept on driving.

23

BEFORE…

She ran along a narrow hall, the light from the bedroom behind her illuminating the way. At the end was a door, slightly ajar, enough for her to see the street outside. She stopped, pulled it open tentatively, wide enough to place her head out, peered up and down the street, at the rows of narrow houses on either side. It was a housing estate, one she was not familiar with. She stepped out, the pavement cold and wet against her bare feet, the air sharp and icy on her flesh, and realised that she was still naked. She darted back inside and stood rooted to the spot.

What now? She would have to leave naked; she had no other choice. As she turned towards the door again, her eyes fell on the staircase next to it, and the pile of clothes on the first riser, as if waiting for her. She recognised a small brooch on the tunic of a jacket as it glinted in the glow from a street light outside. These were her clothes. Quickly, with her hands shaking, listening out for the approach of anyone, she began pulling them on. Beneath the pile was her handbag. She grabbed it and opened the door, ran from the house, this time never once looking back and never once stopping, through a labyrinth of streets, until she eventually emerged onto a main road, breathless, her lungs on fire, as she leaned against a wall, holding on desperately to stop herself from collapsing. After a moment she heard the sound of an engine and looked up to see a car pull in against the kerb, a light shining on its roof.

'Oh God,' she muttered, pushing away from the wall, about to try to stumble on, but unable to. It was all she could do to merely stand.

The window of the car wound down, and a man's small head poked out, a tuft of white hair above each ear.

'Alright, love? Need a taxi? You look like you do.'

Amanda saw now the roof light was actually a taxi sign. She staggered towards the car, pulled open the rear door and flopped onto the seat.

'Where to?' the driver asked.

'Drive. For God's sake. Just drive.'

24

A pain pressed in behind Amanda's eyes as she drove back to Galway. It was almost 3 p.m. She'd been in that garda station for over three hours. She could smell sweat from her body. Her hands were shaking. She'd had nothing to eat or drink. No one at the station had offered her so much as a cup of tea. Her mouth was dry and acrid. They – the gardai – had been through her car with a fine-tooth comb. They had pulled the Mercedes apart, and it didn't feel the same; nothing felt the same any longer. On top of everything she had a new fear now: Fiona. She had also not turned on her phone since Edward had last rang. He would be livid. She would not, could not face him, but she knew she would have to soon. She drove on, trying to block everything from her mind, but everything churned nonetheless, threatening to overwhelm her, as the pain pressed in behind her eyes.

· · ·

She turned from the main road onto Ocean Drive and immediately began to sweat again. She slowed down, right down, her hands becoming clammy once more, her crumpled blouse losing its prickliness and becoming sticky as the moisture from her skin seeped in. A sound began to push through above the noise of the car engine. It was that familiar sound she'd been hearing a lot of lately; it was her heart, pounding as loud as a drum in a deserted auditorium.

She swung the Mercedes in front of the closed driveway gates and stopped, pressed the in-car remote control button, and the gates began to slide open. She did not drive in immediately but remained wary, sitting so far forward in her seat her face was almost pressed against the windscreen as she looked ahead, trying to spot Edward's car. She'd never felt so tense, her body rigid, limbs like wood, stiff and awkward. She couldn't see his car, and exhaled loudly, collapsed back into her seat, arms flopping by her sides. Amanda felt dizzy with relief. Yet it shouldn't come as a surprise, because Edward wasn't due home for at least an hour yet.

She drove through, slowly advancing along the drive-way, her eyes still scanning ahead, sweeping across the house in the near distance, to either side of it, and over the gardens. Watching, noting everything. It no longer felt the same. Suddenly her comfortable, safe, cosy refuge had changed. Ocean View House had taken on a malevolence, a prop in that scary movie she was living through, and it broke her heart. She could not see Edward's car – anywhere. She glanced at the clock in the centre of the console: 4:25. Of course, he was still at the hospital. He very rarely got home before six. But he must have been home at some stage during the day because he'd known she wasn't there, that time he had rung, fuming. He'd said he was at home, but had he been there? And then she remembered the computer, its webcam, the feeling she'd had of being watched the other day.

Was it possible? Could Edward have been watching her? Was that how he had known she wasn't there? And if so, were there other cameras in the house too? No, no, no, she thought, you're losing it. That's not possible. Edward would never do such a thing. If he was to, he would have done it well before now. Why wait?

She was almost at the house now. Her dark, heavy mind churned again, throwing out that memory... of that time. That one time. When he had hit her.

No, you fool, he's not going to do that again; of course not, he wouldn't dare. It was a once-off, a once-off, that's all.

But she could not remember a time when her husband had been as angry as he had been on the telephone earlier. He had scared her, really scared her. And if he had punched her that last time, what about now? He could do it again.

But he'll have calmed down, won't he? Yes, he will. Oh God, he will; please, please let him have calmed down.

She parked the car right next to the front door and got out, pausing again as she listened before striding over, placing the key into the lock, turning it, pushing the door open, standing there once more, listening again intently.

What was that? Had she just heard something? A breeze rustled the trees, and she realised it was just the groaning of the branches she had heard.

She stepped into the foyer. The house was still, quiet, empty... eerie. She didn't like this, being nervous and scared. This was her home. And Edward was her husband. She must not be scared of him, because essentially, he was a good man. Then she thought, sadly, of all that had been happening to her lately. She thought she was not being fair to him. Edward had no idea about any of it; he didn't know what was going on. She reached the staircase and started up it, heading for the office. At the top she crossed the landing and went to the office door, pushed it open, spotted a thick, heavy dictionary on the floor and pushed it against the door with her foot to hold it open. Then she walked across the room and...

Froze.

There was a sound, unmistakable, definitely not the trees swaying outside the window or anything else. The sound was inside the house. Inside the room. Inside this room. It was the sound of the dictionary sliding across the floor and then of the door closing. Still standing, frozen, unable to move, she attempted to rationalise it. Perhaps the dictionary hadn't been strong enough to hold the door open after all? But she knew it was; it weighed the same as a small bag of potatoes.

There was someone standing there. Behind her. She detected a scent and knew who it was. As she turned, she said his name, softly, soothingly, like she would to a child.

'Edward?'

He was dressed in a red polo shirt and beige cargo pants, white sneakers, leaning against the door. He caught her looking at his clothes and read her mind.

'Tuesday afternoon. Remember? I told you. Hospital director's talk on transparency in the delivery of primary care or some bullshit like that. I had a great excuse. I was worried about you. So I came home. As any good husband would do. But I chose to park my car behind the house, I just knew that would be a good idea, and it was. I saw you looking for it.'

He smiled, and she smiled in return. He didn't appear to be angry with her. She had been correct; his anger had dissipated, had exhausted itself. He came to her, opening his arms, about to embrace her. It was what she needed right now, more than anything else, reassurance from her husband that all would be alright, that they would be alright. She stepped towards him but noticed his arms had stopped extending; there was not enough space between them for her to fit. And then she noticed his hands turn upward, palms out, like the buffers of a train, and draw back before springing forward again, each catching her square on a shoulder, sending her sprawling backwards. She fell against something sharp and angular and knew it was the edge of the desk. Her body was at such an angle that for a moment she couldn't move, a ship floundering on rocks, as the tempest that was Edward approached.

'You've been treating me like a fool, haven't you?' His voice was like escaping steam.

'What...? Edward. Stop this. Edward! Please!'

He mimicked her. 'Stop this, Edward, please... Yes, you have been treating me like a fool, haven't you? The way you've been acting. A fever, you said. I even had Andrew O'Shaughnessy take a look at you, as if asking him wasn't embarrassing enough. But you didn't care. You lied. I'll stay home, you said. I won't go anywhere, you said. And then, what do you do?'

Amanda pushed herself from the table and stood.

'For God's sake, what's gotten into you, Edward? What? You're scaring me.'

'Good,' he said, taking a step closer so he was right in front of her. He grabbed her wrist and squeezed. 'Good,' he repeated. With his other hand he pressed the computer to life, brought up Google, typed awkwardly with an index finger, stabbed the return key. 'There. Take a look at this,' he said. 'You just have a look at this.'

He yanked on her hand, hard and sharp, spinning her around so she was looking at the computer, her confusion growing, seeing on the screen a frozen image: at the top the sky visible through overhanging tree branches, at the bottom glimpses of a stone wall running by a pavement next to a road, to the forefront a collection of cars – police cars – haphazardly abandoned. It was then she recognised the road; it was the one outside the King John Hotel, where she'd been stopped. And in the middle of the police vehicles was a lime green Mercedes. She recognised that too; it was her Mercedes.

He scrolled back the video bar to the beginning and pressed play, the screen coming to life. For a moment all appeared tranquil, the trees gently swaying, the rustling sound of the branches, birds singing. Then the sound of sirens – approaching fast. Her Mercedes entered right of screen, moving at a moderate pace as a police car overtook her, travelling very fast, and then she saw two other police cars behind her. One swooped out to the side of her while the other came up close behind, almost bumper to bumper. All the cars came to a stop at the opposite side of the screen, and there were the sounds of opening doors, running feet, and finally agitated voices yelling at her to get out of the vehicle, and, above it all, a female voice, shrill and piercing, 'The seat belt. The bloody seat belt's holding her in... Any sharp objects? Tell me!'

Someone had videoed the entire scene – the whole lot, everything, it was all there, her being stopped and dragged from the car – and had uploaded it to YouTube.

She felt sick. She stared at the screen, scarcely believing it as she watched herself being dragged from the car and plonked onto her arse on the roadway. She noticed a collection of numbers next to a variety of emojis, mostly of smiling faces with thumbs-up icons among them. The numbers represented the number of people who had already viewed the clip. It was 12,456. Really? And they had liked it? What? She couldn't help it as her eyes wandered to the comments box beneath. The first was enough:

> *Rich bitch drug dealer getting what she deserves. And she's a doctor I hear! Unbelievable. No sympathy! Lock her up! Throw away the key!*

'My God,' she muttered.

Edward spoke, his voice low, compressed. 'You know how hard I work? You know how much it took to get where I am? You know how much it takes every single day to hold on to the respect I've built up over the years, that I deserve. And you... you just go along and blow it all away. A drug dealer! A drug dealer! Now that, I'd never have expected. How dare you treat me like a fool. What have you been up to? What?'

He released his grip but swung his open palm through the air, about to strike her. Amanda turned away, cowering, waiting for what was to come.

'Don't even think of it,' the voice said.

She turned her head just as Edward snapped his towards the door too. Pri was standing in the doorway.

'Good job I decided to come over. I was worried about you, and rightly so.'

Edward's demeanour immediately changed, his arm

fell to his side, and his head dropped, shoulders folding. He said nothing for a moment, and the only sound was that of Amanda's frantic breathing, like a bellows on damp kindling.

He smiled, his professional smile, his mask. 'Pri. Ah, look, Pri, this is not what it looks like, not at all, a domestic issue, that's all; everything's fine. Now, will you please leave us to deal with it. Tell her everything is alright, Amanda. Go on, darling.'

'Amy?' Pri said, the word a question mark.

Both women stared at one another. The seconds dripped by in a loud, screeching silence, so loud Amanda wanted to clamp her ears shut against it. She turned to her husband, her eyes lingering on him, giving nothing away.

'No, Edward,' she said finally. 'Everything is not fine. It hasn't been fine for a long time, if ever. I can't stay here any longer. I'm leaving.'

Edward attempted to pull back his shoulders and straighten himself, hoisting up his head a couple of inches.

'What nonsense are you talking about now?'

'I can't put up with it any longer, that's what I'm talking about. And don't tell me you don't know what I mean. I've had enough.'

'I-I don't know what you mean. I don't. And look around you. What could be wrong? You have everything here. This house. Look at it. Everything is here. Tell me what's wrong.'

Amanda dropped her gaze to the floor. 'It's not about that, for God's sake. You just tried to hit me.' And looking up again. 'Think of that. And you ask me what could be wrong?'

His eyes flared. 'I didn't. You're mistaken. I don't hit

women. I've never hit a woman in my life.' He threw his hands into the air. 'I'm not a, a... wife beater.' He glared at her. 'In any case, well, if that's what you want, then go ahead.' His arm shot up as he pointed. 'There's the door... leave, go on, get out.'

'Wait.' Pri came and stood next to Amanda. 'Why should she leave? You leave. Go on. You get out. I witnessed what you just did. And I'll make a statement to that effect. If the police were to come here, that's what they would do. They'd request you to leave, and if that didn't work, they'd make you leave.' She stabbed a finger at him. 'You. Are. The. Aggressor. You get out.'

Edward laughed aloud, and his expression became a sneer. The real Edward, lurking beneath the thin veneer of respectability that he'd been hiding behind all these years. 'Good God, woman, if they were to remove me, I'd be back in the morning. Don't you know that? Are you that stupid? They have no powers to remove me from this house permanently. This is my home.' He snapped his fingers. 'What? You thought they could? Just like that? Honestly!'

He turned and looked at Amanda.

'Come on. Enough of this nonsense. I'm sorry, okay. I don't want you to leave. Tell Pri everything is fine. We'll sort this out ourselves, like we always do.'

Amanda was silent for a moment, then shook her head.

'No,' she said softly. 'I'll leave. For now. But this is only for now, Edward. And I'll be back after you've gone. God, how did I put up with you for so long? How? I ask myself.' She clicked her fingers. 'But no longer.'

Edward went instantly pale.

'You can't leave, you can't, not really.'

'Can't I? Just watch me.'

'But you can't,' he spluttered. 'You can't because I forbid it. I don't give you permission. I am your husband. Listen to me. You do as I say. Me. You can't.'

Then Amanda did something that took even her by surprise. She burst out laughing, releasing some of the tension of the recent days. Edward squirmed. She had recognised something in his voice that she had never heard before, a pleading.

'You're pathetic,' she said, 'all this time, the snide remarks, the put-downs, the gentle asides. Oh, nothing like what you did that one time when you punched me and would have done so again just now if...'

Edward looked at Pri.

'I never hit her,' he said, his voice a whine. 'I never—'

'Don't,' Amanda cut him off. 'Don't you dare deny it. You did. You know you did. We both know you did. But fool me once, shame on you; fool me twice, shame on me. You've been punching me for years, verbally that is, nothing I could ring up about and complain; there were no bruises after all, physical that is, never enough to make me realise for certain what you were doing, but just enough to have me doubt myself, blame myself, have me always think it was my fault. You absolute manipu—'

'And that's my fault too, is it,' he snapped suddenly, like he had to get the last word in. 'Getting stopped by the police was my fault too? Getting dragged from your car and searched like that? That was me too, was it?'

'How do I know? Maybe it was? I would never have thought you were nasty enough to do it before, but I do now.'

'Who the hell are you?' he yelled. 'I don't know you. I don't think I ever knew you. Like I say, if you want to leave, then go.' He pointed once more. 'There's the door. Go on. You... you... bitch. Go!'

'That make you feel better, does it?' she shouted back. 'Telling me to leave, insulting me, gives you some control, does it? Ordering me out of my own house? I'm leaving, but of my own accord, don't make any mistake about that, and like I said, I'll be back; that's a guarantee.' She turned to Pri. 'I'm sorry you had to hear and see all this, Pri. Will you come with me while I gather a few things?'

'Of course I will. What? Did you think I was going to leave you alone?' She nodded. 'All alone, with him? I don't think so.'

Edward's eyes narrowed; he opened his mouth, like he was about to say something, but then closed it again. Amanda looked at him, at the silent pleading in his eyes, the boyish, lost expression, and felt her determination wilt. Had she been too hasty? Edward seemed to sense her crumbling resolve, but then something passed behind his eyes, something she couldn't be certain of, a smugness maybe, but something she didn't like.

'Come on,' she said to Pri, 'let's go.'

25

P ri had insisted that she come stay with her for a while, and she followed her old Jag now in the Mercedes. Pri's home was an ultra-modern glass and steel flat-roofed structure overlooking the River Corrib on the western edge of Galway City. Pri and her husband, Liam, had one child, Marie, currently on a year-long working visa in Australia. Liam was an ecologist and obsessed with all things environmental. He had built the house himself. Amanda drove along the driveway behind Pri to the parking area at the back of the property. Behind that was a small wind turbine – still twice as tall as the house – which, coupled with solar roof panels, provided much of their electricity. The property was straight out of the pages of a Nordic sustainable living magazine, except it was in the west of Ireland. A small orange car was plugged into an electric charging point just down from Amanda by a log woodshed. Despite everything, Amanda allowed herself a small smile. The differences between Pri and her husband could not have been wider and were not hard to spot.

'I rang and told him to get the spare room ready,' Pri said as Amanda got out of her car.

Amanda noted Pri had not even bothered to use her husband's name.

She walked quickly to the rear of the Mercedes, opened the boot.

'I took only what could fit in this,' she said, hoisting out a black roller bag and dropping it onto the ground.

'An excuse to go shopping, then,' Pri said with a laugh, 'out with the old and in with the new.'

Amanda didn't, couldn't, laugh.

'Sorry,' Pri said. 'I know it's not easy; just trying to lighten the load, that's all.'

Amanda looked ahead to the cube-style house. For the first time in her life she had no home to go to. She felt tears well in her eyes as Pri stepped over and wrapped an arm around her.

'Come on inside; you'll feel better,' she said.

'I need to speak with the kids. Before Edward does. To explain being stopped by the guards, everything.'

'Can't it wait?'

Amanda shook her head. 'No, Pri, it can't.'

'Come on then, let's go inside.' She led her towards the house.

The spare bedroom was large and airy, with a bay window that looked out over the river. She was surprised to see Liam out there. He was chopping wood on the other side of the shed, tall and gangly, a mop of dirty, receding blond hair tied back in a ponytail. She sat on the cushioned stool at the dresser by the window and switched on her phone. Her belly tightened as she looked at it, at the multiple missed calls from Edward, fifteen voice messages, as well as calls from Lauren and Danny. But mercifully, nothing else. She didn't listen to any, instead deleted them all. She took a deep breath, brought up Danny's number, pressed call. She spent the next half hour talking to each of her children in turn. She was pleasantly surprised they both accepted her explanation, because their mother being dragged from her car and searched for drugs was so alien, so out there, it could only be the result of a terrible mix-up. Either that or they were too much in shock to express themselves properly. Or perhaps it was a mixture of both. She explained that she was no longer at home and would not be for the foreseeable future either. Danny sounded relieved. 'Best news I've heard in ages,' he said. 'Should have done that years ago, Mum, like I told you. You were never happy, not really. I love Dad, y'know, but still, I think you two are better off apart.'

How prescient, she had thought. She really had underestimated her son.

'As for the YouTube video,' he added, 'hard core, Mum. You rock, girl.'

'Danny, that's not funny.'

'I know, I know. But don't you worry about it, Mum. And I'll see if I can't have it taken down.'

'Really?'

'Yeah, I know a fella had something taken down. I'll talk to him.'

Amanda didn't ask any further questions because she didn't want to know.

She finished with Danny and rang her daughter. But with Lauren it was a different story. She was the apple of her dad's eye, and they'd always been close. The silence when she told her lingered.

'Lauren,' Amanda said, 'please talk to me.'

'I love you, Mum,' she said then. 'But I also love Dad. I hate this. Is it temporary? Please tell me it is.'

Now it was Amanda who was silent, and when she told her the truth, that it probably wasn't, Lauren began to cry, which broke her heart, and as she began to try to reassure her, her daughter spoke. 'Not now, Mother,' she said, 'I don't want to talk anymore,' and the line went dead.

Amanda stared ahead, but could see nothing, too worried about her daughter, thinking, What have I done?

She had slumped low on the stool, and she hurriedly pushed herself upright and fixed her skirt, ran a hand through her hair, thinking of all the reasons why she was here: the note, the message on her computer, being stopped by the police and dragged from her car, the YouTube posting, the confrontation with Edward... and further back, way back, believing that this was all connected... to that one night.

26

BEFORE...

It was a Friday, and for the first time since that night, they both had the weekend off. But it didn't matter. Because it was gone. The laughter they had shared, the laughter that had signalled something else, their friendship. Gone. Amanda and Fiona hardly spoke now. Indeed, Amanda could scarcely bring herself to even look at her. She felt Fiona had abandoned her that night, left her to her fate.

Their apartment was quite large, in a wing of the hospital reserved for student doctors, but with the elephant in the room now living there as well, there was hardly any room left for them to move about, let alone breathe. They both knew it. And the elephant continued to grow, getting bigger and bigger, and still Amanda pretended that everything was as it should be, when it would never be the same ever again.

She carried her small bag of groceries and placed them on the countertop in the kitchen. The apartment felt different somehow too. There was a silence about the place, an empty silence. She stood still, listening for any sound. She had dreaded this weekend, a part of her feeling that, alone together, Fiona would bring up the subject. Fiona was always the more open, studying psychiatry as she was, and Amanda thought she was just biding her time, waiting for the right moment to talk.

She noticed the telephone answering machine blinking. She went over and pressed 'play'. The tinny sound of Fiona's voice came from the speaker.

'Amanda, I've left Dublin, and I won't be back. I know this will come as somewhat of a shock, okay, it's quite a big shock, but I had to get away. I've been transferred to Limerick. I would have talked to you about it, about everything, you know what I mean, but I know you don't want to; you don't want to even mention it. You can't even bring yourself to look at me, can you? It's painful for me too, Amanda, just so you know. Avoiding something doesn't make it go away, you know. Please hear me on that. If you don't deal with this, it will stay with you forever. I know something happened to you. I feel certain it's the same as what happened to me. I really need to deal with this, so I have started seeing a counsellor. That is what the officer recommended when I reported it. It wasn't a nice experience. But it was worth it. I really wanted to talk to you about it, but I could tell that you didn't. I understand. But it doesn't make it easier, for both of us. I've left. Maybe you think I've deserted you, but I would never do that. Get help, Amanda. Report it. At least talk to someone about it. You need to, believe me.'

The message ended, and Amanda stood staring at the phone.

The same had happened to Fiona. The news hit Amanda like a tsunami, literally almost knocking her over. She realised she'd been too caught up in her own turmoil to even consider that something might have happened to Fiona too. But she did now and knew it wasn't just her.

She pressed the delete button on the answering machine and wiped the message – just like that, gone, wishing it was just as easy to erase her own memory. She considered what Fiona had said, that she knew what had happened to her. Amanda shuddered.

27

S he stared ahead, unable to believe that her past had come back to haunt her, unable to move, sitting at the dresser in the spare bedroom of Pri's house.

How was that possible? How?

That everything – her life – had turned to this – so quickly? Did she deserve it all? Was it all her fault? But she knew too, this was not the time for self-pity. This was the time when she needed to be strong.

She ran her tongue over her dry lips as a light knock sounded at the door.

'Yes.'

The door opened, and Pri was standing there, clutching an enormous mug. She smiled. 'Tea, with a drop of something in it.' She crossed to Amanda and placed the mug on the dresser. 'And,' she added, 'whenever you want to talk, I'm here.'

Amanda nodded. 'I know.'

'Right. I'll leave you to settle in.' She turned to leave again. 'You come down when you're ready.'

'Pri?'

'Yes, honey?'

'Thank you. I mean it.'

'I know you do. But you don't need to thank me. I know you'd do the same for me if the shoe were on the other foot.' She smiled and left the room, closing the door gently behind her.

A little later, in the kitchen, Liam's sandals made a flopping noise as he moved about the large room, washing his home-grown vegetables at the sink, moving to the granite worktop, chopping them finely, then to the cooker, piling them into a huge frying pan. He presented his offering a little later, still in the pan, which he set down on the table on a thick wicker coaster.

'It's called Liam's Special,' he said with a smile. 'Just made that up, by the way. Hope you like it.'

Pri threw her eyes heavenward. 'Cringe time,' she said. 'Vegetarian, I suppose?'

He picked up a bottle of wine and began to peel away the foil seal. 'Well, yes, that's okay, isn't it?'

'It'll have to be,' she said, looking at Amanda. 'This is the latest fad, vegetarian.'

'Excuse me,' Liam said, positioning the corkscrew onto the top of the bottle and turning it. 'I've been vegetarian a couple of years now, at least.'

'Oh, how time flies when you're having fun,' Pri said. Liam began to fill her glass. She lifted it and took a long sip. 'Not.'

He said nothing, pouring two more glasses, scooping food onto a plate and passing it to Amanda.

'What do you think?' he said a little later as she ate, looking at her.

'Lovely, really nice,' she replied, swallowing. In fact, it

was delicious, but she couldn't bring herself to say it, not with Pri sitting there silent, picking at her plate.

'And there's loads more,' he added, 'so don't be shy; help yourself.'

Pri refilled her glass, leaving the bottle empty. She got up and brought over another, held it out to Liam.

'Open Sesame,' she said.

Liam hesitated before taking it, long enough to stir something in Pri.

'What? You have a problem with me having another glass of wine now, do you?' She glanced at Amanda. 'What goes on behind closed doors, eh, Amy, you'd never guess. Hope we're not embarrassing you, sweetie?'

'No, of course not.' But actually, it was making her feel a little uneasy.

'I don't think it's me who's embarrassing anybody,' Liam said, twisting his hand around the neck of the bottle. 'Here, it's a twist off; didn't you notice?'

Pri glared at him before snatching the bottle and refilling her glass and, like it was an afterthought, held up the bottle. 'Anyone else?'

Amanda shook her head while Liam just stared at his plate. They finished eating in an awkward silence; then Liam got up and began to clear the table. Amanda started to push back her chair, about to help him, but he shook his head.

'I got it, Amy; it's fine, really.' He smiled, and again Amanda wondered what the problem was with this marriage.

It was getting dark outside, and she suddenly felt very tired. Tomorrow was a busy day. Somehow she needed to get her head in order. Amanda noticed the wine bottle was already empty. Pri had drank it all herself.

'You look tired, sweetie,' Pri said. Amanda noticed her
friend's eyes were beginning to drift, like little buoys
breaking free from their anchors.

'I'm working tomorrow,' she said. 'I'm scared about it. I
don't know what to expect.'

Pri waved a hand through the air. 'It'll be fine, sweetie,
you'll see.'

Amanda lowered her voice. 'I told you my car was
searched, but I never said if they found anything. They
did. And if it turns out to be drugs, I could be struck off
the medical register.'

'No. They have to prove it's yours first,' Pri said and
added cheekily, 'It's not, is it?'

'Of course it's not. This is serious, Pri...'

'I know it's serious. Very serious. That woman,
Fiona...'

'Yes.'

'Well, she sounds like a right loola, doesn't she? You
said she was there, watching, when you were stopped.
Really?'

Amanda nodded. 'Yes. Really. And later, outside the
station. She ran after me; there was something in her
hand.'

'Like a knife?' Pri's wine glass was almost empty again,
her voice rising.

'Maybe.'

'Jesus Christ.' Pri quickly blessed herself. 'You could
still report it, you know.'

Amanda shook her head emphatically. 'No. I just won't
contact her again. That was a mistake.'

'And what,' Pri said, a shrillness to her tone, 'you think
that'll do it, that'll be enough? She'll just go away and
leave you in peace? I have a bad feeling about this, Amy. I

have to tell you, I really do. I don't think she's just going to go away that easily. Sorry.'

'I have to be able to hope. I have to have that, don't I?'

'I still think you should report it,' Pri said, draining her glass.

'Report what, exactly? Remember, they think I'm a drug dealer. Anyway, no. I can't.'

'Because of this bloody secret. You said you'd tell me when you were ready. It must be some bloody secret, Amy, sorry. You didn't kill anyone, did you?'

'Of course not,' she said, getting to her feet. 'I need to get to bed. You're very good to let me stay, but I'll sort something a little more permanent in the next couple of days.'

'No, you won't. You have enough on your plate as it is. You stay here as long as you want. End of.'

I don't think so, Pri, she thought. I can't listen to you and Liam endlessly sniping at one another. And something else is making me uncomfortable – your drinking.

'Thanks again for everything, Pri,' she said, trying not to let her expression show how she truly felt. 'I'll see you in the morning.'

She leant down and kissed her friend on the cheek, the smell of red wine pungent and sour. When this was over, they needed to have a talk.

28

The next morning, Amanda was already awake when the dawn light finally crept into the room, dissolving the black into a drab translucent grey. She'd been awake for hours, tossing and turning. Her eyes were sore and tender, her head heavy, and she felt utterly exhausted. What if I were to just lie here and not get up? she thought. Like, ever again. What would happen then? After a few days, she guessed, an ambulance would be summoned, and she'd be taken to a hospital, and then, later still, she'd likely be transferred somewhere else, to a nursing home perhaps. She liked the idea of a nursing home because she'd be safe in there; she'd be looked after; everything would be provided for her; she wouldn't have to worry about anything.

She pulled back the duvet, dismissing the absurd thought, turned and plonked her feet onto the floor, standing awkwardly, then shuffling to the en suite. Standing over the sink, she turned on the cold water tap, dipped a finger into the flow and ran it over her eyes. They stung, and when she opened them again, the water clung to her eyelids like a viscous invisible cobweb.

Amanda returned to the room and squinted at her watch on the dresser; it was just gone six o'clock. Lack of sleep accentuated her already fraught emotions and stirred up the darkest of thoughts, telling her everything was useless, her marriage was over, and this was all her fault. The past had come back to haunt her, seeking revenge, and overall her life was a battle she could no longer wage. But she knew this was merely tiredness and fatigue talking, and pushed the thoughts away, instead concentrating on her breathing, on the silence of the room, on the beating of her heart, gradually resettling her emotional core. It was more than enough to have to deal with the here and now, she told herself, just this very moment.

It was too early to stay up, she considered. If she ran the shower, the sound might wake Pri and Liam. Likewise if she went downstairs to make a cup of coffee. These were what one had to consider when in someone else's house. She lay down on the bed again and closed her eyes, not imagining for one moment that she might actually sleep. And because she was no longer chasing it, that was exactly what happened; she began to drift off.

She dreamed. In it she could hear a knocking sound, it was not very loud, but still, there was no doubting its insistence. With it came a voice, one she recognised as Pri's, that said, 'Amy, is everything alright in there? Are you getting up today?'

Amanda's eyes snapped open. It wasn't a dream. It was real. It was Pri knocking on the bedroom door.

'W-what? Pri? What time is it? Come in. Come in.'

The door opened.

'It's half past eight, Amy,' she said, entering the room. 'Aren't you supposed to be working this morning?'

'Half past eight,' Amanda practically shouted. 'I have to be at the clinic in half an hour. My God.'

She jumped from the bed, heading for the shower.

'Anything I can do to help?' Pri asked.

'No,' Amanda called over her shoulder, 'this'll take me five minutes. I'll see you downstairs.'

When Amanda got to the kitchen, Pri was sitting at the table, a steaming mug in front of her.

'Would you like some breakfast?' Pri asked. 'I can get you something.' But she made no attempt to move. Amanda noticed that her eyes were bloodshot and her complexion pale.

'No time. I'll grab something later.'

She wasn't hungry anyway. She wasn't anything. The frantic rush to get ready had pushed everything to the side, and although it was no doubt temporary, Amanda was glad for the diversion. Workaholics would understand that logic, she assumed: too busy to feel the pain.

She smoothed down her tweed knee-length skirt and adjusted the matching jacket, complemented with a cream blouse and brown, patent leather pumps. She was about to ask Pri if she looked okay, but Pri was staring blankly into her mug.

Amanda pulled back a chair and sat down. Work could wait. This was more important.

'Is everything alright, honey?' she asked, realising she'd been so caught up in her own problems that she hadn't considered what Pri might be going through. She reached out and rested her hand on the back of Pri's.

Pri looked up and gave a weak smile. 'I have a hang-over, you won't be surprised to hear. I drink too much, and then I end up being depressed and feeling sorry for myself, wondering why I bothered to drink in the first place. But I keep doing it. I'm on a loop. Anyway, I'll survive. You get to work, Amanda; you'll be late. Unfortunately, I'm used to this.'

'You want to talk about it?'

'Maybe, but not now. Get to work.'

'If you're sure.'

'I'm sure. Scoot.'

Amanda stood, bent down, kissed the top of Pri's head, grabbed her handbag and headed for the door.

'See you later,' she called as she opened it. 'And Pri...'

'Yes.'

'I'm grateful to have you as a friend. Thank you.'

Pri raised a hand and twiddled her fingers, looking up. 'Me too, Amy. Now, go get 'em, tiger. See ya later.' But her voice was a flat monotone.

As Amanda closed the door, she couldn't help but wonder just what exactly her friend did all day.

When she met her first set of red traffic lights a little later, all she could think about was how late she was running. Her eyes kept straying to the dashboard clock, as if this were going to speed things along. It didn't; instead it seemed to slow everything down. Her anxiety was like a fizzing, damp firework inside her. She asked herself: Am I crazy going back to work? I haven't fully thought this through, have I? Understandable though, isn't it? What with everything that's been happening. But I should have at least rung Layla, got a heads-up on my schedule for the day. I didn't even do that. I thought I'd be on time, thought I'd be able to go through it all just before I started. Now look at me. I'm running late, nothing done. How unprofessional is this going to look?

The light changed to green, but she didn't notice. A car behind honked its horn, snapping her from her thoughts, and she revved the engine and darted forward. She fumbled with her phone, dialled the White Rock Medical Clinic and switched to speakerphone, listened to the hollow echo as it rang. Layla should be there by now, her starting time was 8:30, and it was now 8:55. Still, her call went unanswered.

Ten minutes later, at 9:05, she rushed through the revolving door of White Rock Medical Clinic. She passed the main security desk and walked quickly along a corridor to her clinic suite. All medical suites were on the ground floor for ease of access. As she pushed open the door, she could see Layla's head bowed behind the desk, her long blonde hair like golden brush strokes. She went to the desk and stood before it, feeling awkward and nervous. She told herself she didn't need to feel this way. Layla was her secretary, not the other way round. She coughed, feeling a little pathetic.

Layla looked up lazily, her eyes settling on Amanda, unable to hide her surprise, her expression like she'd just spotted an overcharge on her Tesco receipt. But still, her cherry red lipsticked lips – which Amanda had always thought too garish for daytime wear but never said anything about – stretched and raised themselves at the corners to give a half smile. But nothing else smiled; the eyes remained the same. Still, Amanda thought, she's smiling, that's something.

Just then, she heard the door of her surgery open behind her. She turned. A man emerged, mid-thirties, she guessed, dressed in grey slacks and an open-neck white shirt. He smiled as he approached the desk, leaned over it to speak with Layla. Amanda couldn't help but stare at what he wore around his neck: a stethoscope. She realised her mouth had dropped open, and quickly closed it again.

'I've a little time,' he said to Layla. 'I'm going to the canteen; be back in a couple of minutes. You want anything?'

'No, thank you, Dr Farrell,' Layla replied, folding her lips into a smile so wide Amanda thought, a little guiltily, that she looked like a horse. As Dr Farrell walked away, her smile receded as she turned to Amanda. 'I'm sorry, Dr Jackson. I was told you weren't coming back until next week. Dr Farrell is the locum sent to cover you.'

Amanda tried not to show her hurt and anger as she took in this news. 'I gathered as much, Layla,' she said with false calm. 'Who told you I was back next week, by the way?'

'Oh, Mr O'Dowd, of course.'

The clinic's director. Amanda could not betray her surprise this time, however.

'Layla,' she said, 'you've seen the YouTube video, I take it. Haven't you?'

Layla looked away, dropping her head, and Amanda was staring at the golden brush strokes again.

'Yes,' she said without looking up, 'everyone has, Dr Jackson.'

'Just so's you know, it's not true. I would never have anything to do with drugs. Anyone who asks, you can tell them that from me.'

Layla looked up now. But her expression had not changed. She was still looking at her Tesco receipt.

'Yes, Dr Jackson, of course.' Her tone was uncertain. She seemed to realise it and quickly added, with a flicker of a smile, 'I mean, of course it's not true.'

'Thank you, Layla,' Amanda said, turning. She strode

out of the surgery, feeling Layla's eyes burning into her back.

The management and operational offices were on the third and top floor of the White Rock, with wall-to-wall glass offering panoramic views across the city. Amanda reported at the reception desk and asked to see Mark O'Dowd. She was told to take a seat and wait. She sat on a bright red fabric chair at a coffee table loaded with glossy magazines, focusing on her breathing, pushing back against her anxiety. She had been to the director's office a mere handful of times in her ten years at the clinic, once when offered the job after having been headhunted from general practice, and a few times afterwards for a variety of mundane, work-related reasons. But nothing like this. Fifteen minutes went by before Mrs Winters, Mark O'Dowd's secretary, emerged from a corridor to the side of reception, heading her way.

'Hello, Dr Jackson,' she said with a beaming smile, stopping before her. Unlike Layla, Amanda could not detect any sign of reserve or suspicion. But then, Mrs Winters had enough experience to be adept at hiding it, unlike the much younger Layla. 'Mr O'Dowd will see you now.'

Amanda stood, forgetting she'd been cradling her handbag in her lap. It fell, tumbling to the floor. She'd also forgotten to close the zipper, so the contents spilled out onto the mauve-coloured carpet patterned with the White Rock Medical Clinic logo of a two-tone blue and white medical cross inside a black circle.

'Oh, my God,' she said, bending, 'sorry, sorry.' She righted the bag, began scooping the contents up and placing them back inside, and stood. The effort made her dizzy, which she knew was a combination of having not eaten that morning coupled with her general tiredness. The room momentarily lurched. She felt something on her arm, realised it was Mrs Winters's hand steadying her. Amanda took a breath, closing her eyes, waited a moment, then opened them again, the dizzy spell having passed.

Confusion pushed through the secretary's mask now, and Amanda could see a certain wariness mixed in there too.

'Are you alright?' she asked.

No, I'm not alright, isn't it obvious?

'Yes, thank you, yes, just, whooo, low blood sugar, I suppose. I haven't eaten, you see.'

'Oh... well, if you're sure.'

'I'm sure.'

'This way, then, Dr Jackson.'

Mark O'Dowd was standing by the window of his office when she went in. The office was huge, taking up a corner of the building. It was an in-house joke that most of the photographs on the wall were of himself. Which was true. He turned, looking at her, dressed in a shirt so white it seemed to reflect the light from the fluorescent bulbs overhead, accentuating his year-round permatan, which probably was the whole idea. He indicated a chair on the other side of his desk, and she crossed the room and sat in it. He remained standing for a moment, then stepped behind the desk and leaned forward onto it, peering down at her, like she was an exhibit of some sort, she considered. She took a slow, deep breath, ignoring him.

'Dr Jackson,' he said, like an announcement. 'Amanda, what brings you in here today, if I may ask?'

He'd spent some years in America, and his vowels in places were slow and stretched.

'To work. It's Wednesday, Mark. I'm due back today... well, am I not?'

He pushed himself upright and slid into his seat.

'No, actually, you're not.' He ran a hand through his thick grey hair. He was mid-fifties, but that grey hair still ringed his head like a miniature forest. 'I' – he stabbed a button on his desktop computer keyboard, stabbed it again three or four more times – 'have it right here. Dr Amanda Jackson will not be returning until further notice. HR will speak to her later, and further details to follow.' His gaze shifted from the monitor to her. 'Right there, from HR. I mean... I've had to arrange a locum, which is costing over two and a half thousand a week, by the way, but no matter.' He paused, his eyebrows knitting together. 'I have to tell you, Amanda, this is highly unorthodox. Why would you think you'd work today? And the, um, I have to mention it, that YouTube video. I know about it. We all do. In light of it, I think it's best, anyway, that you not return to work at the moment, for the foreseeable future at least, until things settle down.'

'Really.' She'd actually forgotten about the video, just for a brief moment. 'What do you mean?'

'Exactly what I just said. That it's best you're not here at the moment. People want to have complete faith in our medical staff; you can understand that surely, can't you?'

His words stung. 'And you mean they won't, not if I'm around, is that it? But I'm innocent; doesn't that count for anything, anything at all? I've done nothing wrong. My patients can have complete faith in me.'

'We'll see,' he said.

Amanda couldn't believe it. Is that what it boiled down to? We'll see. Her ten years of unblemished record at the

White Rock could be summed up with nothing more than that: We'll see.

'By the way,' he added, 'I've ordered an audit of all your prescriptions issued over the past twelve months... Just a precaution, you understand.'

For the first time, she felt it stirring inside her: anger.

'No, I don't understand. What, you think I've been writing out prescriptions, is that it? And for what, and for whom exactly? For myself, you mean?'

He said it again. 'We'll see.'

'Yes,' she said, getting to her feet, 'we will. We will see. When you're proven wrong, as you will be. I have options, just so's you know.'

His forehead creased. 'Meaning?'

'You know what I mean. You're questioning my reputation. That to me is everything; it's sacrosanct. I will defend myself. You don't need me to tell you how.'

He forced a smile. 'Come on, there's no need for that, Amanda. Amanda. Amanda. How's Edward, by the way?'

'Edward, what's he got to do with anything?'

'Have you spoken to him about any of it at all?' He leaned forward. 'Look' – his voice almost a whisper – 'there's no easy way to say this; you're ill, Amanda. Lauren, your daughter, said so when she made the initial phone call... and now, it's very obvious, your mem...' But his voice trailed off.

'Sorry, Mark, my what? You didn't finish.'

'Okay, Amanda. Your memory, that's what I was going to say.'

'What?' she said, her voice rising sharply.

'Can't you remember?'

'Remember?'

'The telephone call?'

'Please' – a pleading in her voice that she hated – 'what are you talking about?'

'Ask yourself, why would I say you weren't returning to work until further notice? Where would I have gotten that from? Would I have just made it up?'

'This isn't a quiz, Mark; just tell me.'

'Right, I will, because you clearly won't, because you don't know. Which, I have to say, proves my point. It was you who rang HR. It was you who said you wouldn't be returning until further notice. It was you, Amanda. You.'

She opened her mouth, but nothing came out of it. She was speechless.

AMANDA COULD NOT REMEMBER a time in her professional life when she'd felt as humiliated. Even as a junior doctor, subject to the whims and moods of bad-tempered consultants and patients, she'd never felt the way she did now.

'Me,' she repeated, 'but that's impossible. I didn't make any telephone call.'

'You can listen back if you want?'

But she didn't want to do that. It would prove nothing. Someone had rung posing as her. That much was apparent. What she wanted was to get away from here as quickly as possible. She stood.

'I can't stand this any longer,' she said. 'I've got to get out of here.'

She left the office without another word, walked out of the clinic in a daze, feeling nothing but the searing heat of that humiliation, which clung to her, burning deep into her soul like napalm.

There was a heavy downpour, shimmering sheets of rain. But she was immune to it, to everything; nothing could penetrate that searing heat of humiliation. As she reached the car and raised the key fob to open it, her eyes fell on what looked like a small grey rag beneath a wiper, the rain sticking it to the windscreen. A sudden, powerful, invisible jolt pushed her, snapping her mind back into the present. The rain cascaded down her face, dripping into her eyes, making her blink. She stepped closer and raised the wiper, realised it wasn't a rag beneath it at all, but a rectangle of saturated cardboard. She peeled it away from the glass, held it by the corners gingerly. Part of her wanted to cast it aside, to allow the rain to disintegrate and wash it away, but she found her hands switching the edges, turning the piece of paper until it was facing her, and she could read the words, the letters resting within cobwebs of smudged ink lines, each one cutting into her as surely as a sharpened blade. Four words:

I KNOW YOUR SECRET.

29

B efore...

AMANDA SAT OUTSIDE on one of the hard wooden benches just down from the staff entrance to the hospital. It was an unusually hot, muggy August afternoon, but the benches had been placed beneath an overhang that offered shade. The aroma of cigarette smoke drifted up to her from a bunch of nurses sitting a couple of benches away. Work had become her refuge from the madness of that night. Sometimes, even at the end of a crushing twelve-hour shift, she didn't want to leave the hospital, didn't want to go home.

'There you are.'

She looked up. Dr Rae Brennan was standing there. The small, petite gynaecologist with an abundance of perfectly coiffured blonde hair sat down beside her.

'It's positive. You'll want to know that immediately. I

just got the result. Looks like you're four weeks gone, Amanda.'

Amanda released a long sigh and sat back, resting her head against the concrete wall behind her. She stared ahead, but saw nothing. The whoop of a particularly loud siren yanked her back into the present.

'I thought so,' she said. 'I didn't want to believe the home pregnancy test. I prayed it was wrong.' She lowered her voice. 'Please, I don't want anyone to know about this. This is strictly between the two of us.'

Dr Brennan raised an eyebrow. 'Come on, you think I'd mention it? I'm a doctor; you're a doctor; you know I can't mention this to anybody, not a living soul.'

Amanda gave a weak smile. Dr Brennan wrapped her arms around her.

'How do you feel? Are you happy with this?'

'No,' Amanda said, beginning to sob, 'I'm not. This is the worst news I could ever get. I'm not ready to have a baby, even if I wanted one.'

She felt Dr Brennan's hands on her shoulders, gently nudging her back so that she could look into her eyes.

'This can be the best time of your life if you want it to be. You have a life inside you, and that's more precious than anything. The number of couples I see every day, heartbroken because it just doesn't happen for them. Sometimes for no reason whatsoever. It's just the way it is, okay? You've got a life inside you...'

'A life that I don't want to bring into the world. A life that was...'

She didn't finish.

'Is there something you want to tell me, Amanda?' Dr Brennan said gently.

Amanda held out her hand, and Dr Brennan took it.

The gynaecologist had been nothing more than a work colleague until now. But one she felt she could trust. Now she had become a friend.

'Just thank you,' Amanda said, 'from the bottom of my heart.'

Dr Brennan smiled. 'You tell him yet?'

'Who?'

'Your boyfriend, of course.'

Amanda shook her head. 'O-oh, n-no, not yet.'

'Well, maybe you should think about it. Listen, I've got to get back. Remember, if you need anything, anything at all, you just shout.'

The gynaecologist gave her a long, searching look. Amanda forced a smile. 'Thank you, I will.'

Dr Brennan got to her feet. 'See you later.'

'Yes, see you later.'

She watched her walk away as a desperate plan began to form in her mind.

Later that evening she rang Edward.

'Yes.'

She could tell immediately by his tone that he was being cool with her.

'I'm sorry, Edward, I haven't been in touch. It's been mad busy... how are you?'

'It's been a while,' he began, and said nothing more for a moment, no doubt allowing that to sink in, 'since I last heard from you. It must be, oh, all of a month. Do you remember? Or had you forgotten? Oh yes, you must be really busy.'

Amanda remembered alright. How could she forget? A glass of wine he'd said, just one, at his place. 'Okay.' But when it was obvious nothing more was going to happen, because nothing was ever going to happen with Edward, ever, she'd decided on that, he'd pouted his lips and sulked, as only Edward could. And then she'd asked herself that question: What the hell am I doing with this man?

Now she was in a blind panic. Now she didn't care. Now she needed him. But he must never know, could never know, the truth.

'I'm sorry,' she said, 'I really am. And of course I hadn't forgotten. How could I? I won't let it happen again. Did you miss me?'

'Aha,' he said, 'is that what it was? A means to test if I missed you? Well, juvenile as it sounds, that does make sense, I suppose.'

'Yes,' Amanda said immediately, grabbing the lifeline. 'I'm sorry, I was being childish. I just wanted to see if you'd miss me. I'm sorry, Edward, I really am, but I wanted to see if you thought about me as much as I think about you. I just needed to be certain.'

There was a soft, dull sound on the line, and she realised he was laughing.

'What?' she said. 'Why are you laughing?'

'It's okay, Amanda, I'll indulge you. I'll go along with your little game. Yes, I have missed you. Of course. So there.'

'Oh, Edward.'

'But you're not to do this again, you hear? I forbid it. And all this talk of being casual, come on now.'

'Of course. I'm so sorry to have upset you; please, it won't happen again. But the truth is...'

'Yes, the truth is...?'

'I've been missing you so much.'

There was a short pause.

'And I've been missing you.' A sudden husky eagerness crept into his voice as he added, 'Meet me, then, Amanda, will you, soon?'

'Yes,' she answered.

'The Templeton Hotel? Tell me when you're free?'

'How about right now?'

30

She drove from the clinic, taking the route to Salthill, the seaside suburb of Galway City, without any will on her part, as if she were on autopilot. When she got there, she sat on a bench in an isolated shelter along the rocky shoreline, staring out at the churning water. A strong wind was blowing, pushing the rain clouds away. For one crazy moment Amanda considered walking out into the ocean, walking in until there was no turning back. That would end it all. She dismissed the thought as quickly as it came.

Ever since she was a girl, it was here that she came when she wanted to be alone, to find peace, solitude, to find herself. She could hear her mother's words ringing in her ears, 'Where've you been for the last two hours? Staring at the water with your head in the clouds, I suppose. Amanda, I worry about you sometimes, I really do.'

In truth, Amanda now knew that, more than anything else, her mother was worried about herself, her own mental health, her own fragility. She likened her mother

to a pretty flower, and her father to poison ivy smothering
it. They should never have married in the first place, as
Danny had pointed out to her about herself and Edward.
Amanda's childhood was one not of mayhem, but of
complete dysfunction, caught between her mother's alco-
holism and her father's dour indifference. They pulled
against each other, her parents, their relationship always
strained and taut, Amanda left to walk the tightrope
between the two. One time she'd yelled at them both,
'Why did you have me, why? Why, when you can't love
her, when you can't even love yourselves?' It was the only
time she remembered the tightrope slacken, when they'd
seemed lost for words, shocked at the visceral observation
of them both by a twelve-year-old.

She'd spent a summer – a wonderful coming-of-age
summer – before taking up her college place in Dublin, in
America on a J1 working visa. At Shannon Airport the day
she flew out, they lingered in the departures area, waiting
for her flight to appear on the board. Her father was more
irritable than usual, because he felt inadequate, she
surmised, standing amongst the streams of international
travellers while he himself had never left the country.
Here, he was out of his comfort zone, no longer in control.
She knew he would hate that, and he did, snapping at
Amanda's mother and saying very little to her. Until it
came time for Amanda to say goodbye and pass through
into the departures lounge. Then he shook her hand
stiffly, and as he released it, suddenly pulled her into a
tight, awkward embrace, an embrace she would never
forget, because it was the only time she could remember
that he had embraced her. Ever. He had whispered in her
ear, 'Please forgive me for everything I've done to you.'
When he stood back, he stuck his chest out, told her to

watch herself, that there were some bad areas of the Bronx, to keep away from the lower Grand Concourse, and to never, ever go to Port Morris. She wasn't going to New York; she was going to New Jersey. She said nothing. She knew he wanted to parade his knowledge, all gleaned from books, designed to show that he was still in charge, that he knew things, standing amongst the stream of international travellers, a man who had never left Ireland. She treasured every moment of it, because he had looked directly into her eyes as he had spoken, giving her his undivided attention.

Now, she wondered, who she'd been fooling? All these years? Herself, that's who. And who had she been avoiding all these years too? Well, she couldn't any longer; she couldn't avoid anything. It had all come full circle, as it always did in the end. She realised she'd been avoiding it, even what Lauren had said about her research into a DNA family tree, because she was probably hoping, deep down, that it would all just go away. But she knew it wouldn't. Amanda was feeling as low as she'd felt back then, her father having been replaced by Edward, her life crumbling around her... because of a secret.

She felt the wind on her face and through her damp clothes. She shivered and stood. But she knew too, she was strong, and she could deal with this; she would deal with whatever was thrown at her. She began to walk away, the anger she'd felt earlier, at Mark O'Dowd, still present. God, it was good to be angry sometimes; it was better than being cowed and scared; anything was better than that. Her anger deepened as she made her way back to the car, as she thought of that note: I KNOW YOUR SECRET.

31

Amanda stepped into the hallway, was just about to call out a greeting, but stopped. Because Pri might be resting. Which was unlikely, it was only just gone eleven, but still. Her Jaguar was outside, so likely she was home. Amanda headed silently towards the stairs and started up it, heading for her bedroom. When she reached the landing, she became aware of a smell, like burnt charcoal, with it a noise, of voices in muted laughter coming from behind one of the closed doors across from her. She hadn't seen Liam's orange electric car outside. But he might have put it in the shed. Anyway, she wondered, why am I even thinking about any of this? It's none of my business. She went to her bedroom door and was just about to turn the handle when the door behind her burst open. She looked to see Pri rush out, giggling. Her head was lowered, and she was running a hand through her tousled hair. She did not see Amanda. She took a couple of steps and looked up and instantly froze when she saw her, her free hand flying to cover her mouth. Amanda noticed her skin was glistening with sweat, and she had nothing on but a pair of stockings and a suspender belt. Behind her, she glimpsed a male body lying on a bed, looking at the ceiling, smoking a cigarette. Amanda realised this was the source of the smell she had detected moments earlier, cigarette smoke.

Pri took her hand from her mouth. 'Oh, Amanda, you're back early. One minute.' She turned and went back into the room, closed the door. Amanda heard her speaking, feeling increasingly uncomfortable. This was none of her business, she reminded herself again. The door opened, and Pri emerged once more, tying the cord of a short satin robe about her.

'Come with me,' she said and nodded towards Amanda's bedroom.

'In there?' Pri grabbed Amanda's arm and led her into the room.

'You need to change out of those wet clothes,' Pri said when they were inside, pointing, 'or you'll catch your death.'

Amanda thought it ironic that Pri thought she needed to change, considering what Pri herself was wearing. Amanda quickly took out a pair of jeans and a sweatshirt from her suitcase and changed. Pri was standing with one ear pressed against the door.

'He's gone. I just heard the back door closing.'

'Pri,' Amanda began, 'I didn't mean to interrupt anything. If I'd known...'

'You didn't interrupt anything; it was time for him to go anyway.'

They were silent. Pri walked to the bed and sat on the edge, clasped her hands together.

'Look, my affair didn't finish, okay. There, you have it. We still see each other when we can, but only the odd time, that's all. I know what I said, that it was over, and it is... except, well, you know, for the...' Her voice trailed off.

'I know,' Amanda said, 'for the odd time.' She couldn't help but shake her head. She sat down on the stool by the dresser. 'But what about Liam?'

'What about him?' Pri shot back. 'He's no angel, you know. I'm convinced he's having an affair too, just haven't caught him yet, that's all.'

'Really?' Utter surprise was in Amanda's voice. 'Are you sure? Liam?'

Pri nodded. 'Yes, Liam. Good ol' reliable stick-in-the-mud Liam. Trust me, he's not all he seems to be.'

Amanda felt a hopelessness descend on her all of a sudden. Could she tell what was real anymore? About anything? Nothing seemed as it was, as she thought it should be, even the lives of her friends. She buried her head in her hands, wanting to cry. But she didn't and wouldn't. What was the point? She'd done enough crying.

'Something's happened, hasn't it?' Pri said. Amanda could feel her hand on her shoulder. 'Why are you back so early? What is it, Amanda? Forget about everything else. What's happened? Tell me.'

Amanda took her hands from her face and tented them beneath her chin, staring ahead.

'My life,' she said, 'is literally coming apart at the seams, that's what's happening.' And she briefly outlined what had taken place that morning.

'Jesus Christ,' Pri said, but didn't follow with the customary blessing of herself. 'What're you going to do? You have to do something, you really do.'

'Yes,' Amanda said, almost in a whisper, 'I know that, but what?'

'It must be her, the loola woman, Fiona. I mean, has to be.'

Amanda nodded. 'It seems the most likely.' Yet she could hear the doubt in her voice.

'And she's connected,' Pri added, 'isn't she? To this... secret?'

Amanda nodded again, her secret, her burden, her calamity.

'Pri,' Amanda began.

'Yes?'

'You asked. What happened, that night, my... okay, secret, if you want to call it that.'

'Uh-huh?'

'Well...' Amanda began, her gaze drifting as her mind stretched back, over the years, to that black cauldron of memories, the flame beneath which had never fully extinguished and was now reignited, the cauldron red hot, the contents bubbling and hissing, spilling out.

Pri was silent, waiting for Amanda to continue.

'When I...' Amanda began, 'was a student, in college, studying medicine – it's where I met Fiona, by the way – one night, when we were out, in a pub, the Merchants it was called, my drink was spiked, and when I woke up, I didn't know where I was. I was in a bedroom, and there was someone there, a man, a man who raped me, raped me multiple times, as a result of which I became pregnant...'

Amanda fell silent.

'What a terrible thing to have happened,' Pri said. 'So you had an abortion. I understand, Amy.'

'An abortion?' Amanda's eyes widened. 'I didn't have an abortion. It was illegal. I had the baby. The baby is Lauren.'

'My God.' Pri's face displayed her shock. She tapped an index finger against her chin. 'Wait. That means Edward's not...'

'Lauren's father,' Amanda finished the sentence for her. 'No, he's not.'

'My God,' Pri said again. 'Does he know?'

Amanda shook her head. 'Of course not. Nor Lauren.'

'Oh,' Pri said. 'Now I understand. Yes, that's some secret, Amy. But, but having a baby like that, after what happened to you, wow, that can't have been easy. I certainly wouldn't do it. Did you ever treat her...'

'Differently? Of course not. In fact, I love her even more because of it; it's not her fault. It would break her heart if she were to know. Really.'

Pri took Amanda in her arms and hugged her tight.

'All these years, you've been carrying this. Oh, Amanda.'

Just then there was a loud, twittering sound. Amanda recognised it as her phone ringing on the dresser top. She went and picked it up, Lauren's name flashing across the screen. 'It's Lauren,' she said, and answered it, 'Sweetheart, how—'

'Mum, don't talk, just listen.'

As Amanda listened, she felt her blood run cold.

'Edward,' she said, taking the phone from her ear, 'he's been attacked. He's in the hospital. My God.'

FIFTEEN MINUTES later she rushed through the doors of Galway University Hospital.

'Ward B,' the assistant behind the front desk told her, 'that's on the first floor. Lifts are right behind you; when you get out, you—'

'I know the way,' Amanda said, cutting her off, turning. She knew a quicker route, from her time spent as a junior doctor here. She pushed open the door at the side of the desk. The assistant was about to say something. This led to a staff-only stairs, but Amanda had disappeared through it before she could speak and was taking the steps two at a time. She emerged onto the ward through the door at the top, right next to the nurses' station. A couple of nurses were behind it, one filling in details on a form, the other, the older of the two, looking at CT scan results on a computer monitor. The older nurse looked up, recognition crossing her face as she smiled.

'Dr Jackson,' she said, standing. 'Now, don't worry, Ed... I mean Dr Jackson, your husband. Everything is fine with him, relatively speaking.'

'Nurse Connor,' Amanda said, 'what happened? My daughter didn't have all the details, just that he was in the hospital, and to come right away.'

The nurse opened the hatch in the nurses' station and emerged from behind it, stood beside Amanda, resting a hand on her arm.

'He drove himself here, presented at A&E. He was dishevelled and a little disorientated. His clothes were torn, and he was bleeding from a head wound. Our first concern was a brain injury. We've discounted that, however. We examined him, and he has lacerations to his head, hands and legs. Also bruising to his face where we believe he was struck with some kind of implement.'

'My God,' Amanda said. 'He was mugged?'

The nurse shook her head. 'Doesn't appear to be the case, but we'll leave that for the guards to decide. Nothing was taken; he said he was attacked, somewhere in the city, not quite sure where. But' – the nurse paused – 'his injuries are superficial. He's fine, shook up of course, but he's fine. We're merely keeping him in for observation.'

'Oh,' Amanda said, 'okay, that's good.'

'Now, my dear, let me take you to him.'

Nurse Connor began walking quickly along the corridor. Amanda hurried to catch up.

'Like I say, Dr Jackson,' the nurse said as Amanda reached her, 'everything is fine. It could have been much worse; these things can turn out very ugly, as you well know.'

Yes, Amanda thought, they certainly can.

The nurse stopped outside a private room. 'Remember,' she said, pushing the door, 'it looks worse than it is. Okay?'

Amanda nodded.

They went in. Edward was lying on his back, his forehead and one hand swathed in bandages, the hair along one side of his head matted to his scalp. The nurse hadn't mentioned that, Amanda thought. His eyes shifted to her, staring. The nurse checked the monitor on the stand, took out the patient chart from its holder at the end of the bed, wrote in it, put it back again.

'Are you comfortable, Dr Jackson?'

He nodded.

'Very good. Your wife is here.' She lowered her voice as she spoke to Amanda. 'Not too long. Ten minutes, okay?'

Amanda nodded as the nurse left. Edward had still not spoken, merely staring at her, his eyes full of accusation. She dismissed it.

'You're going to be okay,' she said. 'That's the main thing, Edward. What happened?'

He turned his head away.

'Bit of a coincidence,' he muttered.

She sat in the chair by the bed, crossed her legs, folded her arms tightly across her chest.

'What's that supposed to mean?' Her tone was sharp. She regretted it immediately. Now was not the time.

He didn't answer. But she knew what he was getting at. Her compassion for her husband in the condition he was in was being eroded by the absurdity that he was blaming her for what had happened.

'I spoke with Lauren,' she said softly. 'Did you give them her number as a contact instead of mine? It would have been better to have given them mine, to spare her the worry; you know what she's like.'

'I know what you're like,' he snapped.

'She and Danny will be down later,' Amanda said, ignoring the remark. 'She's getting the evening train.'

'No.' He turned and glared at her. 'I spoke with her. Told her, both of them, not to come here. Under no circumstances.'

'Why?' She was doing her best to keep her voice calm. 'What do you mean?'

He looked at her, and she felt herself recoil. Never had she seen such venom in his eyes before.

'You,' he said. 'You know what I mean. It's you. You've brought all this on. Yourself. You.'

She was momentarily transported back to the way it had been with Edward, the way it had always been, hanging on every syllable, tuned to his every mood, trying to assuage him, calm him, make him happy, trying to please him. She never could, not then, and not now. She touched her throat, her breath catching. She wanted to be kind, to help him, because yes, despite everything, she wanted that. She did not want to see him like this.

He spoke, and his voice was little more than a rumble, coming from somewhere far below, way down deep inside him, dripping with hurt pride and anger.

'Get out.'

For a moment, she was unable to move. She had not expected this, certainly not.

'Go on, get out.'

She blinked, but got to her feet slowly, wanting more than anything, in this moment, despite everything, for him to be kind to her, and for him to allow her to be kind to him. Because he was right. This was all her fault. Somehow, she was responsible. For everything. She knew it.

'Please,' she said, imploring.

'I said get out.'

She fought back tears, went to the door and pulled it open, stood outside in the corridor, people hurrying by in both directions. How much more of this could she take? Not much, she felt certain, not much. She walked away towards the stairs, feeling like she was becoming more and more lost inside a labyrinth, and the more she sought escape, the more lost and hopeless she became, as the light dimmed, the labyrinth becoming darker and darker...

Soon, there would be no light left at all.

32

'I don't know,' Amanda said. She was sitting in her car, having just come from visiting Edward, on the phone with Lauren: her daughter had just asked what exactly had happened. 'He didn't say,' Amanda added, 'didn't want to discuss it.'

Lauren spoke, her voice beginning to quiver. 'He told me he'd been attacked, that he was walking in town, along one of the streets, a back street, in broad daylight, and he was attacked... But he said these things happen. You know Dad; doesn't want anyone to worry about him.'

Not true, Amanda thought, he's just achieved the exact opposite, but she said nothing.

'He's not badly injured,' she said instead, 'like I told you. But they'll keep him in for a little while, merely for observation. Try not to worry, sweetheart.'

'And then what?' Lauren asked.

'What do you mean?'

'Well, Mum, who's going to look after him? He can't be left on his own.'

Amanda couldn't help but feel a warm glow for her

daughter. She wondered how, as she'd wondered count-less times, someone so beautiful could come from some-thing so evil. Her precious Lauren had always put others first. As a child she'd come home fretting about class-mates or friends who'd seemed sad or unwell, and once with a puppy she'd found on the street. There was a time when she'd considered her daughter might have been too sensitive. But then she came to realise that Lauren possessed an intuition too, the ability to know when others were drawing on her, sapping her energy, when to pull back. She had no doubt she would make a brilliant doctor. Of course, her daughter could not be as objective when dealing with Edward.

Amanda was silent, reflecting her uncertainty. Unlike her daughter, she did not possess the same intuition; it had taken her years, until now, to understand that Edward had been insidiously undermining her, ridiculing her, not so much controlling as subtly ruling her. Whatever the outcome of all she was going through was, she had learned this.

'Dad says it's too dangerous to come down and see him,' Lauren said. 'What does he mean by that?'

'Well...' Amanda began. 'I don't know what he means. I think he's simply confused at the moment.'

'Mum, is there something I should know about? What with all that's been happening to you, the drug search and everything, now Dad getting beaten up. What's happening?'

'I don't know,' Amanda said. And she didn't. But there was something she felt certain of. 'What happened to me was the result of a terrible mix-up,' she said. 'You'll see, because I won't let that go. I'll get to the bottom of it. As for your father, believe me, in my twenty-five years as a doctor, I know all about coincidences. And this is all it is, a coincidence. Please, Lauren, don't worry. Promise me.'

The truth was, Amanda didn't know. She didn't know anything anymore.

'But,' Lauren said, 'there was nothing taken from Dad. He told me. That doesn't make sense, now does it? Mum, I can't help it. I'm worried, for both of you. Is there something you're not telling me?'

'Lauren' – Amanda's voice stiffening – 'I want you to stop worrying about me and your father. Do you hear? We are well able to look after ourselves. This is a coincidence. Do you hear me? That's all.'

Lauren took a slow breath.

'Okay, Mum, if you say so.'

'I do. I say so.'

'Well then, okay, I'll try not to worry.'

'Good. Just concentrate on your studies. I'm going to ring Danny now. I'll talk to you again soon, sweetheart.'

'Okay, Mum.'

'See you soon, darling. Love you.'

'I love you too.'

When she hung up, she had the feeling that Lauren had not asked any further questions because she didn't want to know the answers. As if she knew it was time to stand back, to retreat, to leave her parents to deal with their own problems.

She rang Danny, but there was no answer. She held the phone, pondering, then tossed it onto the passenger seat, started the engine, and drove away.

33

BEFORE...

Amanda vowed not to eat any more peanuts. She had already eaten one bowl and was now halfway through another. But it was like trying to take a bath without getting wet. Impossible. But such were her cravings.

They were sitting in the bar of the Templeton Hotel, an old hotel with an old clientele, but one that Edward liked. The barman was old too, in his white tunic and bow tie, referring to Edward – still a student – as Dr Jackson.

Edward never corrected him.

The hotel suited Edward's prissy style perfectly. Amanda always considered that it would have suited Edward just fine if he had lived during the era when Ireland was still part of the British Empire. She could imagine him in the Imperial Civil Service, a posting to India perhaps, sitting beneath the shade of a karanja tree, being waited on hand and foot by a bevy of servants.

Amanda was desperate. She had a baby in her belly, was prepared to ignore everything that she disliked – even hated – about Edward: that prissiness, his single-mindedness, and ultimately, his narcissism. In the same way that one who is drowning doesn't care if it's a lifebuoy or the floating carcass of a dead dog that offers them something to cling to.

She had not seen him since the Two 4 One night at the student bar. They'd flirted and close danced, then gone back to his place for that glass of wine. Edward was a handsome man – very handsome – everyone said so, with a great body; plenty of girls would like to get it on with him. But she wasn't interested in anything else. As she sobered up, she'd quickly decided on that. She didn't like the way he just expected something, and that pout when he didn't get his way. It would not lead to anything. No way. Edward had rung her a couple of times afterwards, sulking when she said she was busy, trying to put him off gently, even showing up on her apartment doorstep a couple of times. After a week or so though, he'd stopped, seemingly having got the message.

When Amanda found out she was pregnant, every-thing changed.

Which was why she had rung him up, why she was in the Templeton Hotel. Why she was prepared to ignore everything that she disliked – even hated – about Edward.

She smiled now and took his hand in hers, rotating her thumb gently over the back of it. Edward smiled, his shoulders sagging as he relaxed. He rarely relaxed. He said nothing. She continued rotating her thumb, pushing in close against him.

'Edward,' she began, 'I really missed you, like, really missed you.'

She hated herself for it, for trying to dupe this man, knowing what she was doing, knowing that in her desperation she would do anything, because that was what she was, desperate.

Edward was silent, his expression inscrutable. She could feel his hand turning clammy.

'Let's get out of here,' she said. 'What do you say? Go back to your place.'

Edward was on his feet almost immediately. He looked down at her and grinned. 'Well, come on, then, before you change your mind.'

34

W hen Amanda stepped into Pri and Liam's house for the second time that day, she noticed there was no sound. There never was in this house, no TV, no radio, no music, nothing. She thought of that morning again, of Pri and the man in the bedroom, whose identity she didn't – nor wanted – to know. She still hadn't fully processed what she had seen.

None of my business, she thought again.

As she hung up her coat, she looked across the wide hall, could see Pri sitting in the living room, the waning evening sun behind her through the window casting her into a half shadow. She had her head bowed, one elbow resting on the armrest, her chin cupped in the palm of one hand, and was very still, almost like she was sleeping.

Amanda walked across and stood in the doorway, looking in. But something seemed not right. Pri appeared to be so still, too still. She took a breath and held it, listening, trying to detect any sound, any subtle movement, a gentle intake and exhale of breath perhaps, something. Instead, she could hear nothing. Her belly tightened.

'Pri,' she said softly.

There was no reply.

She walked over to her friend.

'Pri,' she said again, but louder this time.

Still, there was no movement and no sound. She bent down, feeling increasingly uneasy, and peered into her friend's face. A terrible thought struck her; was she dead? She reached for Pri's wrist to check her pulse, but a sudden movement caused her to jump back, with it a loud grinding, guttural sound. She watched as Pri's body jerked again, and with it that same noise, but this time the cough was much softer, Pri merely clearing her throat. She opened her bloodshot eyes and stared at Amanda, looking confused. Amanda felt something touch her foot. She looked down, saw the end of a green glass bottle protruding from beneath the settee. Pri rubbed her hands briskly across her face. 'Oh, I must have fallen asleep... what time is it?'

Amanda checked her watch. She was surprised to see it was just gone half five. She told Pri.

'It's okay, it's okay,' Pri said, in a half mutter.

Amanda knew she was saying this to herself, a reassurance.

Pri looked ahead, silent. Amanda felt she had forgotten she was even there. She sat down next to her on the settee. There was a smell, the lingering sweetness of perfume, mixed in with that of old and new wine and stale sex. Pri seemed stranded in the aftermath of it all, washed up, as the tide went out, leaving her floundering. Again, Amanda found a distraction from her own misery in considering Pri's misery. What was happening to her friend? She had known her for many years, but how well do you know a person, really know them? Certainly, in turn, Pri had never known very much about her either. Not until today, that is, because Amanda had presented an image, as had Pri, just as everybody else. Who knew what really went on in another person's head? Yet she always thought she knew everything about Pri. It began to make sense now, those times they had met, the hollow eyes, the pasty skin, the distracted mind, not listening to what she said, having to repeat everything. And her endless harping on about Liam. The classic alcoholic, in this case the secret drinker. God, she reminded her of her mother.

'I need a drink,' Pri said, standing awkwardly. 'And how are you, my dear, dear friend? I was thinking of what you told me earlier. How terrible. Really, this world, is it any wonder a person likes the odd drink, to escape...'

Amanda said nothing.

'Anyway, thank you for not objecting,' Pri said, 'for not telling me that drinking doesn't help. Liam's an old scratched record.'

'You're a big girl,' Amanda said. 'I'm not going to tell you what to do. By the way, where is he, Liam?'

'Gone to Liverpool. He takes the ferry over once a month. A builder's thingy, on sustainable green living or something. Seemingly he's a bit of an expert. Don't ask me. It means I can, okay, drink a little more than I usually do.'

Pri cut a lonely figure as she shuffled into the kitchen. Amanda heard the clinking of bottles, the sound as one was placed onto the granite worktop, then the pop of the cork being pulled, finally the glug-glug-glug of a glass being filled.

'You want one?' Pri called.

Amanda was about to say no, but then thought: why not?

'Okay, yes, I will, thanks.'

Amanda drank quickly, her glass almost empty before she'd realised it, cradling it then in her hands, feeling a little guilty and self-conscious. She looked at Pri, who was staring vacantly ahead, and realised she had no reason to feel self-conscious or guilty for having drank it quickly at all. She thought of her mother again, who at one stage hadn't left the house in over a year, spent the whole time mostly drinking. She had then gone cold turkey and quit alcohol altogether, for a time, that is. Still, even then she couldn't leave the house. Amanda had guessed that some type of intervention was required, because it was clear she wanted to stop drinking, to quit alcohol. In any case, she never got it, the intervention, and returned to drinking and never stopped. She was dead within a few years.

The alcohol coursed through Amanda's body, leaving a warm, light feeling in its wake. She sat back and sighed, trying not to think of anything, just for this one, brief moment, to have her mind free.

'Well,' Pri said, breaking the silence, 'you're probably wondering why I'm like this, aren't you?'

Again, Amanda thought of her mother. The whole world faded into second place behind her needs. And the selfishness of the active alcoholic was something she came across as a doctor almost every day in her surgery. Thinking of her surgery now, the icy edge of the humiliation she had felt earlier cut through into the eye of the storm, into this brief respite.

Pri's head shot round, her eyes glaring. Amanda waited. In her experience, the problem drinker had three settings: endless romancing of the past, belligerent confrontation with the taking of every second word as a slight, or lastly, a removal from reality coupled with a complete lack of any sense of responsibility, i.e., the so-called happy drunk. There were many variants, but one or more of these was usually at its core. Amanda wondered which setting was Pri's, veering towards the second, the belligerent confrontation. But just then, Pri's expression unexpectedly softened. She placed her glass – empty – onto the floor and took hold of Amanda's hand.

'I'm so, so, sorry, my darling. Now tell me. I insist. What happened with Edward?'

She looked at Amanda with intensity, her blue eyes bobbing about.

Amanda told her.

'The bitch,' she exclaimed.

'What?' Amanda said, taken aback. 'What do you mean, the bitch?'

'That woman. Can't you see? What's her name, this Fiona loony tunes person. It has to be.'

'But,' Amanda began, 'how? I mean, Edward was beaten up. Terrible as it is, it happens; he said so himself. As for... okay, maybe... perhaps, I don't know... but not that... I mean, how?'

Pri gave a drunken laugh. 'Oh, sweetie, she could have gotten someone to do it for her of course, paid them, you know. I can't imagine people like that are too hard to come by, if you know where to look, that is. By hurting him, she might think, in some way, she's hurting you.'

Amanda sighed. She knew that normally Pri would have kept such observations to herself, conscious of upsetting or worrying her, or of just being plain wrong. But, uninhibited by alcohol, she had spoken her mind. And now that it was said, Amanda wondered, was it so far-fetched? Anything was possible. And suppose Pri was correct, that Fiona really was responsible for having

Edward beaten up like that... well then. That meant, in essence, Edward was correct; it was her fault.

'Oh, God,' she said as she felt the alcohol's warmth evaporate, leaving her with the beginnings of a pounding headache.

THEY HAD A LIGHT MEAL. Amanda helped Pri prepare pasta with diced ham in a red pesto sauce. Pri's movements were sluggish and exaggerated as she took utensils and ingredients from drawers and cupboards, like she was in slow motion. Once, Amanda tried to pre-empt her, reaching for a ceramic mixing bowl she knew she was searching for when Pri snapped, 'I can get this myself. What? You think I've had too much to drink, isn't that it?' Amanda stood back with an apology, and Pri then smiled. 'Sorry, didn't mean to snap. I can get it. But really, I don't drink that much at all.'

Over the meal Pri rambled on about Liam.

'I love him, really,' she said, 'but it's just he's so fucking sensible, you know? I want a man who's, I don't know, vibrant, who... sets me on fire, in that way, you know what I mean, don't you, Amanda?'

'I know what you mean, Pri.' She tried to keep the wary boredom from her voice.

'And he doesn't do that, not any longer... I envy you in a way, Amy.'

'You do?'

'Yes. You have your career, a doctor. I never finished college, you know? Met Liam in my first week of first year, then got some part-time modelling work, and then I packed it in and left.' She laughed again. 'My parents were soooo angry. But you know, Amy, I'm not a bookish person. I just went to college because that's what everyone else was doing. Liam was besotted with me, and we got married before he even received his degree. Maybe I should have lived a little first.' She laughed. 'I knew I'd never have to worry about money, not so long as I was with Liam. And I never have. My parents changed their minds on everything, by the way, once they saw that. But I'm dependent. I'm the bird in the cage. I need him. Suppose in some ways I'm trying to relive my past, doing what I should have done back then, now, or trying to do things differently, but I can't.' She stared past Amanda in a frozen, unblinking stare.

'You're still young,' Amanda offered, careful to keep her voice neutral, not to sound like she was telling Pri what to do. 'I mean,' she continued, 'night classes, something like that, you could...'

Pri's eyes suddenly narrowed, darkening, as they shifted to take her in.

Amanda inwardly groaned, waiting. But Pri raised an eyebrow and gave a cheeky smile. Amanda watched her carefully.

'So,' Pri said, 'does Edward set you on fire in that way? You never told me.'

Amanda was drinking water. She took a long sip.

'Please, Pri, come on...'

Pri giggled.

'Please, Pri, come on,' she mimicked. 'Aw, how cute, Amy's embarrassed. There's no need to be embarrassed with me, Amy, you know that. Come on, tell me, Pri wants to know everything.'

Amanda got to her feet, pushing her plate away.

'I'm going to bed, Pri, if that's okay. I don't want to talk about this anymore. I'll see you in the morning, okay?'

'I'm sorry,' Pri said suddenly, sounding very sober. Her hand sprang out, grabbing Amanda's wrist. 'Really, Amy, I'm sorry. And selfish. Please talk to me. I want to help. I'm sorry for going on about myself. Tell me about it...' Her voice dropped, becoming conspiratorial, hungry. 'Tell me more of it, your secret. I want to know.'

Amanda felt Pri's hand start to squeeze, the nails beginning to pinch a little. There was a sense of desperation about her, a thirst, her eyes darkening again, yet her mouth was smiling. Amanda recoiled from the wonky expression, pulling her hand free. She strode across the kitchen.

'Goodnight, Pri.'

When she got to her room, she noticed for the first time that there was a key in the lock. She turned it. She had decided she would not tell Pri anything else. She listened at the door, could hear her downstairs as she wandered about the house, her voice muffled, talking to herself.

She realised in that moment that she didn't know Pri at all.

35

1994

It was late April when Lauren was born, just in time for Amanda to sit her final exams as the new Mrs Amanda Jackson. She had the entire summer to stay home and be a full-time mother before her hospital placement began in September. She harboured worries she might not bond with her child, worried she had made a terrible mistake, that she should have gone to England and had an abortion. So when the midwife handed her the little pink bundle, and as her heart swelled and overflowed with a love so intense it made her ache, she was utterly relieved. She decided right there and then that she would put everything behind her. This was her life now, and she was going to make the very most of it.

But no one must ever know her secret.

36

A thought began to formulate in Amanda's head as she lay in bed. Now that she had told Pri, she regretted it, regretted having told her anything. How had she been so stupid? Still, she felt she could trust her on this – at least she hoped she could. In any case, there was nothing she could do about it now.

It was too early to try for sleep. So she lay there looking through the window at the growing darkness, the blue-grey sky slowly fading into the advancing black of night. Her thought was this: to leave the country. Why not? Go to... Spain? Or Italy? Even Australia? Wherever she wanted. The world was her oyster. It was never too late to start again. Doctors were in demand all over the world, after all, and her record was exemplary. Another thought crossed her mind, one so alien considering what she was going through, but it gave her a warm glow: maybe she might find a new relationship, find love, true love next time round. She entertained the notion, imagined walking along a sun-kissed beach with this perfect man, laughing, holding hands, perhaps finding a deserted spot, running up the dunes into it, and...

She giggled aloud, not at the notion of it, but the absurdity. She couldn't even imagine this perfect mystery man; he appeared more to her a shadow, grey and feature-less. She considered this was because she felt she didn't deserve it. It? You can't even say it, can you? Okay, love. She felt she had no right to it, love, from a perfect man, because she felt she wasn't good enough, wasn't worthy. How could she be? She'd never been good enough for the man who'd brought her into this world, who had reared her, who'd been the most important man in her life despite everything: her father.

She turned onto her side, the warm glow having disappeared, in its place the cold reality of having no home to go to, of lying here, in this room, effectively hiding, because she didn't want to be around Pri any longer. But more than anything, it was not that she was being haunted by her past, of what she had done, her secret. It was that she was now living through it, every waking minute of every day. Her past that had come back into her present, both merging, a living nightmare.

Clonk. Clonk. Clonk.

An eruption of bright light filled the room.

Amanda stiffened. The distinctive sound she had heard was of the old brass knocker on the front door, the only bow to history in this temple to modernity. The light was the motion security lamp illuminating outside, flooding into the room. She jumped from the bed and crossed to the window. The front door was directly beneath it. She peered out from behind a corner of the curtain, and... her hands flew to her mouth as her body suddenly sagged, trembling at what she saw.

37

Amanda listened at the bedroom window as Pri opened the front door. Pri's voice sounded remarkably sober, but Amanda could only just about hear it above the pounding of her heart.

'Yes,' she said.

The only sound then was the beating of her heart as she waited for a reply. As her fears were realised. Because outside, when she'd looked a moment ago, was a police car.

'Can I speak to Amanda Jackson, please,' the voice said. 'Dr Amanda Jackson. We believe she's staying here.'

Pri spoke, her voice rising, the words slurring at the edges for the first time.

'Amanda? What's it in connection with, officer?' And added, her voice beginning to slur more now, 'She hasn't gone and killed anybody, has she?'

Pri gave a giggle. Amanda didn't think it was funny, not funny at all.

'Could we speak with her, please? Thank you.'

'Okay, one minute, she's in her room. I'll go and get her.'

Amanda quickly crossed the room and opened the door, went out onto the landing, just as Pri started up the stairs.

'The...' Pri began, stopping, looking up.

Amanda raised her hand and whispered, 'I know. It's the guards.'

Pri took a step back and rested against the banister, crossing her arms, her half-sodden eyes silently observing Amanda as she came down the steps.

'I'm sorry,' Amanda said as she passed her. 'I'm sorry about all this, really.'

Pri pursed her lips and nodded her head back towards the door. 'He's very serious about it all.' Like it was all part of an amusing adventure.

But it's not, Amanda thought, it's not an amusing adventure, but knew that Pri didn't get it; she didn't get anything at this moment. The three settings of the active alcoholic she used for appraisal, well, she guessed Pri possessed a little bit of each of them.

She ran her hands through her hair and smoothed down her clothes, crossing to the door. The outside light was on a timer and had gone out again, so she couldn't see the policeman until she'd reached the doorway. He seemed to loom up out of the darkness. She knew he was there, but still, it took her by surprise.

She wondered if her startled expression might be misconstrued for something else, guilt perhaps?

'Yes.'

'Dr Amanda Jackson?'

'Yes.'

'Can I come in?'

'Of course.'

He stepped into the hallway. He was middle-aged, with a paunch, but, she noticed more than anything, his eyes, they were kind.

'I'm Garda Gerry Lynn. I debated whether it was too late to call this evening, that maybe I should leave it until morning.'

'Please,' Amanda said, a pleading in her voice, 'what is it?'

'The search of your car, Dr Jackson, what we found?'

An invisible force kicked her in the stomach. It took all her effort not to show it, to stop herself from crumpling to the floor.

'What was it?'

'Unscented talcum powder,' he said, 'that's what it was.'

'Unscented... what? Talcum powder?'

'Talcum powder,' he repeated. 'Yes, completely harmless and legal. I thought you'd want to know immediately. So I took it upon myself to call rather than try to ring you, as we were passing.'

The words he'd said sunk in... unscented talcum powder, harmless, legal.

She slumped back against the wall.

'Dr Jackson, are you alright?'

She blinked, her eyes welling up. 'Yes, yes, I'm just so relieved, you wouldn't believe.' Not drugs, not drugs, not drugs. 'Thank you from the bottom of my heart for coming round, for telling me; it's very kind.'

The policeman pushed his cap back on his head, scratched along the hairline, pushed the cap back into position again.

'But,' Amanda said, speaking her next thought aloud,

as if to herself, 'who's responsible, that's what I'd like to know? I mean...'

She fell silent.

'Yes?' the policemen prompted.

Still, she said nothing.

His kind eyes searched hers. 'Would you have any ideas about who might be responsible?'

She shook her head.

'Would you like to make a complaint, officially that is, so we can look into this?'

Again she shook her head.

'No.'

'No? Why not?'

The question took her by surprise.

'Because,' she began, 'I just can't, that's why.'

'Hmmm.' A shadow of suspicion passed behind the kind eyes now for the first time.

Please don't look at me like that, she wanted to scream. Really, I'm a good person. This is something I can't talk about; it goes back, way back, to a terrible event.

'Well,' he said, 'it's completely up to you, of course.'

She felt he was about to probe further, but he didn't.

'I'll be on my way, Dr Jackson.' He turned and stepped out of the house. The security light activated. He paused, spoke without turning. 'But I'd urge you to consider making a complaint, Dr Jackson. Good night.'

Amanda watched him walk away and slowly closed the door.

'Nightcap?' Pri's voice sounded.

Amanda looked to see she was standing on the threshold to the living room, holding up a half-empty bottle of wine. 'It'll make you feel better.'

For the first time, Pri was beginning to irritate her, really irritate her. She went to the stairs.

'No, thanks, Pri, the only thing that'll do is make me feel a lot worse.'

'Ah, come on, one little drink can't hurt.'

Amanda started up the stairs. 'No, thanks, Pri. See you in the morning.' And maybe you should think of going to bed too. She reached the top of the stairs and looked down, but Pri had already disappeared back into the living room.

She sat on the bed in her room, feeling some of the tension of the last few days suddenly melt away from her. This news was important, very important. She did not have to worry about being branded a drug dealer, did not have to face the ordeal of appearing in court, of having her name splashed all over the media, and, most importantly of all, being struck off the medical register. She knew that, and she was glad, grateful for it. But still, this was not over. She knew that. No, this was not over, not over by a long chalk.

Her telephone rang, the sound startling her.

She looked around, having forgotten where she'd placed it. Spotting it on the dresser, she went and picked it up, looking at the number flashing across the screen. She didn't immediately recognise it, but then it struck. She felt herself go cold, an 021 prefix, a Cork number. This had to be Fiona. The cold coiled its way through her. But then the phone fell silent again. Amanda went back and sat on the bed, staring at the phone. A moment later it pinged an incoming text alert. Her finger trembled as she pressed the button and brought up the message.

'We need to talk,' it read.

The phone fell from her grasp and bounced onto the

floor by her feet. She stood and took a step back, rubbing her hands on her clothes, as if trying to clean herself. She took a deep breath and another, tentatively bent down and picked it up again, took another breath, and began to type a message: 'I don't trust you. After what happened. You frighten me. You were watching. I saw you. It was you who told them, wasn't it? The police. Had to be!'

She sent the message, decided she didn't need to deal with this crazy woman any longer, and was just about to turn the phone off when a text came back almost immediately.

'We need to talk. Told them? Told who what?'

Amanda typed out a reply in a flurry of fingers: 'Don't act so innocent. Like I just said. The police, the guards, that's who.'

Again, a reply came back almost instantaneously: 'I didn't tell the police. I didn't know what was happening. None of it made any sense. Still doesn't.'

Amanda considered that was what she would say. Her finger hovered over the turn-off button. Another text pinged in. She looked at it.

'We need to talk. Remember, it was you who contacted me. Think of that. I'll meet you anywhere. I've nothing to do with any of this. Please believe me. We are both haunted by that night. You know what I mean. I know you do.'

That night.

To hell with this, she thought, and pressed the call button, her pulse quickening, her belly lurching as the phone at the other end began to ring.

The same raspy, sing-song voice answered before the first dial tone had finished ringing. 'Hello, Amanda.'

The sound of it struck a renewed fear in Amanda now. Fiona seemed to sense it.

'There's no point in us talking if you continue to think I had anything to do with what's been happening to you. You should hang up right now if that's what you think, and you won't hear from me again – nor do I expect to hear from you. The decision is yours. One way or the other, we need to sort that.'

Amanda said nothing for a moment. Then: 'But you were watching. I saw you. And no one knew I was meeting you, no one.'

'Yes. Yes. So you think I rang the guards and had them do that to you. On what pretext? Why, Amanda? Why would I do that?'

'You know why.'

'Goodbye, Amanda...'

She was consumed by a sudden panic. 'No,' she practically shouted, 'don't. Don't go. Okay. Okay, maybe you didn't. I don't know. I don't know anything. You said that it all went back to that night. As do I...'

'Don't say anything. Not another word. I told you. I don't trust phones. And neither should you.'

'Well, what then, for God's sake?'

'Remember you told me once, the place you liked, where you went when you wanted to be alone, where you felt safest, remember?'

Salthill.

'Yes.'

'There. I'll meet you there. Tomorrow.'

'What time?'

'The same time as our first shift at St Vincent's? Remember. The time we started?'

They'd started late that day, very late, because the

consultant had been delayed. Turned out he had reversed over the family cat in his car when leaving for work. That was why she remembered, why they all did probably.

'Yes, but...' Her voice trailed off.

'Look. Do you want to meet or not, Amanda? If not, like I say, don't bother me again, and I won't bother you. We'll end it right here.'

'I remember the time. Yes, I'll meet you. I'll be...'

But the line went dead before she could finish the sentence. Amanda pulled the phone from her ear, wondering if she hadn't just made one of the biggest mistakes of her life.

.

38

She went to bed, and despite the sounds of doors closing and opening and the mumbling of Pri somewhere as she talked to herself, she drifted off to sleep. But almost immediately her eyes snapped open again. What had woken her? She lay still. There was a sound, like heavy breathing. She turned her head slowly towards it.

Jesus!

And blinked.

No.

Good God.

No.

Someone was in bed alongside her. She screamed, twisting her body, scrambling to the very edge of the mattress, tottering there, then feeling like she was taking to the air, as if flying, but only for an instant, as she realised she was not flying but instead falling to the floor. She landed with a thud. She screamed again, her arms and legs beginning to flail about on the floorboards, moving her towards the door in wild crab-like movements. The diffused light through the curtains cast the room into eerie shadows and pools of black. She knew he was behind her, as she fought against her fear, forcing herself to glance over her shoulder, saw him rising from the bed, starting after her, the stench of his lust scorching the air. She reached the door, and her hand clambered up and found the handle, but it was too clammy to grip and turn properly. Frantically she continued trying, twisting and pulling on the handle, the latch bolt sliding back but never far enough, hitting the strike plate each time she yanked on it, making a clicking sound... click, click, click.

She opened her mouth to scream, but this time no sound came. He was almost upon her, would soon begin to drag her back to the bed, tie her down, do things to her, violate her. A light reflected on his face. She saw it. He was wearing a mask.

NOOOOO!

Again, her eyes snapped open. But this time it was for real. She was on the floor between the bed and the window, bathed in sweat, her breathing fast and frantic. She looked about the room, but could see nothing. She felt a panic take hold, could feel the outline of the bed next to her.

A nightmare.

That was all.

But was there someone here? In the room? Because it had all seemed so real. In fact, was there someone in her bed? It was dark, and she could see little. The panic deepened as she scrambled to her feet, resting one hand on the mattress, frantically fumbling for the bedside light with the other. She heard a dull thud and knew she had knocked the light over. The panic was almost overpowering now, as she braced for a hand to grasp her wrist and drag her back to the bed.

Ahead of her, on the other side of the bed, a pencil line of white appeared, a rectangle of what she now knew was the light from the landing outside. The pencil line began to widen, becoming an ever-increasing wedge as the door opened, and a shadowed shape appeared, stooped, with bedraggled hair.

She sank to the floor as she had done in her hotel room, but she did not cry, instead stared ahead, her chin resting on the bed, waiting for the shape to reveal itself, a silent explosion of light erupting as the light was turned on, dazzling her.

It was Pri. She rushed over, sliding down to the floor next to her, holding her gently by the shoulders.

'I heard you scream. It's okay. It's okay. You were having a nightmare?'

Amanda began to cry.

'Yes. Yes. I was,' she said. 'I don't think I can take it any longer, I really don't.'

'It's late. I don't feel so well either. Let's get some sleep. Come on, into bed. I'll stay with you tonight; you won't be alone. Neither of us will.'

Pri helped her into bed and lay beside her, tucking the duvet about them both, the alcohol fumes hot and stale on her breath. Instantly, Pri was snoring. In the darkness, Amanda found the sound comforting, telling her that she was not alone. She was also comforted by the warmth of her friend's body and the rhythm and sound of her breathing, so that when she went to sleep, she did not wake until the next morning.

39

They sat at the kitchen table, coffees in hand, Pri's complexion a sickly hue in the sharp October sunlight through the bay windows, both their eyes bloodshot. Amanda had just told Pri about the meeting arranged with Fiona for later that day when her telephone rang, Lauren's name flashing on the screen.

She answered. In the heavy atmosphere of Pri's kitchen, her daughter's excitement seemed to fizzle out from the phone.

'Mum. Mum. Some good news. Listen up...'

'I'm listening.'

'I've only gone and won my faculty's gold medal on DNA and Genomes. Remember the thesis I submitted last summer. I won, Mum. I won!'

'Oh...' Amanda began, her voice uncertain, but caught herself and added with false excitement, 'That's great. Lauren. I'm so proud of you. And, darling... what exactly was it on?'

'Us, I told you,' Lauren said, 'remember, the DNA family tree.'

A dart seemed to pierce Amanda, hot and sharp.

'Yes, yes, the thesis.' She could hear the fear in her own voice. Cold fear gripped Amanda, beginning to squeeze, tighter and tighter, as Lauren started to speak. She dropped her head, staring at the floor.

'I had taken Dad's DNA,' Lauren went on. 'Like I told you. And guess what? We share a unique code. It's too technical to get into here, but it's called an ASR strand. So thanks, Dad. It means I can write another thesis on just that; no one else in my class will be able to. And it helped get me that gold medal now. Of course...'

But Amanda was no longer listening, fumbling about, the world starting to spin as Pri looked at her with those tired, jaded eyes.

Amanda opened her mouth to speak, but nothing came out for a moment, then: 'But it can't be? It just can't be.'

Amanda stopped in mid flow. 'What?' Lauren said. 'Mum, what can't be?'

Amanda closed her eyes and opened them, blinked, shook her head a couple of times and clamped her mouth shut, afraid of what she might say, as the truth struck the bedrock of her consciousness, because there was nowhere else to go. It settled there, and Amanda stared at it. Stared at the truth. The truth? The horrible, appalling, inconceivable truth. Could it be? That Edward was Lauren's father? And something else. That he was the masked monster who had raped her?

Edward.

Her husband.

40

A voice screamed inside her, No! as the room began to close in all about.

'I'm sorry, darling, I've just got to go. But well done, yes, yes, well done... no, everything is fine, Lauren. Don't worry... we'll talk soon. I'm so proud of you.' Amanda hung up.

Pri got up and came round to her, rested her hands gently on Amanda's shoulders. 'I heard everything,' she said. 'My God,' and repeated, 'my God,' like there was nothing else she could say. Which there probably wasn't.

In a daze, Amanda said, 'I've got to go. Fiona will be waiting. I've got to go. I've got to talk to her.'

'I want to go with you,' Pri said, her voice suddenly not so tired anymore.

'You do?'

'Yes, Amanda, I do. She's a bit loola; we both agree on that, don't we? And the news just now... Who knows what the hell's happening. I'm going with you.'

Amanda wanted to say that she didn't think Fiona was loola; this was a conclusion Pri had arrived at by herself.

But it would be good to have her along. She pressed a hand to her mouth, suddenly feeling like she was about to get sick, quickly swallowing back the bile.

'Are you okay, sweetheart?' Pri asked.

Amanda got to her feet. 'We'd better get a move on. I don't want to be late.'

Pri pushed away her mug and stood too.

'Right then, let's go.'

They drove in Pri's old Jag and parked in the car park by the Salthill promenade. The time was ten minutes to two. Amanda said she would walk ahead, and it was agreed Pri would follow five minutes later. As Amanda opened the door to get out, Pri said, 'Don't forget, I won't be far away at any time, so try not to worry.'

Amanda nodded, looking at her friend, who appeared much healthier than she had earlier, her eyes clear and her cheeks pink.

She got out of the car and wrapped her scarf around her neck, nodded in a 'this is it' gesture and began walking along the promenade, away from the city suburb, towards the pebbled shoreline about a half mile away. She glanced out to sea, over the buttress of boulders piled against the promenade, protecting it against the wild Atlantic storms. But now the ocean was quiet and calm; it merely lapped and murmured against the grey rocks. The air was bracing, the light pale and soft, but off in the distance a cobweb of black cloud spread out from the horizon like the tentacles of an unseen monster lurking beneath the earth's surface. Which was how she thought of Edward now, as a monster. What was she to do? The terrible news was too much, too overwhelming, to fully comprehend.

She walked quickly; she only had ten minutes, after

all. Reaching the end of the promenade, she hurried down the steps by the Blackrock diving tower. Most people ended their walks at this iconic landmark, but others braved on. She braved on, she had to. She made her way along a rutted path towards the beach. She could not see anyone else about. As she rounded a bend, she crossed onto the marram-grass-stubbled dunes and over them onto the shingled shoreline. She started to walk along it, her feet making a crunching sound. Ahead was the concrete shelter, set back from the beach in a clearing within the dunes, ringed by a necklace of sand. With each step the sky began to darken, the ocean turning a gun metal grey, jarring her mind, the sudden melancholy of this place igniting without warning those memories of that night, bringing back with it something new, something that she had previously forgotten...

There was a voice. 'Thank you,' it said. 'No, no, everything's fine, just, y'know, too much to drink, that's all. I've warned her about it, yes, I did. Doesn't seem to listen to me. It doesn't suit her; told her that an' all' ... 'Well, if you're sure?' ... 'Yes, I'm sure, but thanks anyway. Good to know people are watching out for one another, cos you can never tell these days; never know, someone might'av spiked her drink.' And then a funnel of cold damp air as the door of the Merchants was opened, and Amanda passed through – half slumped against somebody who smelled of fags and antiseptic, a strong, masculine arm tightly wrapped around her waist, as she looked on, a dreamy, detached observer.

Her eyes scanned the deserted beach. She could see no one, and there was no sign of Pri. Where the hell was her friend? She was supposed to be keeping an eye on her. But of course, what was that she had said earlier? Yes, she

would be 'hidden in plain sight'. That was it. Relax,
Amanda told herself, she's probably watching you right
now, from somewhere within the dunes.

Or Pri might not be here at all.

Amanda stumbled on across the rough ground, a
vague sense of wanting, needing, to reach the water's edge.
There, she'd feel safer, would be able to spot any threat
before it had time to manifest, protected on one side by
the sea. When she reached it, shadows were creeping in
over the ocean and across the landscape, passing over her,
taking all colour with them, as if a switch had been
pressed, turning the world monochrome. It was then she
felt the first drops of rain on her face, and with it a sudden
gust of wind, whipping about her, sharp and angry. She
had no coat on, so she pulled the scarf tighter around her
neck as another gust came, barrelling in off the sea, but
this time it did not recede, remained instead blowing at
full force, and with it came a violent downpour, but it was
not rain. It was hailstones as big as small pebbles. She
turned her back against it as the downpour intensified,
becoming an onslaught, feeling a thousand barbs on her
through the thin fabric of her clothing, stinging her body
all over in a furious torment, the wind howling like a
beast. She was suddenly consumed by a terrible fear and
began running across the shingles, away from the water
once more, back towards the dunes. She had only gone a
short distance when she stumbled and fell to the ground
on the slippery, wet surface.

She pushed herself up, stooped against the furious
wind and downpour, peering ahead, her eyes scanning
the dunes. The wind pushed at her back, and she braced
herself against it to stop herself from falling over again, as
her eyes detected something, a movement in the near

distance. She stared, her eyes stinging, her whole body pummelled by the fury of the storm, and saw a fleeting glimpse of a figure, blurry within the incessant rain, emerge from the swirling haze, becoming more distinct as it approached across the beach. Relief and fatigue coursed through her, but her energy was draining like water down a plughole as she began to fall, the shingles rushing to meet her, just in time outstretching her arms, cushioning the impact as she hit the ground.

Thank God, she thought, thank God, it's Pri.

She turned her face up, her mouth tasting of salt and seaweed, taking in the figure standing above her. A figure squat and wide, not petite like Pri. A wave of nausea washed over her as she looked along the short body to the face, a man's face, oddly shaped and strangely oversized, all out of proportion to the rest of his anatomy. He loomed more as a shape, a shadow, than a physical entity, dark, brooding, indistinct, as if one of the very shadows she had witnessed earlier skittering across the landscape had settled to earth. Amanda was overcome by a terrible fear. She turned her head away from the figure, her hands clawing at the ground as she squirmed her body in a half circle, trying to edge away. But to where? The ocean? She inched her way forward, her back slightly arched, like a sea creature trapped on land, awkward, desperately seeking to reach the sanctuary of the sea, as the hailstones continued to pound, a fusillade of miniature hot irons against her face. She could see the churning foam as the water crashed to shore. A hopelessness gripped her. What was she doing? What? Heading to her death? In the cold waters of the Atlantic? She glanced over her shoulder. But no one was there! As quickly as it had appeared, it, the apparition, had disappeared again. She stopped moving, was still, gasping for breath. But then, in the corner of her eye, she saw something, a movement. She swivelled her eyes to the corners of their sockets. And saw she was wrong. The apparition had not disappeared. No. It was still present, standing on the other side of her, right there, a couple of feet away.

'Please,' she screamed, turning to face it, 'who are you? Why are you doing this to me? Why?'

The shape slithered like a ghost towards her. Amanda wondered if indeed that is what it truly was. An apparition... from that night, returned from the dead perhaps? Back to take her with it to hell.

Again she screamed, louder this time, everything she had and more pushed into that desperate sound, but even so, it was tossed aside and lost to the wind. She knew it was of no use anyway; there was nothing she could do; she was alone in this wild but beautiful place. She fell silent, giving in to it all, surrendering, awaiting her fate, sad this place she had always considered her safe harbour had turned out to be nothing more than a treacherous sandbank.

She closed her eyes, and a moment later there was the sensation of being lifted into the air, then of bobbing about, like she was somehow in water, but she could not feel the cold liquid on her body. She opened her eyes and found herself staring down at the shingles from a height, moving swiftly across them. She tried to wriggle free, but the grip on her was too tight. The hailstones beat against her, the wind howling as before, but now appearing as if desperate to devour her.

She was carried off, and there was nothing she could do about it, her eyes closing, just as they had that night, drifting off, everything going black.

41

She opened her eyes slowly, the lids like great weights, heavy and sluggish, as the ropes cut into her wrists, pulling her arms back, stretching them taut behind her. The bed was hard and cold, pressing into her back. She began to cry, her tears mixing with the water bathing her face. She looked up at the grey ceiling. There was a window open somewhere, the wind blowing through the room in a loud, ominous rumble. 'Amanda?'

She shot her head towards the sound of that voice, her name, saw three dark outlines framed within a black border next to her, a background of murky grey sky. Her head throbbed, but she ignored it. She began to shiver. A hand pressed down on her forehead, and she turned her head furiously against it, trying to shake free from its touch.

'She's coming round,' a voice said, a familiar voice, raspy and sing-song. Where had she heard that voice before?

'I know you,' Amanda spluttered in her confusion. 'I know you. I want to go home, do you hear? I want to go home. Are you working with him? With Edward? Have you both done this to me?'

She felt herself being gently pulled to her feet, and she looked about, at the open bedroom that faced the sea... no, no, not a bedroom. She knew this place. Yes, she did. Where? What was it? Yes, of course. The shelter! But who were these people? She tugged against the hands that held her, trying to break free, to get away. 'No. Leave me. I'm not going with you. I'm not. Leave me. Leave me alone.'

'C'mon, Amanda, you're safe; we'll take care of you.' The voice was gentle and soothing.

'You will?' she said, her voice suddenly softening. 'You will? Really? You'll keep me safe from the monster?'

'The monster?' a male voice asked.

'Yes. The monster. It's after me. It really is...'

42

An episode from her childhood played out in her mind. She must have been around twelve years old and had fallen from her bicycle, deeply gashing her knee. She'd been permanently scarred as a result, in the shape of a great big teardrop. She had limped home, her father watching from the living room window as she came down the garden path, waiting for her on the doorstep when she arrived. She remembered the scowl on his face.

'What have you gone and done now?' he demanded, looking at the bike. 'You're not getting another one of those, you know; don't let that thought get into your head. You've only had this one a bloody week.'

'I'm sorry,' she said, fighting back the tears, her knee an explosion of pain. 'I'm so sorry, Daddy, I really am; please don't be mad at me.'

'Don't sniffle,' he snapped. 'Don't be mad at you? You're completely hopeless, you are... I mean, why couldn't I have had a boy?' He shook his head. 'Why oh why? Someone I could be proud of instead of, instead of...'

His voice trailed off as he turned and went back into the living room, slamming the door shut.

Amanda ran straight to her bedroom, the pain in her heart smothering the physical pain in her knee. She stayed there more or less for three days, until the wound had begun to heal, but she would never forget the words her father had said. The physical wound was never stitched, the ugly scar the result. The emotional wounds, even after all these years, had never even partially healed, were still as raw and tender as ever.

Her eyes were moist, and she wiped a hand quickly across them, the images receding. Had she been dreaming? She couldn't be certain. She had a scattered recollection of what had happened on the beach, of falling, the water coming closer, of being lifted up and carried away, a darkness descending, then nothing. She must have blacked out. Amanda felt warm and comfortable though, a bright light bathing the room she was in. She stared across it through a window and could see the tops of trees outside.

She looked about for the first time, taking in her surroundings. A blue curtain was pulled halfway around her bed, leaving a vista through the open portion of a beige wall and the window with the trees outside. She heard voices and sounds, familiar sounds. And knew where she was. It was an A&E cubicle at Galway University Hospital. She was dressed in a hospital gown, and a health service regulation pale blue blanket covered the bed. A nurse came round the corner of the curtain and smiled.

'Dr Jackson, how are you feeling?'

Amanda didn't answer, aware of someone standing behind the nurse. Her eyes darted in their direction.

'Yes,' the nurse said. 'You have visitors.' The nurse glanced over her shoulder as the two guards entered. A dart of fear struck Amanda, radiating out from her chest, with it the feeling like she had just put her foot out for a step and found it wasn't there, a hollow, disconcerting sensation. One of the police officers she recognised. The one who'd called to Pri's house the night before, but it seemed so long ago now. His name escaped her. His colleague, a young female, nodded, but neither guard spoke.

Amanda opened her mouth, but nothing came out. All she could think was, Why are they here?

The police officers silently observed her.

'My name's Imelda Daly,' the female guard said, then, 'community policing; this is my colleague, Gerry Lynn.'

'We met,' Amanda said.

'Really?' Garda Daly's voice lilted a little in surprise.

'Yes, I met Dr Jackson,' Garda Lynn said. 'I went round to tell her last night that the search of her car was negative. How are you, Doctor?'

There was something about his tone that struck Amanda. She remained silent.

'It's okay,' the female guard said, 'if you don't want to talk about it now.'

'Talk about what now?' Amanda asked. 'What do you mean?'

She noted the exchange of glances between the two.

'Tell me,' Amanda said. 'Why are you here?'

An expression settled on both their faces, similar to Layla's on Tuesday when Amanda had called to the White Rock to discover another doctor was working in her place.

That look, like they'd just found an overcharge on their Tesco receipt.

'Dr Jackson,' Garda Lynn said, those kind eyes of his boring into hers, 'don't you remember?'

Amanda was silent again, fearful of what was to come. 'Remember what?'

'There's no easy way to say this, but don't you know that you just tried to kill yourself?'

Amanda's mouth dropped open.

'I-I... what?' Her voice was a strange grumbling sound.

'Yes,' Garda Lynn said, 'we received an anonymous call,' and went on to outline what had happened; a call had been received at Mill Street station in Galway City. 'I'm not certain whether it was male or female,' he continued. 'They said Dr Amanda Jackson had gone to Salthill with the intention of ending her own life, she was heading for a location on the beach just past the Blackrock diving tower, and we were to hurry, before it was too late; she was going to go into the sea. A unit was dispatched immediately.'

'And there wasn't a moment to lose,' Garda Daly chipped in. 'When we got there, you were disorientated. It looked like the tide had pulled you back to shore. A local man, name of Paddy Ferguson, saw you on the shoreline and went and carried you to safety. You can thank that man that you're alive today, Dr Jackson. He probably saved your life. The ambulance crew brought you round.'

'He found me, this Ferguson man, carried me to safety, you say?'

'Yes, if he hadn't, you could have drowned on the incoming tide, a high tide, by the way, Dr Jackson, coming in very rapidly.'

The odd-shaped figure, Amanda realised, the sensation she had felt, of being lifted into the air, of bobbing about. It was him, this Paddy Ferguson, as he carried her to safety.

'But,' Amanda said, 'the tide did not pull me back in, because I never went into the water in the first place. I never tried to kill myself, okay?'

Again, the exchange of glances between both officers.

'For God's sake,' Amanda said, looking at each in turn, her voice creeping up an octave, 'I didn't try to kill myself. Okay? Please. Believe me. And even if I did, it's not against the law, is it? So why're you here?'

She knew by their expressions she shouldn't have said that, her comment about suicide not being against the law. She felt certain it entrenched their view that she had been trying to take her own life.

'In actual fact,' the female guard said. Amanda immediately disliked her tone, like she was talking to a child. 'We have to ascertain if you are at risk. It's why we're here.'

'At risk? At risk from who?'

'From yourself, Dr Jackson,' Gerry Lynn said. 'That's who.'

'At risk from myself? That's absurd. I'm not at risk from myself. Who decides if I am? You?'

'No,' he said, 'of course we don't. The doctors. And until they do, until they give us their verdict, we have a responsibility, a duty of care. The initial call was made to us, after all.' He smiled. 'We want to do what's right, Dr Jackson; can't you see that? We want what's best for you. If you weren't trying to, you know, end your life, what were you doing there on that beach? Tell us, please?'

'And if I don't? What then? You'll arrest me, is it?' Amanda was surprised at her belligerence and knew it wasn't helping matters.

Garda Daly pursed her lips, hooking a wayward strand of hair dangling in front of her eyes behind an ear with an index finger. 'Um, yes, Dr Jackson. Actually we can. For your own safety, that is. If we deem you to need the appropriate care and if you don't want to receive it. Certainly, yes, under those circumstances, we can arrest you.'

In other words, have her committed to a psychiatric hospital. Amanda dropped her head. 'I know how this must sound,' she said softly, 'but I can't. I can't tell you... I just can't.'

Garda Daly sighed. 'We know something's going on,' she said. 'We're not stupid. But if, just say, we were to believe you, that you didn't try to kill—'

'I didn't,' Amanda interjected. 'I didn't try to kill myself.'

'Okay,' the female officer went on, 'then why would someone ring us and tell us that you were? Why would someone go to all that trouble to say it if it wasn't true? And the same for that call we received that you were carrying drugs in your car? It's stacking up, Dr Jackson. You have to agree. Isn't it? Something here's not right; it's all a bit off.'

Amanda gripped the edges of the blanket and squeezed tight. 'Yes.' Her voice compressed, trying to keep it, and herself, measured. 'I have to agree, it is stacking up, and you know what? I can't take it anymore. Okay? I don't know what's going on. I don't. Can I leave? That's what I want to know. Can I?'

'That's not up to us. Of course it's not,' Garda Lynn said. 'That will be a decision for the doctors.'

'Yes, I know, but it seems it's for you to decide if I'm a risk to myself. That's what you said. Well, am I?'

Garda Lynn shook his head. 'No, like I said, that's for

the doctors to decide. We just want to be certain you're not going to leave here and make another attempt...'

'I didn't make any attempt.'

'... on your life, Dr Jackson, that's what I'm saying. We're waiting on the consultant psychiatrist to come and speak with you, to make the final decision.'

'Dr Andrew O'Shaughnessy... I know, I've already spoken with him.'

'You have?' Garda Daly asked. 'Where? When? We couldn't find any record of you speaking with him.'

Amanda was about to explain, but instead said nothing. Of course they wouldn't find a record; it had been an informal chat, in her own home, nothing more.

'Why did you speak with him?' Garda Daly asked, studying her much closer now than she had done before. 'What was the reason for it?'

'I-I...' Amanda stuttered, knowing they would ask Dr O'Shaughnessy about it anyway, that there was no point in her trying to hide it. 'I had a bit of a meltdown, okay, that's all.'

That's all? A bit of a meltdown. Like it was an everyday occurrence.

'My family,' she added, 'they were worried about me.'

'I see.' It was Garda Lynn, his kind eyes not so kind anymore, and Amanda knew there was no point in her saying another word, not one, because his mind was already made up.

'Where's Pri, by the way?' she asked. 'My friend.'

Garda Lynn nodded back over his shoulder. 'Outside in the corridor.'

'I want to see her. Please.'

Daly nodded. 'Okay, I don't see any harm in that. But

we'll be right outside, Dr Jackson, and we'll be right back again.'

Like, what? she thought. I'm going to try to kill myself right here in this hospital bed? I don't think so. She merely nodded her head and said nothing.

43

P ri entered the cubicle and stood beside Amanda's bed. She'd been sobbing.

'I'm so sorry, Amy, that I wasn't there for you. Really, I'm sooo sorry...'

'It's not your fault. But what happened, Pri? I don't remember much. I blacked out. Tell me.'

Pri looked about for somewhere to sit, but there were no chairs, so she stepped over to the window, leaned against the sill, folding her arms. 'I'm not quite sure myself,' she began, her voice cracking. 'What I know is that I watched you walk away from the car, remember? You went along the promenade, as you said you would. I waited a while, until you were almost at the end, and then I got out myself, to follow. I didn't want to catch you right up, just keep an eye on you, but I'd forgotten how much faster a walker you are than me. I followed, but really, Amy, we both hadn't thought this through, now had we?' She paused, took a breath before continuing, her voice a little stronger, 'When I got to the dunes, the storm just blew up. Jeez, where did that come from? We should have checked the weather forecast first. We both know what the weather's like there, how suddenly things can change. And change they did. Anyway, I made my way onto the beach, but I couldn't see you. I panicked, Amy. I hadn't even brought my phone. I'd left it in the bloody car; can you believe that? I started walking along the beach, I knew you couldn't be far away, just couldn't, and then I saw you, off in the distance, but you were too far away... I'm so sorry, Amanda, I really am, that I couldn't stop you from going into the water, that I couldn't get to you in time...' Her voice began to falter again. 'It must have been a cry for help, really, it must. I should have known. Is that why you brought me along? You know? To stop you? Because it was a cry for help? Oh, Amanda.'

'What?' Amanda's tone was incredulous. 'A cry for help? You think I was trying to kill myself as well? That's what you're saying?'

Pri arched her eyebrows and stepped over to the bed. She rested a hand on Amanda's arm and gently stroked it. 'It's okay, Amanda. Really. I understand. Believe me, I've thought about it a couple of times myself. But I was too caught up in my own stuff to notice. I mean, to really notice what was happening with my friend, what was happening with you. I was selfish, but I'm not going to be selfish anymore. I'm going to change.'

Amanda tried to keep her voice calm but was unable to. 'I didn't try to kill myself,' she said, the words much louder than she'd intended, adding quickly, lowering it, 'I'm sorry, Pri, but really, I didn't. You know me, if I did, if I were thinking like that, don't you think I would have told you? Of course I would.'

'Is everything alright in there?' A nurse's head appeared around the edge of the curtain.

Amanda nodded.

'Yes, nurse,' Pri added, 'of course. Everything's fine.'

'Okay then, keep your voices down, please.'

'The police received a phone call,' Amanda said when the nurse had gone, 'anonymous. Saying I was about to kill myself. Who the hell even knew I'd be on that beach?'

Amanda stared at Pri. The answer was obvious.

'Fiona,' Pri said, saying it for her, 'that's who.'

Amanda nodded. 'Yes, it doesn't make sense. I mean, why?'

Pri shrugged. 'Who knows. The drugs search didn't make any sense either, did it?'

Pri folded the fingers of one hand and peered at her nails.

'I met her,' she said softly.

Amanda blinked. 'What? You met her. You mean, she was actually there?'

'Yes, Amy.' Pri looked up. 'I met her. She was there.'

'I thought that voice was familiar, but I didn't know, thought I was imagining it. I wasn't. Where exactly? I didn't see anybody. The shelter was deserted.'

'It all happened so quickly,' Pri said. 'I tell you, I got the shock of my life. She was actually standing right beside me, just down from the dunes. I don't know where she came from; it was like she was just, well, there. She came up to me and asked me if I was with you. There were a couple of other people there, on the beach. What could I say, Amy? I said yes. In hindsight, maybe I shouldn't have let on to that. But I think she knew. I think she'd been watching all along, maybe even saw us arriving in the car, I don't know. But she was watching, had to be. I asked her if she was Fiona, and she simply nodded, then said yes, that she was Fiona, Fiona McBride Crowley.'

Amanda said nothing for a moment, thinking about this information.

'I see. And what then?'

'And then, well, nothing. I left. I was too worried about you. I wanted to be with you, so I started running. That's the last I saw of her.'

Amanda's expression was grim as she was consumed suddenly by a renewed sense of hopelessness.

'Isn't it time?' Pri said softly, nodding to the corridor. 'To tell them, the police.'

'I told you before. I can't.'

'You can't. Or you won't?'

'I can't. I won't. Both.'

'Why not, for God's sake? This has gone on for long enough. Edward needs to be...'

'You think I don't know that,' Amanda snapped. 'Sorry, Pri. I didn't mean to snap. I have to think of Lauren and Danny. God, Lauren, how will this affect her? I need a little time, that's all.' She dropped her voice, so low it was barely audible, 'because it would destroy her. I have no doubt. Can't you see that? Well, can't you? I'm doing this for my daughter, for my children. I need to protect them.'

Pri cocked her head to one side, looked at her friend. Then her face crumpled as she began to cry softly.

'You poor thing, Amy, you poor, poor thing. How selfish of me. Of course. It's just so terrible, you know, that I can't, I just can't fully comprehend it. It's like I forget about it sometimes. I put it out of my mind, like it doesn't exist, simply because I can't deal with it, if that makes sense.'

Oh yes, Amanda thought, that makes sense, perfect sense.

'I'm sorry,' Pri went on. 'How can I...' But her voice trailed off as they entered the cubicle again, taking up position, one either side of the bed. Officers Lynn and Daly.

44

Amanda didn't immediately notice Dr Andrew O'Shaughnessy following the two police officers in. But when she did, she knew immediately by his expression that something was not right.

'Can I ask everyone to leave,' he said gravely, looking about at Pri and then at both police officers, his eyes lingering on them. 'There's no threat. Just step out for a moment while I speak to the patient? Alone. Thank you.'

Amanda did not like the sound of this, did not like the sound of this at all: There's no threat... while I speak to the patient. What was happening here? She could guess.

'Amanda,' Dr O'Shaughnessy said with that grave tone again when everyone had left the cubicle. He pulled the curtain, sealing them in. In his right hand was a ballpoint pen. He scratched the side of his head with it, a nervous gesture, she felt, rather than one that had the purpose of satisfying an itch. She knew it wasn't like the psychiatrist to be nervous. If it was, he hid it very well. She waited for him to continue. Dr O'Shaughnessy looked at her for what seemed an eternity before he spoke again.

'I'm sorry, Amanda, but you'll have to spend a little time at St Catherine's. It's in your best interests.'

St Catherine's, what was one time known as the County Mental Infirmary, a dour, sprawling, gothic affair of grey stone, turrets and gargoyles, a couple of miles outside the city. Everyone knew it. Nowadays much of it had changed, the building split into various sections, combining general medicine outpatient clinics catering to overspill from the University Hospital, as well as an annex of the regional technical college and a Department of Enterprise business incubation centre. Yet a small part still remained as a mental health facility, or the Lock-Up ward as it was known, or officially the Regional Mental Health Facility. That was where she was going, the Lock-Up.

She fumbled about, pushing herself up in the bed, her hands gripping the side railings.

'Andrew,' she said, her voice surprisingly calm. 'You can't be serious. Please think about this. You can't. You know me. We spoke about it, remember?'

He smiled, a weak, uncertain smile, the smile he used many times each day no doubt, when faced with difficult situations such as this.

'It's for your own good.'

My own good!

He must really think I'm crazy, she considered, if he thinks I don't know what's for my own good, yet he seems to think he does. She realised it was no good pleading with him, that indeed, it might make matters worse. Still, she couldn't stop herself from trying.

'But,' she said, 'we spoke about it. Remember? Andrew, we did. You said I was fine, your words, not mine. You said that I was in a "condition of most robust mental health, with a refreshing lack of reserve in talking truthfully about myself". I remember it clearly. You said that. You. And we would speak about it again. Yes. We never did. And now... this, you're committing me? Come on now.'

He folded his arms, his tweed jacket suddenly appearing too small for him, the stitch lines along where the arms met the shoulders revealed as the folds of his neck were squeezed above the collar of his shirt, and his cheeks glowed.

'Yes, yes, I know I did, but circumstances change. You know that yourself, being a medical professional too. But I felt there was more. I intimated as much, didn't I? Amanda, the truth is, you are a risk – a risk to yourself, and that's my final conclusion. I can't allow you to simply leave this hospital. And for what? For me to wait and hear of what happens to you next? Because something will happen, I have no doubt. No, I can't take that risk. I am responsible for you now; you are my charge. My fear is that you might try it again. And you might succeed next time in killing yourself. That's a risk I simply can't take. And I won't.'

She took a breath, scarcely believing what she was hearing. 'I tell you,' she began tentatively, 'I didn't... I didn't try to kill myself.' And, noting his expression, added, 'Oh, what's the use?'

'The last time,' he said, 'you almost fooled me, Amanda.'

'God, I didn't almost fool you. I didn't almost fool anyone... except myself maybe, that is.'

'And what does that mean?'

She shook her head. 'Nothing.'

Again, that look she'd been getting a lot of lately.

'I know you're not telling me the truth,' he said.

'Amanda, come on, enough fun and games. It's me you're trying to make a fool of. Because you told me, and you know it. I just want to hear you actually say it, that's all.'

'I told you? I told you what? And you want to hear me actually say what? Andrew, I'm sorry, but what are you talking about now?'

His eyes were still, his expression pensive.

'Please, Amanda, talk to me. Tell me what this is about. Then I can help you.'

'I told you what? You tell me.'

'Okay. You told me about the police and the search of your car and your attempt to kill yourself. You told me. Come on now, don't take me for a fool, not for a second time. Please.'

'And how exactly did I tell you?'

He exhaled in a long, low breath, shaking his head, unfolding his arms and reaching into an inside jacket pocket, taking out an envelope.

'You wrote to me. This is it. The letter.' He held it up.

Amanda froze.

'You don't remember, do you? Or you're acting like you don't.'

'I don't.'

'You sent this, Amanda, come on.'

The sensation was like a trapdoor opening beneath her, and she was tumbling through.

'I didn't send it.' A pleading in her voice that she loathed. 'Look, I know how this must sound. But I didn't send it. I didn't.'

He paused, those same still eyes, that same pensive expression. 'It must be obvious,' he said calmly, in that way she herself had spoken to very ill patients, 'to even you, Amanda, but you need help.'

'No, I bloody don't,' she snapped. 'Okay, okay, I'm sorry. I didn't mean to snap. Just show it to me, please, the letter I mean. Will you?'

He held it just out of reach. 'You won't tear this up or anything, I hope.'

'Andrew, I just want to read it, for God's sake.'

He stretched, and she took the plain white envelope, just like the one she had found beneath the windscreen of her car. But envelopes such as this were ten a penny. It was addressed, in block letters, to:

*DR ANDREW O'SHAUGHNESSY, GALWAY
UNIVERSITY HOSPITAL*

She opened it and withdrew the single sheet of paper. The same type of paper too, just as before, thicker than copier paper, but not quite board paper either, somewhere in between, a type of card paper. Her sense of déjà vu was palpable. She opened it and studied the writing. She had the sensation of looking at herself in a mirror for the first time. She never could remember reading her own hand-writing, not once, ever, without a recollection of actually having written the words in the first place. But now she had no recollection. None whatsoever. And yet, there it was...

My handwriting.

'I,' she began, 'I...' and fell silent as nothing came out. She began to read what she had written, in her slightly askew, irregular, and typically sloppy doctor's handwriting:

Dear Andrew – I've been finding things very difficult lately. Very difficult. Indeed. Sometimes I don't know

what I'm doing. I mean. My thoughts. I don't know
what I'm thinking. It's all. Just. Just. Too much. If you
know what I mean. I hope you know what I mean. I
mean. I'm sure you can. You are such a good psychia-
trist after all. But. My thoughts. They're very erratic. I
do things on impulse. I don't know why. Hey, did you
hear? You probably did. I was stopped. By the police.
My car was searched. It was all over YouTube. I don't
know why. I mean, I don't know why I did it. I really
don't. But I was the one who rang the guards. Explain
that? Me. Can you believe it? Well, I hardly can. And
now... Oh, and another thing. I've left Edward. Yes,
poor, poor, Edward. He was assaulted, you know.
Somewhere in the city. I might have had something to
do with that. Yes, terrible, isn't it? Me. But I might.
Nothing more than a feeling. On my part. But still...
Look, I never wanted him to be part of this. Part of my
insanity. Okay? You see, something happened. To me.
Years ago. Something he doesn't know about. No one
does. It's ground me down I can tell you. It's left me
hopeless. It's left me. It's left me... which is why I've
decided to end it all. I can't take it anymore... Andrew, I
want to tell you. But I don't want my family to know.
Please. Well, I do, but not until it's finished. Until it's
too late. Until I'm free. And they can't stop me. Oh God,
I want to be free, I really, really, do. And, by conse-
quence. So will they. My family. They will be free too.

Amanda put the letter down, stared at it, then picked it
up again, folded it carefully, placed it back in its envelope
and handed it to Andrew.

'There, you can have it back, no problem.' She added,
with a slight smile, 'I doubted myself for a minute there. I

mean, so much has been happening, I really, actually did doubt myself. The handwriting is very convincing. But it's not mine. And I'd never write anything like that, too flowery, and that punctuation? No, it's not me. It's someone else doing this to me. Andrew, I think it's rather obvious, and you're falling right into the trap.'

'A trap,' he said, 'you see it like that? A trap? What trap?'

She knew she had to be careful; every word was being scrutinised.

'It doesn't matter. You don't believe me. Let's just leave it at that. Anything I say will be too much.'

He gave a slight shrug. 'Fine, we can do that, for now... but we'll talk about this later. About everything. I'll give you plenty of time, Amanda; there's no rush.'

'If only you knew the truth, Andrew, the whole truth, you wouldn't treat me like this.'

'Like what? Have I not been courteous and professional with you at all times?'

'Oh yes, Andrew, you have. Certainly.'

'Well. What then? And don't worry, Amanda, this is a safe environment. You can talk to me. About anything.'

'Right then...' She paused, deciding. 'It's this. Edward raped me. Many years ago, before we were married. I was on a night out with a friend of mine, Fiona. He spiked my drink and raped me. I became pregnant. I never knew it was him. I married him because I felt I had no choice. I needed a stable environment for my daughter. All these years I never told anyone about that night. But now... I've found out, Lauren's DNA thesis. I found out that he is the father of Lauren; he is the one who raped me. Yes, you heard correctly. He spiked my drink, wore a mask, and raped me.'

She stared at him.

'Edward is Lauren's father,' he said gravely.

'Yes.'

'Your husband, the man you married, is the father of your daughter?'

'Yes.'

Amanda now realised how that must sound.

'I became pregnant that night. When he raped me. He spiked my drink and raped me.'

She reached out and took hold of his arm.

'Please, Andrew, you've got to believe me.'

Dr O'Shaughnessy patted her hand gently.

'Amanda, release my arm, please.'

'You don't believe me.'

He pulled on his arm and took it away.

'I have to go,' he said, and left the cubicle, but this time, pulling the curtains behind him.

Amanda could only think: he thinks I'm barking mad.

She rested her head back against the pillow, closing her eyes. A moment later footsteps approached, unusually slow and ponderous, stopping right outside the closed curtains. She looked up as a hand appeared, pulling the curtain aside: a male hand; she assumed it was Andrew O'Shaughnessy. He pushed through into the cubicle.

But it wasn't Dr O'Shaughnessy. Her belly lurched when she saw who was standing there.

Her husband smiled, leaning on an old blackthorn walking stick she recognised: a gift from somebody or other years ago.

'I needed something to help me get about. They were going to give me a walking stick at the hospital, but then I remembered we had this. Perfect.' He smiled again and

nodded towards her. 'How are you bearing up, eh, darling?'
Darling. He knew of Lauren's DNA thesis by now. He knew
the result. Had to. What it meant. Amanda studied him.

'You knew about this before I did,' she said, 'didn't
you? Lauren told me she asked you for a DNA sample, but
you were reluctant. No wonder. Of course you were
reluctant.'

He limped over to the bedside and stood above her,
resting his weight awkwardly onto the stick. A dressing
covered a corner of his forehead, and purple and yellow
bruising streaked his face. Amanda looked around, edging
away from him.

'Just so you know,' he said, 'no one's going to believe
you. Think about it. You just tried to kill yourself,
Amanda, for God's sake. You need help. You really do. Just
remember...' He reached out, and she winced as he rested
his hand against her cheek. 'I'm here for you, Amanda. I'll
always be here for you. Okay, darling?'

Amanda raised her hand for the call button. She was
just about to press it when Edward grabbed her hand,
squeezing tight.

'No, don't disturb the nurses; they're run off their feet.
I'll see to it that you get all the help you need, Amanda. I'll
make sure of it.'

All sound seemed to cease in that moment, background noises, of voices, of rushing footsteps, gurneys and
medicine trolleys, occasional cries of pain, all gone. And
in that moment their eyes locked together.

She stared at him.

'I only want what's best for you, Amanda, truly. And it
would be best if this remained our little secret.' His hand
came and brushed her cheek again. 'Otherwise... well,

who knows what might happen. I mean, look what happened to me.'

'What did happen to you?'

'I was hoping you could tell me. The guards interviewed me, you know. I told them that you seemed to have gotten mixed up with some dodgy people. That episode with the car and all, stopped and searched like that. I said you just weren't... right lately, and maybe, just maybe, my getting attacked was some kind of message to you. I don't know. But it's all very odd, and I told them that. And you know what? They agreed with me.'

'It's you, isn't it?' Amanda whispered. 'Doing this. Doing everything. It's you.'

Edward smiled. 'Amanda, Amanda, you're not well, saying such things. Now, I'd better be going. Andrew told me not to stay too long.'

She watched as he left the cubicle, and became afraid, very afraid.

She thought she knew her husband, difficult, self-righteous, condescending Edward. But she was wrong. So very, very wrong. She didn't know Edward. She didn't know him at all.

A nurse came in almost as soon as he had gone.

'Just to let you know, Dr Jackson,' she said, 'you'll be remaining here until the morning. Someone will be with you at all times, so don't worry.'

'I'm not worried,' Amanda said. 'I feel fine.'

'Yes, of course.' The nurse's tone patronising, Amanda considered. 'You don't have your own bathroom facilities,' the nurse added. 'As you know, the loo is right outside.'

'I've already been.'

'Well, if you need to go before the special comes on duty, just press the call button.'

A special: term for a nurse or assistant assigned to a patient requiring round-the-clock observation.

The nurse turned, about to leave again.

'But,' Amanda said, 'I don't need anyone. I don't need a special. I just told you. I can manage by myself.'

'Of course. But I wasn't talking about that.'

'You weren't? What were you talking about?'

'The cubicle door, Dr Jackson, it will be locked.'

The nurse was gone before the full impact of those words sank in. Amanda heard a short snapping sound. She knew it was the bolt sliding across inside the door lock.

She felt an urge to scream, took a deep breath, opening her mouth, her vocal cords constricting, poised to send out a piercing, desperate sound. But at the last moment she snapped her mouth shut again, fighting back against the rising panic and the fear that made her feel hollow inside, like she might break and fragment into a thousand pieces. This was the closest she had come to completely losing it, abandoning herself to a swirling vortex where she might be lost forever should she fall in, and even if she did re-emerge, she would never be the same again. It wouldn't take much for her to break, she knew that. She really was skirting the edges right now – the edges of a nervous breakdown.

She thought of Lauren, dear sweet Lauren, who cared about everyone else more than she cared about herself, and Danny, her surprisingly responsible, caring, beautiful son.

She couldn't allow this to happen. She wouldn't allow it to.

She clamped a corner of her lip between her teeth and bit down, felt the hard, sharp incisor pressing against the skin, the pain wrenching her back into the present, onto the correct side of sanity. She flopped her head back against the pillow, staring up at the ceiling.

She would get through this.

She could get through this.

She had to get through this.

45

Amanda knew that A&E beds were always at a premium. Yet they had allowed her to remain here, not only in A&E, but in an A&E cubicle, of which no hospital had very many. She wondered if they would move her onto a ward later? Possibly. She concentrated on this and other practical questions, successfully halting her mind from wandering to where it wanted to go, to a place of hopeless fatalism.

She'd had an omelette and salad for supper – surprisingly good – and sometime later that evening, just after darkness had fallen on the world outside the window, the orderly came round again, pushing a tea trolley, and poured her a cup from a great big urn. After this she was alone, the sounds of the A&E department outside a constant backdrop. She didn't know where her phone was, and not having it compounded her sense of isolation.

The main light in the room was off; in its place a night light along the wall gave off a weak, yellow glow as the moon crept high in a clear sky outside the window, the tops of the trees spindly against the washed sky, appearing like hands as they moved about in the breeze, as if about to tap on the window. She dozed after that, which is the best that can be hoped for in a hospital, and her last images were of those spindly hands outside the window before she slumbered.

She dreamt. Of running across an open field. It was a scorching hot day, yet she was dressed in a long woollen skirt and turtleneck jumper. Someone was chasing her, but each time she looked over her shoulder to see who it was, no one was there. She reached the other side and tried to jump a wide ditch. She fell short, managed to gain a grip as she slid down, her legs scrambling wildly for footing and then finding it as she began to clamber up again. She hauled herself over the top and ran on, through a tunnel of tall bramble, at the end a corner, and then another, and yet another, before she realised what this was: a maze. She was becoming increasingly frantic, the tall bramble squeezing in on either side of her. She knew she should turn around and go back, yet she seemed unable to, just couldn't stop running... The bramble continued to press in, now beginning to tear at her clothes, at her flesh. But she persevered, pushing forward until the space was too narrow to move, and she became trapped like a fly in a web, the light dwindling all around her, and then everything was pitch black. Behind her she could hear the footsteps of her pursuer, slow and steady, louder and louder until they stopped right behind her. There was a hot, heavy breath on her shoulder, and with it a smell, of alcohol and sweat – male sweat. But at that moment she was free; the thick tangle of bramble was gone, had simply disappeared. She bolted forward, scarcely believing it, lunging into the darkness. But only for a short distance before she was viciously yanked back, the binds cutting into her flesh, a dead weight pressing down, that stench of alcohol and sweat intensifying, making her gag, threatening to smother her, as Edward leered down from above, moving closer and closer...

Her eyelids snapped open, and she was awake again, back in the A&E cubicle, her body bathed in sweat, her breathing frantic, the bed sheets sticky against her skin.

She heard something, what she thought was the sound of someone speaking. It came again. And she knew. It was the sound of someone speaking. She strained her ears to hear what was being said.

'How are you, Amanda?'

She turned her head, but there was no one there.

'How are you, Amanda?' the voice repeated.

She looked again, in the other direction this time, and could now discern a shape moving about a short distance away. It approached her and stopped next to the bed. Amanda felt angry at the special for creeping around like this. Didn't she know it would alarm her? At the very least, she should have introduced herself.

But Amanda said nothing about this, instead answered, 'I'm fine.'

'Good, because we have a lot to do.'

'We have a lot to... what do you mean?'

Amanda felt goosebumps forming on her skin. Something was not right here. Not right at all. And the voice was familiar.

A beam of light sliced through the air, a pencil torch, swinging wildly for a moment before settling in a pool of white onto the centre of the bed. Amanda was numb, her body, her mind, everything; she was unable to even blink. And then, in a sudden flurry of movement, she raised an arm, fumbling about for the call button. And just as suddenly, a hand clamped onto her wrist, a small hand, but surprisingly strong and cold.

'Don't,' Fiona commanded. 'Don't.'

The torchlight had shifted, shining onto a portion of her face. Amanda could see ribs of pale grey hair draped across the forehead. For the first time in a long, long time, twenty-two years or more, she was looking into the face of Fiona. She noted, even in the partial light, that same anxious expression, but the face gaunt now, the cheeks sunken, the flesh lined like crumpled paper.

Amanda felt her body slacken, sinking into the mattress, as the cubicle door opened, and she turned her eyes to see someone enter.

'Turn on the light,' Fiona snapped.

The harsh fluorescent ceiling light flickered into life.

Amanda stared at the person who had just come in, her eyes bulging. It took a second for her to process the image, so inconceivable was it.

'What are you doing here?' she spluttered.

'Hi, Amanda,' Pri said.

46

Threatening stimulus to the brain, if extreme enough, can sometimes result in what is known as the Matrix Effect. Amanda was experiencing this right now. Everything slowing down as she looked on, an observer, Fiona leaning towards her, placing a finger against her lips, her expression a silent communication. Amanda gave a slow nod of her head, an exaggerated, sluggish movement, and stayed silent.

'Trust me?' Fiona said, her voice an echo from somewhere far off, though she was standing right in front of her.

Amanda shook her head, not in reply, but in an attempt to free it from what felt like an invisible shroud draped around it. A glass of water was held to her lips, and she drank from it greedily, almost emptying the glass. She felt a little better.

Pri spoke quickly. 'Amanda, listen. We were speaking. Fiona and I. I believe her. You've got to believe her too. That's why I'm here. We came to get you... Amanda, have you heard me? We've come to get you. Before they take you to St Catherine's.'

Amanda raised a finger and pointed at Fiona. 'We never spoke. About that night. I'm sorry. I tried to fool myself it had never happened.'

'My life was destroyed that night too,' Fiona said. 'We're in this together. And we're close, Amanda, so close...'

Amanda raised her eyebrows in a question mark.

'To the end, Amanda. I feel it. That's why I came. Because it's come back. It's come back for you. We need to do this. We may never get another chance.'

Amanda blinked.

'Us,' she said, the word settling for the first time in sync with the movement of her lips, 'what do you mean us?'

'That night,' Fiona said, 'it happened to me too. We were both raped, Amanda. Yes, me too. You tried to bury it, but you can't; you never will. Amanda, we don't have much time. Come with us.' She looked to Pri, then back to her.

'How did you get in here?'

'Does it matter. I know the procedure; I worked in the system for long enough. They think I'm your special. The real special will be here shortly.'

Amanda said nothing, a part of her retreating, too overwhelmed to know what to do.

'Not a sound,' Fiona said to Pri, who kicked the trolley brake off and tugged on the end as Fiona went behind the headboard and pushed. Together they began wheeling the trolley from the room.

It's quite normal for trolleys to be wheeled through A&E

departments; patients are continuously being conveyed to wards and other departments. No one took any notice. Pri's Jag was parked just outside the boom barrier to the ambulance bay. There, they helped Amanda from the trolley and into the Jag, pushing the trolley to the side and out of the way.

Amanda peered from the rear window as the Jag sped from the hospital. Fiona was sitting beside her. She suddenly remembered a time before that night, a time of laughter, fun and adventure, before it all came crashing down. A particular episode, forgotten until this moment.

'God, he's cute, isn't he? So gorgeous.' Fiona was giggling like a schoolgirl.

'He's not so bad, I suppose,' Amanda said.

'Is that all you can say?'

'Okay. He's more than cute. He's beautiful. He's Rudolph Valentino incarnate. God, what am I saying? The man is' – she lowered her voice, a little embarrassed – 'sex on legs, okay?'

They were lying sprawled on the sofa, Amanda's head on the armrest. It was 5 a.m., and they had just come in. Fiona giggled again.

'El Dorado,' she said. 'That's some club. Oh yes.'

And it was. A pulsating, grinding audio and visual extravaganza, the number one play pit for the A listers of Dublin city, the bankers, the media lovvies... everybody who was anybody, the big fish in a small pond.

'Edward,' Fiona said, and Amanda's ears pricked up.

'What about him?'

Fiona's voice had taken on a slushy tone that Amanda had never noticed before. 'Okay, be like that; you know what I mean, girl.'

'Know what?'

Fiona sat up, looking at Amanda intently. 'Did I ever tell you?' she asked.

It was Amanda's turn to giggle now. 'Tell me what?'

'Girls who like boys who like girls who like girls... or something like that.'

'What's that mean? That you like girls?'

Fiona's eyes blazed. 'Is that what you think? Seriously? Like, is it?'

Amanda took a breath. 'Is there any more wine?'

'No. There's not.'

'Okay... what's the question again?'

'You just said do I like girls. You asked that. Why? Do I look like a dyke to you?'

Amanda gave another giggle. 'Come on. I was only messin'. Don't get so serious. I know you don't like girls.'

Fiona's face was hard, expressionless.

'Really, come on,' Amanda said, 'I was only joking.'

And then Fiona burst out laughing. 'Fooled ya. You thought I was serious. Ha!' She fell silent. 'Maybe I do like girls.' Fiona placed her hand on Amanda's. 'Maybe I like you...'

Amanda laughed. 'Woohoo,' she said, and puckered her lips playfully, closing her eyes, 'gis'a kiss, then.'

Which Fiona proceeded to do. Amanda turned her head away.

'Okay, okay.' Her eyes opened. 'This's gone far enough.'

Fiona burst out laughing again, pointing. 'Look at you. Would ya get a grip, girl. I'm only winding you up. Jeez, and you thought I was the uptight one.'

But Amanda wasn't sure about that, not sure at all.

'I know,' Fiona said, 'let's go out and get something to eat. Someplace must be open.'

'It's five o'clock in the morning. We need to get some sleep. What's got into you? I've never seen you like this before. Did you take something at that club I don't know about?'

A guilty look crossed Fiona's face. She giggled, got up and started wobbling towards her bedroom. She opened the door and turned.

'Maybe,' she said, taking a step backwards, closing the door slowly, looking at Amanda all the time. 'Maybe Fiona's been a naughty girl.' She laughed again, and the door closed, the sound of her laughter echoing from the other side.

Amanda squeezed her eyes shut, turning off the memory, and realised she didn't fully trust Fiona and never had.

47

She listened to the drone of the powerful engine, felt every pitch and roll as the car took bends and corners at high speed. Amanda was sweating again, her whole body stiff and tense. She fumbled for the window button on the door console and pressed it, felt the cool air flood in. The road noise was a flat, constant background monotone. Pri was talking rapidly, and Amanda tried to concentrate on what she was saying... 'We went to the beach shelter and spent over an hour there talking... Fiona told me everything, about what happened to her that night...'

'Where're we going?' Amanda asked.

'To a house I own,' Fiona answered. 'Outside Limerick city. No one will find us there.'

'Pri,' Amanda said, staring ahead, 'what if you're wrong? What if this is a trap?'

Pri looked back at her in the rear-view mirror, the headlights of a passing car making her look like she was peering through a letter box. Her eyes were bright, alive, more alive than Amanda could remember ever having

seen them before. This was an adventure to her, Amanda
thought, a break from the monotony of her stay-at-home
boring life and her husband. But she saw too in that
fleeting moment a flicker of doubt, because Pri hadn't
fully thought this through either. Neither had Amanda, of
course, but the difference was Amanda didn't have a
choice.

Amanda turned back to the open window again, felt
the cold air on her face, closing her eyes, taking a deep
breath, doing her potato-sack routine. But it was too late.
Everything was too late.

There was no going back now.

SHE MUST HAVE SLEPT. When she opened her eyes again,
she saw a high, red-brick wall running along the side of
the road outside her window. She looked to the other side,
and there was a row of terraced houses. As they continued, the houses gave way to fields crossed diagonally by a
line of huge electricity transmission towers. On her side of
the road the high stone wall continued, however, and up
ahead she could see a gap appear in it. As they
approached, Fiona pointed to it and told Pri to slow down.
'Turn in there,' she said.

The car swung through the gap, a rough track
stretching ahead in a long gently sweeping curve, disappearing into a thicket of trees.

They continued on, and in the middle of the thicket of
trees was a clearing. In the middle of the clearing was a
small, red-brick cottage, little more than a dark outline
squatting before them. Pri drove along the side of the
cottage and turned the Jag in a wide circle until it was
pointing back the way they had come. She cut the engine.

The silence was sudden and disconcerting. Amanda stared through the windscreen, through the gap in the trees, just able to make out the track they had just come down stretching off and disappearing into the darkness.

'No one knows about this place,' Fiona said, and something about her tone struck Amanda with apprehension and fear. She suddenly felt there was no escape, like she was never going to get out of here... alive, that is. And worse still, a part of her didn't care.

Pri opened the driver's door and was about to get out.

'Wait,' Fiona said. 'Listen.'

Amanda held her breath, not daring to move. She thought she had heard something: she listened, but could hear nothing, nothing at all. She looked at Fiona beside her, but could only make out her outline in the thick, syrupy light.

'Okay,' Fiona said, 'I thought I heard something, that's all. Let's go. Come on, let's get our stuff and go inside.' She opened her door and climbed out. Amanda followed. Fiona fumbled for the key at the front door while Amanda's eyes adjusted to the darkness. She could see a scaffold fixed to a gable wall at one end, and the sash windows along the front of the cottage were sandpapered down to bare wood in preparation for painting. Building debris lay scattered about on the muddy ground by both sides of the door. Amanda heard the lock slide back as Fiona turned the key. She pushed the door open and stepped into the inky blackness of the cottage. But Amanda didn't move. She heard the clip of Fiona's shoes on the floor, a stone floor by the sounds of it.

Pri came from behind and stood next to her.

'Go on, Amy, get inside,' she said. Pri nudged her, a little roughly, Amanda thought. 'It's okay, go on.'

Amanda stepped into the house, and Pri followed. The door closed behind her, and a light came on.

'I'm sorry, Amy,' Pri said, catching her look, 'if I was a little rough just now, but we needed to get inside.'

The air was cold inside the cottage, and there was a musty smell, a mixture of damp and wood. They were standing in a short hallway, and ahead of them Fiona was standing in a room. Pri led the way in. It was a combined living room-cum-kitchen, furnished in retro style, lots of pinewood, a couple of worn fabric sofas and a couch, an old-fashioned range cooker, bare rafter ceiling. It took a lot of money to have a place look this simple.

'Thank God I have the interior finished,' Fiona said, moving to a back door and sliding a heavy bolt across it. 'At least we should be safe until...' She walked back across the room, passed Amanda and Pri, went along the hall to the front door and did the same here, sliding the bolt across, the sound a metallic whip crack, carrying a sense of ill will with it, and so too, a latent violence.

Sounds that brought Amanda back to that night, back to that room and to that bed. She could smell that mixture of alcohol and sweat again, male sweat, overpowering, consuming her, as Fiona turned and smiled. But something about that smile struck fear in Amanda. She took an involuntary step back, as if trying to escape. But there was no escape. Not now. They were all locked in this house together.

48

'A re you afraid?' Fiona asked. 'Uncomfortable? Of me?'

Amanda said nothing.

'Understandable if you are,' Fiona added. 'We have a lot to talk about, Amanda. Let's get a fire going.'

THEY SAT around the open fire a little later, mugs of steaming tea in their hands. Fiona had to go back outside to fetch a bucket of logs. When she came back in, she pulled the curtain tighter about one of the windows because the light could be seen from outside. Amanda's wrists suddenly hurt, and she ran a hand over them, feeling what she thought were welts, and with it a numbness, but when she looked, there was nothing there. Slowly, the numbness receded, and she pushed forward in her seat, feeling the welcoming heat of the flames on her face.

'You want me to make myself scarce?' Pri asked, as if

sensing the solemness of the moment between both women.

'No, Pri,' Amanda said. 'I want you here.'

Pri nodded.

Amanda sipped from the piping hot tea and cradled the mug in both hands. She detected the faint aroma of body wash and remembered that Fiona had always liked gels, soaps and bubble baths. The bathroom in their apartment had always been full of them.

For some moments no one spoke, the only sound the crackling of the wood logs in the open hearth.

'I didn't think it so unusual,' Fiona said then, her voice very low, like a baritone, as if a different person were speaking. Her expression had altered too, distant, removed. Amanda knew in that moment that this was how she had dealt with everything, by removing herself from it. 'I mean, in my professional career I've dealt with countless similar cases. But this one is unique.'

Amanda glanced to Pri.

'I told her,' Pri said. 'I told her, Amy, how you got pregnant. I had to.'

Amanda nodded, but said nothing.

'Yes,' Fiona said. 'I coined a phrase, nescius, from the Latin, pronounced ness-shoes, for unconscious, or not aware, in this case an unconscious violation. Probably, knowing what I do now, by the symptoms that I certainly exhibited, and I presume you too, Amanda, my, our drinks were spiked with Rohypnol.'

'I know that,' Amanda said, 'or something similar.'

'No. I'm certain that's the one,' Fiona said. 'By the way, you know that that drug has never been approved for medical use in the US?'

'No,' Amanda said, shaking her head. 'I didn't. Look, wait... how do you know the same happened to me?'

'Well, didn't it?'

'That's not the point. You said you knew. The message you left on the answer machine. How could you... unless you were there.'

Fiona laughed. 'Oh, give me a break. Is that what you think? That I was there? What, looking on from the shadows?'

Amanda thought it sounded very silly now that she'd said it aloud.

'Hm, it made sense... at the time.'

'Of course, because nothing made sense. You were looking for answers. Well, you can forget that one. To me, it was obvious it had happened to you. And it had.'

'Yes, yes, it had.' She could hear an anger creeping into her voice.

'Because we never spoke about it,' Fiona said softly. 'Remember? Your now husband back then was a medical student; he would have had little trouble getting hold of that drug... You're going to report this, aren't you? Even now?'

Amanda was silent again. The reflection of the flames danced across her face.

'I'll come with you,' Fiona pressed.

Amanda ignored that question for now. 'If Edward assaulted me,' she asked instead, 'did he assault you too?'

Fiona shook her head. 'I can say with certainty that he did not. I've seen his graduation photos. They're online, on the college website. His build is all wrong. The man who raped me was taller, heavier.'

'But it happened at the same time,' Amanda said, 'so someone he knew? Were they working together?'

Fiona nodded. 'Probably.'

Amanda looked down, folded her arms tightly. 'My God, two of them,' she said, looking up. 'I never stopped to consider it might have happened to you as well. And that we never talked about it. I didn't talk about it. I had the feeling that you wanted to; that's why I avoided you. Can you believe it? I was too caught up in my own shame to even begin to think about what might have happened to you. I just wanted to forget. I'm sorry, Fiona, truly.'

'Yes,' Fiona said, 'I know. But you had nothing to be ashamed of, and neither did I. We were victims. We were not responsible. But like many victims, we didn't see it that way. Did you think it was somehow your fault?'

'Yes,' Amanda said, 'sometimes I did,' her voice rising. 'But it wasn't my fault. I know that now. But, over the years, when I was alone sometimes, feeling particularly low, I'd think about it and think about it until it would consume me, with no release, no one to talk to about it, to share it with, and then, during those times, well then, I could believe anything, yes, that it was my fault, and yes' – her voice dropped – 'that I even deserved it.'

'But it's not,' Fiona snapped. 'You understand that now, don't you?'

Amanda nodded.

'I want you to say it,' Fiona said. 'Don't just nod your head. I want you to say it, "It's not my fault." Go on.'

Amanda noted the fire in Fiona's eyes.

'It's not,' she began, but fell silent, feeling the anger building in her again, rolling through her, a snowball, getting bigger and bigger, as she suddenly shouted, 'It's not my fault. No! It's not. I didn't deserve it. It's not my fault!'

Fiona smiled.

'Good,' she said, 'that's what I wanted to hear.'

'But,' Amanda began. Once more she fell silent.

Even now, that instinct, that need to keep everything quiet, hidden, was overpowering. But now, she knew, she could no longer stay silent; now she had to face up to it.

'I will report it,' she said, her voice low but determined. 'I have to. It's Edward. I have to do this.'

'But we need to be careful,' Fiona said. 'He's probably capable of doing whatever it takes to keep this whole thing quiet. It will destroy him, you know, his career, everything, when this gets out.'

Amanda nodded. She knew.

'After that night,' Fiona continued, 'I also had to be honest with myself. But first I went through a process, a craving to belong, to be accepted. Every night I would wake up consumed by guilt and self-loathing, and that's always the barometer to me of what matters in my life at any one moment, what I have to deal with, what I must deal with, even if I'm trying to deny it myself, to avoid it.'

'And that's me,' Amanda said. 'The only difference is I never got beyond it.'

'Yes, that need to belong, to be accepted, to be' – she raised her hands and used a couple of fingers to apostrophise – 'normal, to blend in.' She lowered her hands again. 'I got married. His name was Alex Crowley, the last man I ever had a relationship with, before I became honest with myself, that is. The marriage was a disaster. Poor man. When I told him a couple of months later that I was leaving, I could see the relief on his face. He subsequently married again, to a woman who this time appreciated him, because he really was a lovely man. He has three lovely children now, and we still keep in touch. Anyway, I kept his name; it helped me fit in, took suspicion from me I felt; the fact that I'd been married, it removed the need for explanation and gave me that sense of belonging I craved. And it forced me to become honest. I stopped trying to fool myself and everybody else, which I'd been doing all along. I said to myself, "To hell with it." So I became true to my own sexuality, and it was a liberation, I can tell you. Ireland back then was such a different place, wasn't it, Amanda? You know what I mean, don't you?'

Amanda nodded, thinking back to the stifling religiosity that had controlled every aspect of life back then. Even now, in an age of relative enlightenment, when the prime minister of the country himself was gay, for God's sake, it was hard to believe that back then, having a child out of wedlock or being gay meant being socially shunned, being an outcast, ostracised by everybody, even your own family. She thought of her own parents and had no doubt that was how they would have treated her had they known. Indeed, those were cruel times for anyone who in any way was an outsider.

'But,' Fiona continued, 'if I may put it like this, I always, well, leaned the other way, didn't I, Amanda? You picked up on it, right?'

Amanda thought back again to that night, when they had come home from the club, and Fiona had kissed her. She nodded.

'I tell you this for a reason,' Fiona said. 'Because I lived with a partner for a number of years. We eventually split. She had been married, to a man of course, and had one child, a son, Shane. I have to say, those years I spent with her were the happiest of my life. But it didn't work out. Anyway, when the relationship finished, I was brokenhearted, not so much for what had been lost between myself and Angela, that was her name, by the way, but with Shane, her son. He was six years old. I was absolutely broken-hearted. I was so close to him, I had to pinch myself that he wasn't really my child. Can you imagine how that feels? I mean, really?'

Amanda nodded. She knew how that felt.

'Yes,' Fiona said knowingly, 'I know you can. It's so, so... visceral, like having your heart ripped out. I never forgot him, how could I? Some years later, he was a teenager by then and I had lost all contact, a person was referred to me by Social Services. It was him. He never made the connection. How could he? But it was him, Shane.' Fiona paused, her eyes misting over. 'I should never have allowed it, I really shouldn't, because it was a conflict of interest; it was never going to be possible for me to be impartial. But I was so delighted to be able to spend time with him, and I looked forward to seeing him once a week, every week. I never revealed the connection to him, I couldn't. He had a lot of issues, and I was very concerned; it obscured my professional judgement. He took his own life, and I was struck off because I was deemed, correctly, not to have acted professionally. I enabled his deviant behaviour, his drug taking, other things too, allowed him to do what he wanted rather than doing what was right, giving him what he needed. There is a crucial difference. But at the time I couldn't see it. I chose the easier option because I didn't want to challenge, to upset him, told myself it would be alright, he would be alright. Unbelievable, really, for a mental health profes-sional to do such a thing. In other words, I fooled myself. They said I caused his death. In any case, I lost my career. Why do I tell you this? Because that boy had been raped too; his drink had been spiked; it had happened to him just as it happened to me, happened to us. But he couldn't deal with it. It set up a rage in me. It was obvious I was angry. I was angry with everyone, friends, relatives, assistants at the supermarket, everybody, you name it. Until eventually, people would have nothing to do with me; can't say I blame them. I was angry towards you too, Amanda, when I heard from you, until I realised why you were contacting me, and it gave me something for the first time in years. It gave me hope. If I could try to understand what happened that night, then I might find peace; we both might.'

A log in the fire crackled, throwing up a shower of sparks that fell against the fire guard and extinguished.

A sudden, loud, shrill voice could be heard, 'Go on, Go on, Go on.' Amanda snapped her head towards it, saw Pri pick up her mobile phone from the table. She couldn't help but smile; it was just another of her wacky ringtones. Pri placed a hand over the phone, muffling the sound, not answering it. She turned to Amanda. 'It's Lauren; she's been ringing me. This is the third call. She wants to talk to you. You okay to take it?'

Amanda stretched out her hand. 'Yes, Pri, thanks.'

Pri handed her the phone.

Amanda cleared her throat, took a breath, and pressed the answer button.

'Lauren, sweetheart, it's late, shouldn't you be—'

'Mum!' Lauren cut her off, her tone urgent. 'Where are you, for God's sake? I couldn't get hold of you on your mobile. What's happening, Mum? Tell me.'

Amanda wondered, did her daughter know about the hospital? Had Edward or somebody else told her?

'Everything is fine, Lauren.' She hoped her voice did not portray the lie.

'Where are you?'

'I told you. I'm with Pri.'

'But I rang Pri's landline. Liam answered. He doesn't know where anybody is, Mother.'

'Oh, well, um, that's because myself and Pri had something to do. Liam doesn't know about it. I'll tell you all about it later. But everything's fine, Lauren, honestly. Please don't worry.'

Lauren fell silent. Amanda crossed her fingers.

'Well, if you're sure,' Lauren said.

'I'm sure.'

The line crackled with static.

'Please, Lauren, everything is fine... I need to go. I'm tired, talk to you tomorrow, okay? Goodnight, sweetheart.'

She finished the call before Lauren could reply, sat holding the phone, thinking of her daughter, who was now thinking and worrying about her. How was all this going to end? And, more importantly, when?

Suddenly, the lights flickered and then went out, throwing the room into darkness save for the glow from the open fire. The three women silently looked to one another, the flames dancing over them, catching their startled expressions, like images in a gothic painting. There was a sound, so soft it could have been a breath of wind. But it wasn't – it was a noise from outside; it seemed to have come from the other side of the front door. They waited, but nothing followed. Amanda exhaled the long breath she'd been holding, relaxing her tight shoulders, turning her gaze from the door. Just then, something flickered at the very edge of her vision. She returned her gaze, staring, and saw that Fiona had forgotten to slide the bolt back into place after bringing in the wood.

Or had she? Could she have done this on purpose? To make the task easier for whoever it was outside to enter.

She saw it again, what had attracted her attention, and blinked. Was she seeing things? Then it came again, and now there was no doubt. She was not seeing things.

The handle was turning.

49

As the door opened, Amanda felt an icy blast of wind blow in. For a moment it seemed that no one was there, but then she saw something, a movement, sudden, indistinct, featureless, an apparition, an orb of bright light; it seemed to float into the cottage and move along the wall from the door.

Fiona jumped to her feet, and Amanda stiffened. Beside her Pri raised her head and just stared. Fiona took a step forward and froze. Amanda could see why. The apparition was holding something in its other hand, revealing itself as a dark malicious outline, but unmistakable nonetheless: a shotgun.

Time seemed to stand still. Then a voice spoke.

'Sit,' it commanded, a male voice, calm and icy.

Fiona went back to her seat and sat down, and for a moment there was nothing but silence, a surreal, deafening, evil silence.

The light swung across the three women; it seemed so bright. Amanda raised a hand, shading her eyes against it.

Then she understood what it was, it was the light from a powerful torch, and it was pointed directly at her.

'You. Drop your hands.'

Amanda realised the voice was speaking to her. She dropped her hands. The light shifted again, settling on Pri, who bowed her head away from it, looking at the floor, wrapping her arms tightly about herself, as if trying to become smaller, to hide, to disappear.

'Look up,' the voice boomed, a frightening, jarring contrast to the silence that had just gone before, impacting all three women as surely as a physical slap. 'I said look UP!'

If its intention was to intimidate and cow, then it had succeeded.

The light shifted once more, onto Fiona this time, who seemed to have quickly regained her composure, sitting up in her chair, staring ahead, unflinching, defiant.

Amanda thought: Oh Christ.

She began to shake, everything from the last twenty-two years, all her fear, anxiety, stress, that entire cesspit, coming to the fore now, threatening to drown her. She could feel herself slipping into it, her grip along the edges of reality tentative and fading. She knew it would be so easy to just let go and drift off.

No. No. No. Hold on. You must. You need to be strong.

The light suddenly shifted away from them, and Amanda could see the shape for a brief moment as it moved back to the door and kicked it shut, the shotgun visible in the light of the fire, its barrel pointed at them. As if she was morbidly mesmerised, Amanda forgot about everything but that one question, wondering... Is that Edward? In the dim light, she couldn't be certain. Now she saw something in the belt he wore around what appeared to be a pair of overalls. Was that...? Amanda couldn't be certain, but it appeared to be the blackthorn stick from her home, the one Edward had been using at the hospital.

And then the shape was gone, hidden again behind the beam of light, which widened now, taking in the three women sitting in a half circle in front of a roaring fire, like a spotlight in a macabre play. The dancing flames of the fire gave brief glimpses of him as he came and stood next to it, revealing more detail, and one in particular. That his face was covered by a mask, cling-wrapping the ears and nose, buttressing the lips, cobwebbing the eyes behind a fine mesh.

Amanda's body began to spasm at the sight of it, her belly contracting like a concertina, tighter and tighter, as she tried vainly to stop what was about to happen, but it was no use, the liquid coming, forming a puddle on the chair between her legs, warm and strangely comforting, before dripping onto the floor, the sound loud and out of all proportion to its source, plop, plop, plop.

But then, like her fear had exhausted itself, she felt an anger begin to stir deep within her, gaining strength, in turn making her feel psychically stronger as she thought: How dare he. HOW FUCKING DARE HE!

Her hands moved, pressing down onto the corners of the chair as she began to rise from it. Without stopping, she ran forward blindly, extending her hands, her long nails like talons ready to tear through that mask, into the flesh beneath... But then, she felt a searing pain across her cheek and stumbled, as with lightning speed the blackthorn stick made impact, rising into a high arc and pausing at the top, ready to come down and strike again.

It didn't need to. Amanda fell, outstretching her arms

at the last moment, cushioning the impact as she hit the floor. She lay there, dazed, feeling no pain at all, strangely.

There was a silence, a thick, heavy silence. The firelight flickered on a pair of shoes to the side of her, fawn leather, a crow's feet of black crease lines across the middle. Something about those shoes seemed vaguely familiar, but she forgot about them as her mouth opened and emitted a low croaking noise. They looked like Edward's old golfing shoes. She turned her eyes up, peering at the shape towering above her, but couldn't be certain. Was this him? Then she heard a voice, realised it was her own, pleading, 'Who are you? Edward?'

Her question was ignored, and she asked again, louder this time, 'Who are you, I said?' as she began to crawl forward, wincing with the pain. She suddenly reached out with a speed that would have surprised her if she'd even been conscious of it. But she wasn't. All she was aware of was the gritty texture of the fabric of the trousers he, this person, was wearing, between her fingers as she grabbed it. Her breathing seemed to pulse through the air.

'Tell me?' she screamed, summoning all her energy. 'Who are you? Are you Edward? And why... why have you come back? Tell me.'

Something moved, the dancing flames revealing an abstract of flesh that she knew then to be his hand. A noise, similar to that of the buzzing she had heard all those years ago, but this time softer, not an electric razor, more like a zipper. She stared, discerning in the soupy light that he had unzipped the overall to roughly his navel. He laid the torch on the ground, and his hand disappeared inside, emerged again clutching a large plastic bottle. He twisted the cap off and discarded it; she heard it tinkle across the floor. One of the fawn leather shoes moved, swinging back into the darkness before emerging again – at speed, heading straight for her face. She gasped and jerked her head to the side just in time, felt the wash of air on her skin as it passed.

For a moment she was unable to move, frozen to the spot, but then realised he had not sought to kick her; he was merely stepping by. She laid her head down, pressing her cheek against the cold floor, watching as he approached Fiona, holding the bottle out to her. Now the light was sufficient for her to see something else inside his belt, the coil of rope. And she knew, just knew, with a sickening clarity, what that was intended for. She calculated that she was being ignored – merely for now – because she was injured and, probably, because she had pissed herself. Amanda was certain of something else too, that none of this would be enough to save her.

An inexplicable sense of calm started to spread through her, with it a feeling of detachment; she could feel the regular beat of her heart through her chest against the floor; it was almost hypnotic. She was calm, because in this moment she didn't care what happened to her, because there was something she sought, and she would do whatever it took to achieve it: revenge.

She used the darkness to conceal herself just as he had done. There wasn't a lot of time. He started to nudge the bottle against Fiona's closed mouth, some of the contents spilling down her chin. It would not be long before Fiona succumbed and was forced to drink some or all of the contents.

He spoke, his voice low, like a distant rumble, but crystal clear: 'Drink. I made this cocktail especially for you. Drink, I said. You won't need much. Go on, drink.'

Amanda crawled across the floor, hidden within the

darkness lying beyond the pool of torchlight. The fire was ahead of her, mere feet away, and soon its light would cast itself onto her too. But for now she was safe. She continued as a tentative plan began to form in her mind, feeling the growing heat on her body as she approached the flames. The heat became intense as she stopped in front of the fire, glancing back, knowing that if he turned now, he would see her. But he appeared too busy to notice. Fiona's head was yanked back, the bottle pressed so tightly against her lips that she could not even move her head. It would not be long now before those lips parted. In his other hand he held the shotgun, resting it against his chest on top of the belt buckle for support, trained on Pri, the finger resting on the trigger. One false move. That was all it would take. Pri sat completely still. A rage began to burn in Amanda, as intense as the fire now clawing at her skin. She looked ahead again, squinting against the heat, saw the fire shovel with its wooden handle leaning against the wall by the hearth. Her plan became complete. She quickly reached out and gripped the shovel handle, stretching up her other hand, gripping the edge of the stone mantel above. She began to pull herself up, the heat mercifully moving from her face to her clothes, which acted as a temporary shield, and pushed the shovel into the flames. At that moment he spoke, a gruffness to his voice, an insistence, a command, repeating it over and over, 'Open your mouth. Open your mouth. Open your mouth...' his voice masking the sound of the shovel.

She pulled it from the flames loaded with burning logs. But it was too heavy to lift with one hand. She took her other from the mantel and used both to hoist it into the air. Her heart pounded like a drum, and she expected at any moment to feel his hand on her shoulder, flinging her back from the fire, across the floor. She began to turn awkwardly, her raging endorphins masking the pain in her cheek, convinced she would find him standing behind her, waiting for her. But he was not, too preoccupied dealing with Fiona. Amanda knew at any moment Fiona would be forced to give in.

She crept up behind him, seeing nothing but the outline of his back; there was nothing else that existed in the world but that. Closer and closer she came, the heat and smoke from the logs shrouding and stinging her face, forcing her to partially close her eyes, her vision like looking through blades of grass at twilight. She was almost there, his outline filling her limited vision. He suddenly leaned forward, growling, 'Take this. I said take it,' the movement causing his overall to billow. It was just what she needed. She paused, calculating, gaining a crucial sense of perspective, because she would only get one attempt at this. She stepped to the left and then one step ahead, into the pool of torchlight. All his attention was on Fiona, with evidently no concern his two other captives posed him any danger. Amanda swung the shovel, keeping the motion fast but measured. Immediately she felt it impact his chest, and she felt the teeth of the partially open overall zipper along the edge of her palm before she flipped the shovel handle up, the burning logs sliding down inside the overall, getting trapped around his crotch area.

His roars sent shock waves through the air as the shotgun and bottle fell from his hands. Amanda opened her eyes wide to see him scampering like a wounded animal towards the door, trailing smoke and flames... He pulled the door open, and Amanda immediately felt the merciful wash of cold air over her. He flew out into the night with a feral howling sound, slapping at his crotch area, sparks and smoke billowing up into the night.

And then he was gone, the horrible howling sound fading to silence. If it hadn't been so deadly serious, it might have been funny.

Amanda flopped down onto the empty chair next to her and looked at Pri in the wedge of light from the torch lying on the ground. Without a word her friend reached down and pulled out her mobile phone from her handbag lying on the floor next to her. A light illuminated on it as she brought it to life, capturing the mixture of fear and shock on her face. Amanda watched as she stabbed a button three times, a voice answering almost immediately: '999, what's your emergency?'

As Pri began to speak, Amanda looked past her, the rest of the room in darkness. 'Fiona,' she called, 'Fiona, where are you?'

She strained to hear an answer while Pri continued talking frantically into the phone, but there was none. Amanda looked to the open door. Fiona had slipped out without her noticing. And where was the shotgun? That had been on the floor. But now it was gone. As if in answer to her question, the air filled with an ear-splitting boom, one she recognised immediately as the sound of a firearm being discharged somewhere close by. And then a voice sounded, high pitched and desperate. It was Fiona's as she screamed one word: 'Help.'

50

Pri took the phone from her ear as her mouth dropped open. She stared at Amanda, who stepped towards the door. Her jaw had started to hurt, a sharp stinging sensation.

'Don't,' Pri said, her voice quivering.

'Don't? We – I – have to. Fiona... she's in trouble.'

Pri reached out and grabbed Amanda's wrist. 'Don't. We can't... go out there. We can't. We wait. That's what we do. The police are on their way.'

'No,' Amanda said, pulling her hand away. 'Not this time. This time I fight back. This time it's different.' Pri wrapped her arms tightly around herself again, squeezing herself, and dropped her head: Everything just go away and leave me alone.

Amanda knew how that felt and thought, But this time I can fight back. I can. And I will.

She went to the doorway and looked out, the moon high in the sky, the ground coated in a glistening frost. What should be a pretty picture postcard was instead a poster to that horror movie she was living in.

Her eyes searched through the moonlight-diluted darkness. She detected the faint aroma of cordite and burning flesh on the air.

From the corner of her eye, she saw something glint by the gable wall to her left and turned towards it. It was the reflection of moonlight on the steel chamber of a shotgun. In Fiona's hands. Amanda gasped. A body was lying on its belly on the ground a short distance in front, a curl of smoke rising from beneath it into the air. She must have taken the shotgun, Amanda considered, when it fell from his hands, followed him out and... shot him!

'My God,' she said, running out into the night.

Fiona turned lazily and watched her approach, shifted the shotgun. Amanda stopped.

'I didn't kill him,' she said, her voice surprisingly calm, 'just winged him in the shoulder. But he hit his head on the way down, so I'm not so sure of anything anymore.'

Amanda eyed the shotgun warily, turned her gaze onto the body.

She suddenly felt like throwing up, and swallowed quickly a couple of times.

'Maybe he's dead,' she said softly. 'Look how still he is.'

'Do I care?' Fiona said. 'I hope he burns in hell, whoever he is, the bastard... Here, take this shotgun, will you?'

'Why?'

'Because I want to check if he's dead. Just in case. Not taking any chances with him, not now.'

Amanda looked at the body. She wasn't certain of anything anymore either. Is that Edward lying there?

Amanda took the shotgun. It was lighter than expected. Fiona helped her press the butt-stock against the wall so that she could balance against it and aim at the same time. Amanda watched as Fiona began walking over to the body, feeling the outline of the trigger against her finger, hoping she had the courage to pull it if required. Fiona took a couple of paces before she paused, glancing back at Amanda. She looked very uncertain all of a sudden.

In the distance there was the sound of sirens, barely audible, but growing louder with each passing second. Amanda felt overcome by a fear that this opportunity would be lost. It was suddenly important to her that she be the one who unmasked this fiend. Was it Edward?

'Fiona,' she called, 'wait; come here,' her tone authoritative, in control, her medical professional's voice. 'Take it.' She nodded towards the shotgun.

Fiona seemed to sense Amanda's determination. She didn't object, came and took the weapon from her. Amanda walked towards the body, the sound of the sirens much louder now. She knew she had to be quick. The body was completely, deathly still.

Amanda stood over it and looked down, then knelt onto one knee. From the corner of her eye she saw Fiona raise the shotgun and aim it at the body, staring along the barrel. Amanda had no doubt that she would pull the trigger without hesitation – at the least provocation. A trickle of moisture ran down the back of her neck, her hands turning clammy. But her determination did not waver, even as she reached out a hand and saw that it was shaking.

Time seemed to slow down again. But she knew. She had to do this. She held her hand over the mask before lowering it, running her fingers along the gritty surface. What she thought was a coating of tiny particles of some sort, dust maybe, was, in fact, finely textured rubber. She hooked a couple of fingers beneath it, but immediately pulled them back again when she touched the flesh, wrinkly and brittle like it had been left in water too long. And it was cool to the touch.

She swallowed, gritting herself, a part of her wanting to go back to Fiona and not have to do this, wanting to return to the house and wait for the police, have them deal with it. But her fingers seemed to move of their own accord, squeezing under the mask again.

The sounds of sirens were ear splitting, and she could see headlights in the distance, blue flashing lights, bouncing through the air along the track to the cottage.

She took a breath and pulled.

51

'My God.' Her voice was hushed, like escaping steam. 'It can't be.' She turned her head before looking back again. Just to make sure.

Amanda could not believe it.

Yet.

There it was. In front of her. The proof.

How was it possible? It wasn't. It couldn't be. But it was. Because she was seeing it with her own eyes; she was staring at it. That face. His face. That benign, gentle face, that gentle soul, lifeless now. But he wasn't gentle or benign. He was none of those things. She reached out and touched his skin, making sure that this was real, that he was real, desperately needing to reassure herself of it. And he was, it was, it was all real.

How dare he? How dare the bastard? Fool me. Fool everybody. Her anger continued to build, reaching such a climax that it threatened to devour her, that she couldn't take it any longer, as she grabbed a fistful of her hair in each hand and started to scream, releasing just enough of twenty-two years of pent-up rage that it was sufficient to shore her up, to hold her together, was just enough to stop her from falling apart. Because it was all beginning to make sense. They had always been friends, such good, evil, twisted friends. She knew they must have been together on that night, operating in tandem.

Jesus!

She stared down at the body, at him, and it took her a moment to realise that his eyes were open, and he was staring back at her. She felt a pressure on her hand and looked to see his hand was resting on hers. She yelped and tugged on it, but his grip instantly tightened as his lips parted into a cruel smile, and in a rumbling whisper he spoke her name. 'Amanda.'

She screamed again and did not stop, the sound briefly drowned out by what seemed like a huge explosion, loud enough to make her ears ring. It was that of gunpowder igniting, hurling out its load of buckshot from the barrel of the shotgun in Fiona's hand. On her right side, Amanda felt a sensation like hot sparks against her flesh as she watched Andrew O'Shaughnessy's face rupture, spouting a geyser of blood and skin and God knows what else, some of it raining down on her, vile and sticky. She screamed harder than ever, and with one final, desperate tug, yanked her hand free from his death grasp and plopped onto her back, falling silent, staring at the sky, at the moon...

She became aware of the sirens again and an engine growling, of the scraping of tyres on gravel as a vehicle skidded to a halt metres behind her, headlights turning night into day. She pushed herself up onto her side, stared ahead in the harsh, glaring light, heard the pounding of feet rushing towards her, and voices, among them Fiona's,

all shouting at the same time: 'Jesus, she's got a shotgun'...
'I shot him' ... 'Shot who?' ... 'Him' ... 'Give me that' ...
'Sorry, sorry' ... 'What the fuck happened here?'

To Amanda it was merely background noise, chaff.

She was aware of someone leaning over her. She
looked up to see a policeman unclipping a radio mouth-
piece from his jacket. It made a squawking sound as he
raised it to his lips, and then he began speaking into it
rapidly, requesting an ambulance and other units to
attend. He quickly pulled on latex gloves when he'd
finished and squatted down beside O'Shaughnessy. The
geyser had stopped; in its place was what resembled a
thick red stew, white fragments of bone and one intact eye
floating on the surface of it.

The policeman looked at her briefly – he was scarcely
more than a teenager – as he stood. He turned away,
began to get violently sick.

52

The clock on the mantelpiece read 12:15 a.m. Amanda, Pri and Fiona were sitting by the window next to the front door of the cottage. The curtains had been pulled, and the door was open. The lights were on; someone had discovered that the main switch in the electricity service box had been turned off. Outside, there were lights all ablaze too, and the generators providing the power for these gave off a constant humming noise. Officers were coming and going, consulting with another who was sitting at the kitchen table, an epaulette on each shoulder; clearly he was the one in charge. Amanda could not stop glancing over at this heavily built, bald-headed man, and each time she did, she found his gaze was already upon her.

The realisation began to dawn: they were being treated – all three of them – as suspects.

The clock read 1:05 when this officer finally approached, stood before them with hands on his hips, silently observing them for a time before he spoke.

'Inspector Myles McDonald, ladies. If you could be so kind as to tell me what went on here tonight?'

'It's a long story,' Fiona said.

'Then shorten it,' he snapped. 'Who shot the victim, Andrew   O'Shaughnessy,   Doctor   Andrew O'Shaughnessy?'

'Me.'

He stared at Fiona.

'Did you now? Torture him too, or was that a group effort?'

'Torture?' the three women said in shocked unison.

'His balls were like used coals from a charcoal grill.'

'He wasn't tortured,' Amanda blurted. 'It was an act of self-defence. He was going to drug us. Rape us. You saw the mask. And the bottle, it's somewhere around here. He wanted us to drink from it... analyse the contents, you'll see.'

'An act of self-defence,' he repeated.

'Yes.'

He raised an eyebrow. 'Yes, I'm beginning to see. Indeed, it must be a long story. It always is. One that we're not going to make any sense of tonight, I can tell. You'll be coming to the station, all of you, pending interviews in the morning.'

'You mean we're being arrested?' It was Pri, who up to now had been very subdued and silent, so much so that Amanda was certain she was in a state of shock. She looked at her, but thought that, by her voice and clear-eyed expression, she probably wasn't. Pri glanced furtively back to her, then to Fiona, and Amanda could see something pass behind her eyes. 'Well, I've done nothing wrong,' she said slyly.

Amanda's mind whirled. Pri was trying to distance

herself from them at a time when they all needed to stick together?

'What do you mean by that?' the inspector asked, his voice rising. 'That you've done nothing wrong? By inference I take it to mean that these two' – nodding his head – 'have. What exactly do you mean, please?'

Pri said nothing, dropped her head onto her chest in that way of hers that she'd been doing a lot of lately.

'I don't know,' she muttered. 'I'm just saying. I did nothing wrong. That's all.'

The inspector was about to say something when an officer suddenly entered the room and rushed over to him. He spoke in a voice so low that Amanda couldn't hear. Then the officer turned. Amanda recognised him. It was Broderick, who had interviewed her along with Kinsella at the station in Limerick. Amanda had a feeling that, as far as he was concerned, connections were continuing to build up. The look on his face said it all as he turned to her: villain.

'So,' Inspector McDonald said, looking directly at Amanda too, 'you didn't mention any of what this officer has just informed me of, did you now? Thought we wouldn't find out, did you? Thought we wouldn't enquire? Silly. You, Dr Amanda Jackson, are a runner from protective custody at the University Hospital in Galway, specifically psychiatric services. You were to be committed, Dr Jackson, weren't you, for your own good? And I can see now, for the good of others too. Well, they're not getting you back until we talk to you first, and I don't care how mad you are.'

She stared at him, stung by the comment, pressing herself against the wall, as if trying to escape through it, from this place, from him. In all her professional life she'd always understood the importance of empathy, no matter what the circumstances. It shocked her that a policeman – a senior policeman – could display such a lack of these same qualities now.

'I'll remember that,' she said, her eyes blazing. 'I won't forget it, I promise you that. And neither will you. I'll make sure of that. You're making a big mistake.' She looked to Pri and Fiona. 'Because we're the victims here. Us.'

'Yes of course,' he said, condescension dripping from his tone, 'you would say that, wouldn't you? Now, Broderick, take them away, for God's sake. I'm getting a headache.'

But Broderick hesitated.

'Where will I take her?' He pointed at Amanda. 'There's a signed committal order for St Catherine's for her. If she's...'

'Yes, I know, mad, then we can't lock her up at the station. Yes, yes, I know. Take her to St Catherine's, then. Makes no difference to me; we still interview her in the morning, only we now do it there. Take the other two to the station; arrest them on suspicion.'

'You can't—' Fiona started.

'I can,' he cut her off. 'And I just have. You've a history too, my lady, don't you? Yes, I know all about it.'

'Who signed the committal order?' Amanda demanded.

'None of your business,' the senior officer retorted.

'O'Shaughnessy, wasn't it? Jesus, don't you get it?'

'Oh, I get it alright. Dr O'Shaughnessy signed the committal order, and now he's dead. Get them out of here, Broderick,' he snarled. 'I told you. I'm getting a headache.'

53

Broderick sat in the back of the patrol car alongside her. He said nothing on the half-hour drive to St Catherine's. The hospital was in darkness when they arrived, no exterior lights, no lights along the driveway either. Nothing, except, that is, for a single bulb glowing above the heavy wooden main door. They drew up outside, and the driver went and rang the bell. When the door opened, a tall, hulking man, dressed in a white tunic and trousers, was standing there. The officer spoke with him, gesturing towards the car. The man, a nurse Amanda presumed, nodded, then emerged, and they both approached. Broderick got out and went round and opened her door.

'Out you get,' he said.

She got out of the car slowly.

The nurse immediately came and assisted her gently.

'This way, please,' he said. 'We have a room ready, Dr Jackson.'

She felt his hand on her back, and with his other hand he indicated to the door. 'This way, please,' he repeated.

She heard the officers getting back into their car behind her. But only when she'd passed through the doorway into St Catherine's and the thick heavy door had begun to close did the patrol car pull away.

She'd been to St Catherine's a couple of times in the past. Now, with most of the lights off and shafts of moonlight coming through the high, narrow, arched windows, it seemed to exude its gothic soul, its true self, so that she hardly recognised it.

The nurse seemed to read her thoughts.

'Yes,' he said, 'it's very quiet at night here. Our patients sleep best when the whole building is silent and in darkness. They're very sensitive to any light or noise.'

She nodded, noticing his name tag, 'Kevin'.

'Let's get you to your room,' Kevin said, the sounds as they moved towards the elevator in a corner echoing in the empty foyer. They took it to the third floor, got off onto a long corridor with numbered doors on either side. They stopped outside 243, and Kevin used a key card to open it.

'I left a nightshirt and a few things on the bed for you,' he said, 'slippers too, and fresh towels in the bathroom. Anything else, you let me know.' He turned on the lights, the sudden brightness forcing her to squint her eyes against it. When her eyes had adjusted, she saw that the room was not too dissimilar to any to be found in any mid-scale, branded, high street hotel chain.

'It's not what you thought, is it?' he said.

And it wasn't, but more especially for the bars across the window.

She didn't answer.

He walked to the window and held the cord dangling from a corner and pulled the slats shut.

'Your face is swollen, I see. Is it giving you pain? You need me to have a look at it?'

He lowered his gaze, and his eyes seemed to linger on her chest area before slowly moving down, over her body...

'No,' she said, 'I don't,' starting to feel uncomfortable.

'Are you sure?' A curdling to his voice as he stepped closer. She could smell his stale breath. 'Because I think you need a good seeing to, Dr Jackson, I really do.' He ran his tongue slowly between his lips.

She felt an invisible kick to her stomach, a mixture of fear and shock. What the hell is happening here? 'I want you to leave this room. Now.'

He smiled, revealing small, yellow, crooked teeth.

'Of course, Dr Jackson, anything you say.' But he made no effort to leave, instead reached into a pocket of his tunic and took from it a small vial of pills. He opened it and took out two, offered them to her between two chubby fingers. 'Here, take these.'

She peered at them. 'What?'

'They'll help you sleep, stop you thinking about things; they've been prescribed, Dr Jackson.'

'No. I don't want them.' Amanda felt so tired she would not need anything to help her sleep. But that was not why she wasn't taking them. She would take nothing this man offered her.

'You have to. They've been prescribed, Dr Jackson, I just said.'

'By who?'

He sighed. 'The chief psychiatrist, that's who. When the committal order was signed. Any other questions?'

'Oh, Dr O'Shaughnessy, that's who you mean.'

'Yes, of course, Dr O'Shaughnessy.'

Amanda edged backward. He was speaking like he didn't know O'Shaughnessy was dead. Or maybe he didn't care. In any case, she wasn't going to tell him. She really wanted to sit down. But she wouldn't, not until he had left. She was motionless, then reached out a hand. He smiled.

'That's it. Good girl.' He placed the pills onto her palm. 'Now, down the hatch.'

But Amanda turned her hand over so that the tablets dropped to the floor. She quickly squashed them beneath her foot.

'If you don't leave now,' she hissed, 'I'll scream, and I'll wake this whole fucking place up. You have five seconds, one... two...'

He raised the palms of both hands into the air, smiling again, displaying those horrible teeth once more. His eyes rummaged over her, like she was stock in a market, making no attempt to hide his leering. Amanda felt violated, crossing an arm tightly over her chest.

He turned and loped over to the door with a slow, cocky gait. Stepping out into the corridor, he turned again. 'Feisty, Dr Jackson, aren't you? Just the way I like them. Yes, just the way I like them.' He gave a little laugh.

The door shut, and Amanda felt the energy evaporating from her body, leaving her on the verge of collapse. She just managed to hobble to the bed, stretching out on it. She would not undress. She would stay like this, fully clothed. The words he'd said repeated in her head. She thought of his leering too. He was a predator, no doubt, as was O'Shaughnessy; such creatures always sought each other out, no matter where they were. But in here, amongst their helpless victims, gathered like sheep in a pen, they had their pick of easy prey.

Her eyes felt heavy, so heavy, and she fought against

the urge to close them, knowing that to do so meant she would fall asleep, and then she would be vulnerable.

'I must not sleep,' she muttered. 'I dare not, not here, in this place. I must...' But she could no longer resist, her eyes closing, clamping shut, and instantly she was taken down into a deep, dreamless void.

54

'When we went to church, hey ding dooram day, when we went to church, me being young, when we went to church, he left me in the lurch, maids when you're young, never wed an old man...'

The voice was so sweet that Amanda thought she must be dreaming. She liked that voice, and the ballad was familiar, the mighty Dubliners had made it popular years ago, a bawdy, rousing, funny song. But then another song entered her head, and she heard the chorus shouted out as it had been that night, when her voice was one of those half singing, half shouting along, 'Alice, who the fuck is Alice.'

She opened her eyes. Daylight was flooding into the room. She looked down, saw that she was still lying on her back, with a blanket half pulled around her, which she'd probably done in her sleep. She glanced about the room, saw an over-bed tray next to her, a tray with a bowl, a teapot, cup and saucer on top.

'Sleeping beauty has awoken, just in time for her porridge.'

The voice came from somewhere close by, but Amanda couldn't see anyone. She turned her head both ways, straining her eyes to see behind her. The woman stepped forward, as if from the wall, into Amanda's field of vision.

'Hello,' she said.

'Hello.'

The woman pointed. 'I was just taking down the name, removing it. From the wall. Of the last person in here.' She glanced at something in her hand. 'Mary, that was her name. Mary, Mary quite contrary. You're not contrary, are you? I don't know your name. They told me, but I forgot. That's why we have name tags on the wall, so people don't forget, you see. Do you like porridge? I hope you do; it's all we have.'

Amanda observed her. The woman wore a pale yellow smock with white trim, an embroidered patch on the front that said, 'Ursula, Special Catering Assistant.' She was small and thin, the body of a child, but the weathered face of an old woman, sunken cheeks and thin, flat hair.

'You come in last night?' she asked.

Amanda nodded. She needed to use the bathroom.

'You met Kevin, then.' Ursula pointed a finger and laughed, displaying her gums and a few teeth, lopsided like gravestones in an old graveyard. 'He's alright, but I much prefer Tommy. Tommy's nicer. He says he might marry me, if I'm good that is, and if I do everything he says. But he says I'm naughty. I don't think I'm naughty... well, maybe a little.'

Ursula laughed and began pressing the fingers of one hand into her groin area as she sang in that sweet voice of hers that did not belong in a place like this... 'Maids when you're young, never wed an old man...'

She continued singing, stepping towards the door.

'Ursula,' Amanda called, and she stopped, smiling, angling her head in curiosity as she looked at her. 'What about Dr O'Shaughnessy, Ursula, what's he like?'

Her smile disappeared. She shook her head, pursing her lips, and didn't speak.

'Tell me, Ursula, what was he like? You know he died last night, don't you?'

Ursula blinked, but her expression remained, like she couldn't process this information.

'Yes, Ursula. Dr O'Shaughnessy. He's dead.'

'Dead?'

Amanda nodded.

'Ghostface, dead?'

'Ghostface?'

'Yes. His nickname, silly. Cos of the mask he wears.'

Amanda shuddered. 'Mask? He wears a mask?'

'Yes. Scary. He's dead? Really? Ghostface?'

'Yes.'

Ursula laughed suddenly, stopped again just as quickly. And then that sound came once more, of her sweet voice singing, as she left the room. Amanda could still hear it in the corridor outside, slowly fading until it was gone, as she closed her eyes again.

IT TOOK her a moment to make sense of anything. Of the voices around her, of the memories from the night before. She tried to open her eyes... but was unable to. Was she trapped in this nightmare now? Forever? A fear consumed her, that she would never be able to open them again. Maybe I'm dead? Or maybe these people think I'm dead. Maybe I'm in a coffin, and maybe they are the congregation gathered round my grave. But I'm not dead. I'm here. I'm breathing. I'm not dead. I just can't open my damn eyes, that's all. Look at me; look, I'm breathing.

She felt a hand on hers, soft, gentle, and another on her forehead, brushing across it, and over her hair. 'Amanda, how are you?' a voice just as gentle asked. 'You seem agitated, Amanda. Is everything alright in there? Are you awake? Your eyes are flickering.'

And just like that, as if determining that it was safe now, her eyes opened, and she was staring into the face of a woman, a woman in a white tunic just as he, him, Kevin, had worn. Amanda jerked her head back into the pillow at the sight of it. She was wrong; she wasn't safe.

'No,' she said, 'no, go away...'

'Don't be alarmed, Amanda, everything's alright. My name's Jill O'Leary, head nurse... You do know where you are, don't you?'

Amanda nodded and took a gulp of air, looked about. She'd been asleep.

'Of course,' she said. 'I'm in the bloody loony bin.'

'We prefer to call it a psychiatric facility, Amanda.'

'Yes. Of course you do.'

The nurse peered down, her gaze searching.

'You've been through a lot. It will take time. Now, I want to look at your face, and you must then shower. You agree, Amanda?'

'What about him? The one who works nights.' Amanda could scarcely bring herself to say his name. 'Kevin. I don't want him near me. I don't want him touching me – ever. Do you hear me?'

'And did he?' Jill asked, no surprise or shock in her tone, merely a sense of resignation.

'You know about him, don't you?'

The head nurse didn't answer.

'Yes, you do. And O'Shaughnessy. You know about him too. What is it, the dirty little secret? Brushed under the carpet. I thought those days were over. You should be ashamed of yourself.'

'I tried,' the nurse said softly. 'I really did. It's not what you think, Amanda, just trust me on that, will you?'

'And what does that mean?'

'So this is our patient.' A male voice suddenly sounded, and Amanda looked to see a young man dressed in a grey suit, white shirt and red tie enter the room, come and stand by her bed. 'Dr Talbot, Dr O'Shaughnessy's registrar.' He gave a weak smile as he added. 'How are you, Amanda?'

'As well as might be expected.'

'The police are anxious to speak with you, but I wanted to get to you first.' He glanced to the head nurse. 'We both did. Is that alright?'

'You both did?'

He looked over his shoulder, like he was checking that nobody was standing there. 'I've been going over your notes. This may be a lot to take in, as events are happening so quickly, and I hope it doesn't all overwhelm you.' He fell silent.

'Why should it? There's nothing wrong with me apart from this.' She pointed to her cheek, then tapped her forehead lightly. 'But in here, I'm all there, believe me.'

He smiled again. 'Yes, I have no doubt.'

'Don't you? Then why am I here?'

'Let's get you sitting up first.'

When she was sitting up and comfortable, the head nurse standing on one side of the bed, Dr Talbot the other, he began.

'I need to be quick. Long story short, as I say. I've been going over your notes, all of them.' He glanced to the head nurse. 'In the absence of Dr O'Shaughnessy, after the tragic events of last night, I am in charge now. Yes, I've been over your notes, Dr Jackson, and your medical history too. I've looked at everything carefully. I really can't understand, no, I can't...'

He fell silent.

'Can't understand what?' Amanda prompted.

'Just as you say, there's nothing wrong with you. So what the hell are you doing here?'

'Is THERE anything you want to add?' Garda Broderick asked after he'd filled three foolscap sheets of paper with his neat cursive script. She had hesitated just a moment too long so that he looked up, his eyes narrowing ever so slightly.

She nodded emphatically, compensating for her hesitancy. Reassured, he smiled, replaced his pen back into the loop on the arm of his fleece and folded the statement carefully.

No, she had not lied; she had just not told him the whole truth.

'What about Fiona?' she asked as he got to his feet. 'Did you get a statement from her?'

'Yes. I did.'

She noted the way he looked at her had changed: his eyes no longer held dislike or accusation; instead – and she wasn't sure she liked this either, but she much preferred it – they held pity.

He stood still, holding her gaze. And in that moment, Amanda was certain that Fiona had told the policeman everything, her own complete story. And she felt certain too, that he knew that she had not.

'There's something else,' Broderick said, his tone lowering.

'Yes.' Here it comes, she thought.

'She has quite the CCTV set-up there, at the cottage. We were surprised at how elaborate it was, and the fact that she had it in the first place.'

'Really?' Amanda said, unable to hide her surprise, not surprised at this news, but surprise that Broderick wasn't pressing the matter of her statement – not for now in any case. As for Fiona having CCTV, that wasn't a surprise, not in the slightest, and not because she'd already mentioned it, she hadn't, but because it was just the sort of thing she'd expect her to have.

'And it provides evidence,' Broderick went on. 'It captures Dr O'Shaughnessy very well... suffice to say it provides a clear sequence of events.' He paused. 'I'd like to apologise, Dr Jackson. I got this one wrong. I'm sorry, if you can accept my apology. I have no doubt O'Shaughnessy is behind it all.'

Amanda looked away. In the brief time it took for her to look back again, she'd gone through everything. It wasn't just O'Shaughnessy. Yet... could she say this now? She knew Fiona hadn't mentioned that part. Because if she had, Broderick would have said. Fiona was leaving this up to her.

'Yes, Dr Jackson, is there something else?'

Broderick had that look again; he knew there was
something else.

'Not now,' she said. 'I need a little... time, that's all.
After all, I've waited this long. Might as well try to get it
right.'

'What do you mean?'

'I don't have enough is what I mean. To tell you
anything else. Not yet. But I will.' I hope.

Broderick seemed uncertain. 'Better to get it all out
now and let us decide.'

That's what I'm afraid of. If I get it all out now and let
you decide, you'll decide there's not enough. Because
there isn't enough. I need evidence, proof, something. My
testimony alone will not be sufficient. She could imagine
the scenario, Edward's word against hers, and after all this
time, contesting dates, proving dates, whatever, it would
be impossible. And watching on everything would be
Lauren. No, she needed more.

'Fine,' he said, getting to his feet slowly, like he was
reluctant to leave her, 'but don't hesitate to contact me if
you change your mind, or you want to talk to me further
about this. Understand?'

'I understand,' she said.

He nodded, and she watched him leave.

It was just after lunch when the young woman came into
Amanda's room, dressed in a smart navy-blue skirt suit
and holding a clipboard. Her name was Marie, and she
was a senior official with the Health Service. She was
friendly and efficient and spent some time taking all the
details that Amanda could remember from her experi-

ences in St Catherine's and everything she knew about Dr
O'Shaughnessy.

When she was finished, she stood and said, 'Our
investigation is only beginning, and we will be in touch
with you again soon. I've contacted your family. Your
husband asked if it was okay for him to come and collect
you later today. I said I was sure it would be. He also said
to tell you that things can change for the better when we
least expect them, and that you'd understand that too. He
said he wants to make amends.'

Amanda felt her head spin, and spin again faster and
faster, like she was on a carousel and about to be tossed
off it.

'He actually said that?'

'Yes,' the official said, 'he did... oh, another thing.' She
reached into a pocket of her jacket and took out something. 'I'm sure you'll want this back. I had it sent down.'

It was her mobile phone.

Amanda held out her hand, but not for the phone.
Instead, she grabbed the official's wrist in a tight grip.
'Don't let my husband in here; don't let him near me, do
you understand?'

The official glanced down, then up again. Amanda saw
it, that look, like checking an overcharge on a Tesco receipt.

'Y-yes, of course, Dr Jackson. Whatever you say. No. I
won't.'

'And someone else will collect me,' she said, letting the
hand go. 'I'll make sure of it.'

THAT SOMEONE WAS PRI. Amanda rang her, and she came
and collected her from St Catherine's an hour or so later.

'What an ordeal, Amy.' They were on the motorway travelling back to Galway City in the Jag.

'But it's not over yet. Not until Edward's dealt with. You know he rang the hospital, wanting to come and collect me, to work things out, like nothing is wrong.'

Pri was silent, and Amanda could see her grip tighten on the wheel.

'Yes,' Amanda said, 'unbelievable, isn't it?'

'What now?' Pri asked. 'Maybe you should just forget about Edward. Live your life, Amy.'

'What?' The word was delivered much sharper than she'd intended.

'Well...' Pri hesitated, then: 'Think about it. He's never going to trouble you again. Not after this, is he? Just saying.'

Just saying, Amanda thought. Just saying. But she wanted to shout, Don't you get it, Pri? Don't you? After everything I've – we've – been through. Don't you bloody well get it?

But instead she said calmly, yet with a hard, resolute edge, 'You can't ignore a monster. And I don't intend to.'

'Of course,' Pri said quickly. 'Of course, I was...'

'I know...' Amanda said, but didn't finish, instead, thinking... I know. You were just saying.

Pri's big Jag ate up the miles. When they reached Ocean View House, she stopped the car just in front of the driveway.

'Are you sure about this, Amy?'

Amanda nodded. She'd never been so sure about anything in her life. She looked down the driveway, could see at the end the autumn sun reflecting on the front of the house, making the windows sparkle. She was home. This was the place she had raised her children; this was the place that held beautiful memories, not just for her, but her children too. Despite everything, she'd always loved this house, thought it looked like something from the pages of a fairy story, that it was magical, innocent almost.

But she knew, as long as Edward lived here, it would always be stained; he did not belong in such a place. He had to go, and it was up to her to make sure he left, to preserve that beauty and innocence, to wrestle it back, return it to what it was, a loving, warm, beautiful home.

She glanced at the time, a little before 3:15 p.m.

'Yes, I am sure,' Amanda said. 'I need to check something. Edward won't be back for hours. Drive ahead, please, Pri; this won't take long.'

Pri swung the car through the gateway and went down the drive, turned in a wide arc so it was pointing back the way they had come, next to the door. Amanda got out, but went quickly along the side of the house first, peering round the back. Edward's car was nowhere to be seen. She came back again and stood by the driver's door. Pri wound down the window.

'I'll stay here,' Pri said. 'Just in case. If I see him coming, I'll beep the horn. You never know... you think that's a good idea?'

Amanda nodded. 'Thank you, Pri, yes, I think that's a good idea. But I don't particularly care anymore. What can he do? The cat's out of the bag. He'll soon know all about it.'

Amanda turned and let herself into the house. It was cold inside, and although everything looked the same, she got a sense of something forlorn, a sadness that had taken hold in the short time she'd been gone. She pulled the collar of her coat up and headed for the stairs.

. . .

SHE WENT TO HER BEDROOM, their bedroom, and stood in the doorway before stepping in slowly and walking around the bed onto Edward's side. She crossed to the window, turned and leaned against the sill, looking about the room as if for the first time. In some ways she was looking at it for the first time, the way she was seeing it now.

This had been a prison cell, she decided. Despite the deep-pile floral carpet – Amanda didn't like carpets; she much preferred wooden flooring – and the €80-per-roll wallpaper, the gilt-edged prints on the wall, and by square footage, the size larger than many six-figure single-bedroom apartments that she could think of. But to her, that was what it was, a prison cell. She hadn't realised it before. But she did now. She'd been living in her very own Truman Show, brainwashed, a prisoner of Edward, prepared, up until now, to fool herself that everything was good between them. She glanced to the phone on the dresser next to his side of the bed.

For instance, how many times had she used that? Not without it being handed to her first by Edward, that is. Never. That was the answer. How many times had she actually gone round to his side of the bed to pick it up? Again. Never. Not once. She lived on the other side of the bed, rose each morning and walked the same path to the en suite on that side of the room, then back again, the same path to the wardrobe, using the left door only – never the right, or heaven forbid, both of them – selected what she needed, and closed it again, rejoined the path back to the bed, where she stood on a piece of ground, probably on closer inspection to be found worn by her endless trodding. Is this how animals survive in a zoo? I never realised before, but that is what I was – an animal in a zoo.

Her eyes wandered to his side of the bed again before diverting to the opposite side of the room, staring at the picture of a Clydesdale horse hanging on the wall there. She could feel a tightness in her belly, but her eyes wandered back to the bed, taking in Edward's pillow – an orthopaedic one that he had ordered specially from a hospital supplier – and the dresser. The exact same dresser as on her side of the bed, white with gold-coloured handles.

She couldn't take her eyes from it. The more she stared at it, the more she wondered... what was in there? Still, she held back, like an explorer who had discovered the outcrop to a new world, hesitating before venturing in. All her married life she had never encroached on Edward's half of anything. There was fifty per cent of her husband that she knew nothing about.

The dresser.

The fucking dresser.

It intrigued her.

It felt like a no-fly zone surrounded it. What would happen if she were to go over and just open a drawer? Instant vaporisation?

Her belly tightened, and her breathing, short and shallow, made a clicking noise at the back of her throat.

She thought of Fiona, liberated after shooting a man to death.

Amanda strode over to the dresser and grabbed the handle, pulled it open.

. . .

AND WAS SURPRISED. Because the drawer was messy – by Edward's standards, that is: block of cling-wrapped Post-it notes carrying the logo of a pharmacy company on it, no doubt given to Edward by some salesman or other; a couple of telephone chargers; paperback novel of some description; various pens; couple of loose buttons... the usual detritus to be found in any drawer in any house anywhere in the country. She was about to close the drawer again when she noticed something lying at the bottom, white so that it appeared to be a part of the actual bottom itself, but shorter so she could see the gap between the side of the drawer and the edge, and knew it wasn't the drawer base... it was something else. She pushed aside the telephone chargers and Post-it notes bundle, took hold of a corner and pulled. It was a sheet of paper, and it came out easily. If it had been thinner paper, it would have torn, but it wasn't. It was thicker, like card paper.

She held it up by a corner edge and stepped back, turning from the bed, a ray of cold autumn light through the window catching the paper, highlighting faint trails across it, like a tiny twig pulled through sand to form a message. She angled the paper, but the light reflected directly onto it, and the outlines disappeared. She walked round to her side of the bed, sat down and opened her dresser, rummaged through it and found a pencil, placed the paper onto the dresser top, deftly began running the pencil across the page, holding the lead flat, shading it in quickly and evenly from top to bottom. She purposefully did not concentrate on the white, wormlike outlines that appeared until the whole page was completely shaded in. Then she held it before her.

But she already knew. Just knew. What it would say.

She looked.

She felt the breath being literally sucked out of her body as she stared, placing a hand onto her chest, above her heart, gasping for breath. With it came a heaviness in her upper chest, getting heavier, like a big rock was sitting inside there – Jesus, am I having a heart attack or a stroke? Then the heaviness began to recede as she started to breathe normally again.

A pen had pressed the outline of the words through a sheet of paper that had rested on top of the paper she was now holding. Those same four words. Fifteen letters in total, combining into four words, combining into one sickening belly punch:

I KNOW YOUR SECRET

55

Amanda felt the energy drain from her body. She slumped onto the bed, lying there, curled, an arm over her face, shutting out the light, retreating into the darkness, a cave, that she wanted to swallow her up. Her body did not seem like it belonged to her, like it was separate, a hollow vessel, one she was merely hiding within now. Her mind fissured and sparked, like miniature electrical short circuits, with nothing connected, and nothing making sense.

Her arm began to feel heavy after a time. Heavy like back then, during the opening scene to the movie, the camera panning to reveal a woman tethered to a bed, the woman: her. She could hear music, a building crescendo of screeching violins and pounding drums, as she opened her eyes and peered ahead to see a masked figure approach, with the head of a goat – or was it a mask? – and hoofed feet – or were they boots? With an enormous penis, erect and quivering, like it was scenting the air, as it came to within inches of her face. She writhed about on the bed and screamed. She could hear footsteps advanc-

ing. No, no, no, not again... She knew the monster was
standing next to her, by the bed. This time its mask would
not protect it. This time Amanda knew who hid behind it.

Her eyes snapped open, releasing her from her dream.

'Thank God,' she said, noticing the person who was
standing there. 'I nodded off. I was dreaming.'

Amanda got up. Pri was standing by the bed.

'Everything alright? Why've you come in?'

Pri gave a vague shrug. 'Fine, fine.'

'I'm going to ring Lynn. Tell him what I found. It won't
sound so crazy now.'

'Lynn?' Pri said.

'Yes. The guard, remember? From the other night, at
your house? The time has come.'

'What do you mean, the time has come?'

'To report Edward, of course.'

Pri looked at her oddly.

Amanda stepped towards the door, but stopped. She
heard something.

Dutt...

The sound seemed to be coming from outside on the
landing.

Dutt...

'You hear that?'

'Hear what?'

'That sound. Listen.'

But it didn't come again. What came was a different
sound, the slight creaking of the floorboards. Someone
was standing on the landing outside the room. Amanda
detected a movement, looked to see a pair of feet appear
in the doorway. She stared at them, ignoring the rest of
the person for now. As if fascinated by the crepe-soled
shoes, folded in the middle, the dark crow's feet in the

white leather along the crease line. Similar to the shoes at the cottage that he had worn, O'Shaughnessy. Golfing shoes. She ran her eyes slowly upward, knowing as she looked that it shouldn't come as a surprise. Because she knew now. Yes, she did. But still, it did come as a surprise. It was a gut-wrenching kick-to-the-stomach surprise. Now that he was standing before her.

'Tut, tut, tut. Amanda, Amanda, Amanda...'

That same, familiar, condescending tone.

Amanda drew back her shoulders.

'Come on, Pri, we're leaving, and there's nothing he can do about it. Step out of the way, Edward.'

But he didn't move.

'I said get out of the way.'

For the first time in her life as she looked at him – apart from that night, that is – she felt she was seeing the real Edward. There was a look in his eyes, the layers he had been hiding behind stripped away, leaving two hard, lifeless, cold orbs staring at her. Strangely, she was not afraid, now that the beast had slunk out from the shadows into the open. His hands were in his pockets – had he something in there? – as he very subtly began to rock back and forth on the balls of his feet. Why is he doing that? She felt a slight breeze from somewhere, a window or a door must be open, and with it came the sound of the distant, hoarse chatter of a magpie just at the moment Edward opened his mouth, making it seem like the sound was coming from him. Edward, she saw, was laughing.

Now she became afraid, turning her head to glance at Pri, but pausing, because she was nervous of turning her back on him.

'You've left me no choice,' he said, taking a step forward.

Amanda stepped back in response, bumping into Pri, as she felt a pressure behind her knees – like when she was a child, bumping into the back of each other's knees in the schoolyard, losing balance; one slight nudge was enough to send you falling over: great gas.

As she lost her balance, she felt a sharp push into the centre of her back and went tumbling to the floor. In that moment she fell, her mind tumbled too, trying to make sense of it all, and she did, realising that it was Pri who had pushed her.

Pri pushed me!

She hit the floor and looked up just as Pri glanced to Edward, a strange mixture of desperation and affection in her eyes.

Then she ran to him.

'Please, Edward. We don't need to do this. We can just leave. Leave now. Come on.'

Pri went to wrap her arms around him, but Edward writhed against her, turning his head away, his eyes all the time trained on Amanda. His hands, Amanda saw, remained in his pockets.

'Go away,' he shouted to Pri, swinging his body, pushing her away. Pri seemed stung as she fell back, her mouth opening, hanging like that, her arms outstretched, frozen and empty.

Yes, it all made sense to Amanda: how O'Shaughnessy had known they were at Fiona's cottage, the incident on the beach, everything... because Pri was keeping them one step ahead. She remembered how Pri had appeared in the office at the top of the house just as it seemed Edward was about to strike her. It was all an act, part of one carefully choreographed performance.

'You sick bastard,' she hissed, sitting up and pointing at Pri. 'What is it with you, huh?'

Pri looked like she was about to burst into tears.

Edward smiled, regaining his composure.

'Answer my question. You'll go to prison for this. What is it...? You two?'

His smile only widened, goading her. 'How do you work out I'll go to prison? Who's going to send me there? Anyway, it was all Andrew's idea. He said we could have you committed for the rest of your life, that he'd done it before, that we only needed to sign the forms. Andrew devised the whole plan. And it almost worked. It's surprisingly easy to hack a computer, you know, and writing notes, leaving them on your car was nothing; neither was popping a bag of talcum powder into the boot of your car, mere child's play. Oh, and the malarkey on the beach with your suicide letter... mere semantics, they really thought you were losing it. Except hitting myself with a shoe to support my story that I was mugged. That might have been a bit over the top, granted. But even so, I took pleasure from it all because it meant I was getting back at you, Amanda, for making such a fool out of me.'

'What?'

'For not telling me Lauren wasn't my daughter – which is what you thought. You said nothing about it; you married me for convenience. Yes, you took me for a complete fool, didn't you?'

Amanda shook her head, incongruous. He was blaming her for what had happened, what had happened to her; it was all her fault.

She shuddered, tried to get to her feet.

'Don't. I didn't tell you get up, did I? Stay where you are.'

She sat down again.

'Andrew's sexual peccadilloes,' Edward went on, 'my friend had some very specific, if extreme, tastes. That night was all his idea too...'

'Is that what you call it?' she said, cutting him off, forcing herself not to shout. 'Peccadilloes? Tastes? His fault. To hell with you.'

'I went along with it that one time, that's all. With you. That one time.'

'You sick bastard. You mean I should feel honoured? I don't believe a word out of your mouth. Not a word.'

'I wanted you. I did what was required to get you. I got you pregnant. Surprisingly easy once I worked out the dates. You wouldn't have been interested in me otherwise. This way, I was your knight in shining armour. I saved you from being ostracised, from disgrace and exile, from losing your career. Come on, you have to admit, it all worked out in the end. Well, didn't it? Until now, that is. Still, I expected you to tell me, I would have understood, you see, and you would have loved me even more. But you didn't; you kept that your secret.'

That smile of his was beginning to infuriate her. She thought of what O'Shaughnessy had said: I can safely say, Amanda, you are in a condition of most robust mental health, with a refreshing lack of reserve in talking truthfully about yourself. I'll tell Edward if I may; he will be greatly reassured. She could only assume this was some sort of bluff, a red herring, designed so that when his true, final verdict did come, it would be less likely to draw suspicion. How deviously clever, wanting to make it look like it was her fault.

'Her.' Amanda stabbed a finger towards Pri. 'I asked you. What about her?'

'Please, Amanda,' Pri whimpered, 'I'm sorry...'

'Well, where does she come into it?'

'How can I put it?' Edward said. 'We're friends, with benefits... it's been going on for years, Amanda. You hadn't a clue, had you?'

And she hadn't. Not a clue. The room suddenly lurched, and she reached out to steady herself, but there was nothing to hold on to. She felt Pri's hands on her shoulders.

'Get your hands off me, bitch.'

Amanda closed her eyes and swallowed a couple of times. How had she not noticed? How had she not suspected? Surely she would have noticed... something?

'She has addiction issues,' Edward added. 'No surprises there; you know the way she knocks back the wine. But she likes the pills best. She'll do anything for a few of those little yellow happy pills... won't you, Pri my dear, hm? I'm always happy to help out.'

'Enough!' Amanda shouted. She couldn't take this any longer.

'Yes. I agree.' Edward advanced, his hands finally emerging from his pockets, one holding a syringe, the other a small glass vial.

'What? What're they for?'

'I told you. You've left me no choice. Don't make this difficult, Amanda. Please.'

He stood, towering above her. In the corner of her vision she saw Pri step closer behind her. Dear old Pri, acting helpless but going along with it anyway. Zoned out, not thinking. Pri was a master at that.

In one quick movement, Pri leaned down and pulled Amanda back by the shoulders, making her virtually helpless, the top half of her body acting as a counterweight to the bottom half, hinging on her arse, with Pri balancing her like a swing. Edward had already extracted the contents of the vial into the syringe.

'We have children, Edward; you can't kill me.'

He replaced the empty vial back into his pocket.

'He's not going to kill you, Amanda,' Pri said with a nervous twitter. 'Don't be silly.'

You stupid bitch, Amanda thought, of course he's going to kill me; that's only what he told you.

Edward stooped and gripped her upper arm. Amanda immediately tried to yank it free again. But it was no use; his grip was too firm; he probably didn't need to be precise, just plunge that syringe anywhere into her arm muscle. She felt the tip touch her flesh, and she pulled back, her arm pressing against the floor, nowhere else to go, the tip following... She turned her head away; she didn't want to watch.

'Edward!'

For a moment Amanda thought it was her voice, but it wasn't. It was clipped and authoritative, so unexpected that Edward paused, glancing over his shoulder.

Amanda knew that voice: Emily O'Shaughnessy. She took her opportunity and yanked on her arm with such force that it shot free from Edward's grasp. Behind Emily someone else appeared, a figure running into the room: Fiona. She barged in between Amanda and Edward.

'It's all over, you. Stand back. Leave her alone.'

Amanda quickly scrambled to her feet.

'Come on now, Edward.' Emily's tone could cut granite. 'This is enough nonsense for one day. We know everything, Edward; it's no use.'

He looked at them each in turn, and it melted right

away before their very eyes, all that arrogance and smug self-assurance disappearing, gone.

There was the sound of feet pounding up the stairs, then a blur of blue uniforms barging into the room. Amanda recognised one of them, Lynn. A police officer stood before Edward. She was young, female, which Amanda thought appropriate. Amanda listened as the officer spoke: 'Edward Jackson, you are under arrest on suspicion of kidnap, rape and false imprisonment. You are not obliged to say anything unless you wish to do so, but whatever you say will be taken down in writing and may be given in evidence. Do you understand?'

Edward didn't speak. Amanda saw his eyes slide to the corners of their sockets, flaring with renewed arrogance, scarcely believing what was happening.

'Do you understand, Dr Jackson?' the officer grunted, her tone and demeanour out of character with her petite appearance.

Edward appeared stung by the comment, by the lack of respect. He narrowed his eyes, looking at her. 'That's impossible,' he said, his composure returning. 'You're making a terrible mistake. And how dare you speak to me like that.'

'Yeah, yeah, you can save that for the judge,' she retorted.

'We searched the home of Andrew O'Shaughnessy,' Lynn chipped in. 'We can thank Emily for giving us the heads-up. We found videos, diaries, even a handwritten manuscript, a memoir, in a hidden safe. The man was a meticulous note-taker and chronicler of events. And in that there is enough to put you away for a very long time, Dr Jackson.'

For the first time in his life, Amanda's husband was

speechless, his expression one of confusion, utter confusion. And in that moment, Amanda could not help but feel... well, what exactly? She wasn't sure: pity, sorrow, a mixture of both?

'Come on,' the young guard said, tugging on his arm.

'Wait, I want to say something... Amanda.'

Their eyes met for a fleeting moment, yet in it she had a feeling of something passing between them...

Edward opened his mouth to speak.

... of time, of years spent together, moving quickly, and then, like a comet across the night sky, puff, gone.

Edward closed his mouth without saying another word, like he knew it was no use; his power over her had been broken.

Amanda watched him go, feeling the invisible chains falling from her, realising in this moment just how much a prisoner she had been. Suddenly there was no doubt about how she felt.

She was free.

EPILOGUE

EIGHTEEN MONTHS LATER

The TV studio was hot, very hot, beneath the rows of LED lights suspended from the ceiling. Amanda was just about to reach for the glass of water on the table between her and the host, Brian Sullivan, when he spoke to a camera, and she quickly pulled back her hand.

'Good evening, and welcome to tonight's episode of The Topic. My guest is Dr Amanda Ryan, whose book, Living A Nightmare, has become a global best-selling phenomenon. Welcome, Dr Ryan, and what can I say? What a book.'

'Thank you, Brian, and thanks for having me.'

'Um, I still can't get my head around all of this though. I mean, I'm going to jump right in here, but your husband...'

'Ex-husband, Brian. We've divorced. Which is ironic because it's what he wanted, just not the way he wanted it. That's why I go by my maiden name now, which is Ryan, of course.'

'Oh, of course, Dr Ryan. Yes, of course. Apologies.'

Amanda gave a wry smile. 'That's alright, Brian.'

'As I was saying,' he continued, 'I still can't get my head around all that's happened. Quite unbelievable. I mean, this sort of thing happens in movies, doesn't it? Not in real life. But that's not true, because it happened to you, didn't it, Dr Ryan? It actually happened to you.'

Brian Sullivan looked at her in that way of his she'd seen countless times on the ratings-topping TV show; faux concern she'd always called it, except now she wasn't so sure; he seemed genuine enough.

'Thing is, what happened to me is, I'm not going to say it's common, but it does happen, and more than you'd think. I've had countless letters from readers who've had similar experiences.'

'Really?' Brian Sullivan leaned back in his chair and pressed a finger against his cheek. 'Countless letters. Really? You mean women who have married the men who have done such a thing to them...'

'No, I'm not saying that. No. Most women don't marry their abuser. In that sense I am unique, yes, but I didn't know that the man who'd drugged and raped me was the man I'd been married to for more than twenty-two years. What I mean is that women are drugged and raped more than you'd ever think. Most don't even report it. I didn't. Which I am ashamed to admit to now, by the way. I'm lucky to live in a democracy with a rule of law. In some countries in the world they don't have that, and women in such places have little or no rights. In that sense, I would urge anyone who has been abused to report it to the police; no ifs or buts, do it.'

Brian Sullivan nodded. 'Yes, shocking, utterly shocking, and people should report it, male or female.'

'As I say, I didn't report what happened to me. I was trying to protect my daughter. I didn't want her knowing anything about it. It was wrong. I should have reported it. But as I say in the book, I also felt dirty and sullen. I was ashamed. I just wanted to put the whole affair behind me.'

'Until you found that note on your car, isn't that right? That's when it all started up again.'

Amanda nodded. She suddenly felt like she might cough, reached for the glass of water and took a long swallow.

'Yes,' she said, putting the glass back onto the table. 'And what my ex-husband started was eventually his undoing and also the demise of his co-conspirator, Andrew O'Shaughnessy.'

'And the reason,' Brian Sullivan said, his voice rising with each word, adding tension, 'was that your ex-husband knew his secret was about to get out. Isn't that it?'

'Yes,' Amanda said. 'So he set up this elaborate plan to have me declared mentally unstable. It almost worked. I came close to it for a time, I will admit, because I was in a terribly dark, hopeless place, all alone. I was really close to the edge on occasions, I can tell you, close to crossing over to the other side.'

'And that's where Andrew O'Shaughnessy came in, isn't it?' The TV host looked directly into the camera. 'For the benefit of viewers who may not know, an investigation is underway to try to establish the number of victims he abused. Also, members of staff at St Catherine's Mental Health facility have been suspended and are currently under investigation too.' Looking away from the camera, back to Amanda, he continued, 'And that might just be possible, isn't that right, Dr Ryan? Because it appears he kept records. In fact, the level of meticulous detail reflects a clinical approach; he carefully planned things – one of the reasons, I suspect, he managed to get away with it for so long.'

'Yes,' Amanda agreed, 'and clearly he was an extremely cruel and manipulative individual, his victims in the main vulnerable women at the lowest points in their lives, women who had been incarcerated into the mental health system and had no voice whatsoever. And then there were the others, women like me, who were drugged and effectively kidnapped, raped, but I suspect few of us want to be reminded of what happened then. The women in the care of the psychiatric services, in the care of the State, you have to remember, sought help, safety and protection, but instead, well, as we are beginning to find out, they were exploited in the cruellest possible way by that man. As I would have been exploited once again too, I have no doubt, if I had remained committed to St Catherine's for any longer than was the case.'

Brian Sullivan shook his head gravely. 'I can only say the title of your book sums it all up, Dr Ryan, doesn't it? Living A Nightmare.' He fell silent, allowed it to percolate a moment for effect, then: 'Andrew O'Shaughnessy was shot dead by Fiona McBride Crowley... our researchers contacted her, to at least try to obtain a comment for tonight's show, ideally have her appear, but she refused, and refuses, to talk to us. Are you still in contact with her?'

Amanda shrugged. 'Yes. On and off.'

'And she was acquitted of all charges?'

'Yes, indeed she was. It was determined, quite rightly in my view, to be a clear case of self-defence.'

A look crossed Brian Sullivan's face. Was he going to

probe further into that night? It had been agreed before-hand that her appearance on the show would be brief, the conversation a mere sketched outline of her story. This was her publisher's idea, who had agreed to the terms, seeking merely to wet the public's appetite, that they might actually go out and buy the book. Which suited Amanda fine, because she didn't want to be on this show at all. The book had been written as a means of cathartic release for herself, but, as she was beginning to realise, from a publisher's perspective, marketing was as important as the writing. So she was going along with it.

But if he had been considering this, he had changed his mind. 'And your friend Pri?' he said instead.

Amanda pursed her lips, shaking her head slowly. 'Pri did not receive a custodial sentence, but she is receiving the help she needs. I'd like to leave it at that. Despite everything, I do respect her privacy.'

'But they'd been having an affair for years, behind your back.'

'Yes, but Pri was in a position to be easily manipulated; she was in a very dark place. Addiction can do that.'

Amanda had made scant mention of Liam, Pri's husband, in her book. She considered Pri's husband was entitled to his privacy too. They were still together, however, as even now, Liam was there for his wife. Without Pri's active addiction issues, maybe things could work out between the two. And there was little mention of Emily O'Shaughnessy in the book either. Amanda suspected Emily could write a book of her experiences with her husband – experiences she wasn't ready to talk about – yet, that is.

In any case, this was Amanda's story, no one else's.

Again, the faux look of concern crossed his face, and this time it looked anything but genuine.

'Your kids, Dr Ryan, this can't have been easy on them. How are they bearing up?'

Amanda smiled warmly. 'They're in the audience; you can ask them yourself if you like?'

'Oh, really.' Shading his eyes with a hand, in faux surprise again, because he already knew they were there.

A camera on a remotely operated boom swooped down from the ceiling and picked out Danny and Lauren easily. Amanda saw their faces appear on a monitor.

'Hi... Danny and Lauren, isn't it?' Brian Sullivan said.

They both nodded.

'This can't have been easy, guys.'

They looked at one another, uncertain, before Lauren looked ahead to the presenter again.

'No,' she said, 'it hasn't.'

Amanda wanted to get up, go down to her kids, and hold them close.

'But especially for you, isn't that right, Lauren?' Brian Sullivan asked.

Lauren stared ahead blankly for a moment.

'For both of us,' she said then, glancing to her brother, smiling warmly at him, 'but you're correct, especially for me. It was a lot to take in, your father' – pausing, taking a breath, before continuing with resolve – 'a father you're particularly close to drugged and raped your mother. I mean, if that doesn't...' Her voice trailed off. 'But I've received help from an excellent therapist, and I'm coming out the other end. Because I have my life to lead, and I can't lead it if I allow this to drag me back. I can't allow it to. I know my mother loves me dearly, and that's all that matters at the moment.'

'And your father?' Brian Sullivan said. 'You keep in contact?'

Amanda watched her daughter's pained expression and wanted to go to her, to protect her, but knew she couldn't.

'No,' Lauren said, 'neither of us have. I don't think I, we, either of us, can ever forgive him... but still, he is my father. I don't know what the future holds, maybe in time, a lot of time, but not now.'

'Andrew O'Shaughnessy was a friend of the family too, wasn't he?'

Amanda's head swung towards the presenter. She hadn't expected that question to be asked of her children. None of that had been discussed beforehand.

'Yes.' It was Danny, a note of defiance in his tone. 'And I feel sorry for them, really, his family. But what else can I say? What can anyone say? We're all victims.'

'Indeed,' Brian Sullivan said, turning back to Amanda, 'there is nothing anyone can say. You've returned to work, Dr Ryan?'

'I've resigned my position, but I will be continuing as a physician. I'm considering setting up my own clinic. First, I want to take some time out. There's a big world out there, and I want to see some of it. Make up for what I've missed. This is my time to live, to explore. I'll start back after a little travelling; a new beginning, you might call it.'

A fake laugh and a wave of the hand. 'Yes, a new beginning. Sounds amazing. I wish you, we all wish you, the very best with that.'

Amanda could not help but give a curt nod. The truth was, Brian Sullivan, in his well-cut suit and chipped dictation, his dyed hair and made-up face, was beginning to irritate her. She wanted this interview finished with. The

TV host, attuned to the nuances of guests from over a quarter century of presenting, immediately sensed it. His smile widened as he looked to the audience and swept his arm towards Amanda.

'Dr Amanda Ryan, ladies and gentlemen, and her book Living A Nightmare. It's out now. And I can't recommend it highly enough.'

A large screen hanging from the ceiling announced 'Ad Break', a clock beneath running down the seconds from two minutes.

A voice through an intercom announced, 'Anyone need the bathroom, do so now. Thank you.'

'That wasn't so bad, was it?' Brian Sullivan said to her with a lingering look.

'No, thank you, it wasn't,' she lied.

'I don't bite, do I, Dr Ryan?'

'No, you certainly don't bite.'

'Okay then, see you in the Green Room in a little while? We can have a glass of champagne maybe.'

Amanda stood. 'Unfortunately, I can't. I have an arrangement to meet a friend. But thank you again, for everything.'

The TV host did not reply, his attention taken up by his schedule card and the next guest who was walking onto the set, a small, young man, dressed in jeans, boots and sweatshirt.

'Ted Breen, up-and-coming country star, how are you? Pleasure to meet you, sir; take a seat.'

Amanda stepped away, and a headphoned assistant pointed towards a door at the back of the studio, smiling as she passed. Brian Sullivan said nothing, like he had already forgotten her. Danny and Lauren met her by the door. It led out to the rear car park and was the one she had come through earlier.

They group hugged.

'You were brilliant,' Lauren said.

'Yes, Mum, brillo,' added Danny.

Amanda pulled back, resting a hand on each of her children's shoulders, looking at them both in turn.

'I'm so proud of you; you've dealt with this amazingly.' Her eyes lingered on Lauren. 'Especially you, Lauren.'

'I have Fiona to thank for that. She's been amazing, Mum, really.'

Yes, Fiona had been amazing. When Amanda had told her she was appearing on the nation's number one talk show, she'd been very specific: she did not want it mentioned that she was counselling her daughter. 'Keep it vague; just say we stay in touch occasionally; leave it at that.'

And Amanda had. Fiona, after all, had been struck off the medical register.

'What are you two up to now?' Amanda asked.

'We're catching a late-night movie,' Danny said. 'Actually, it's kind of a double date.'

'No, it's not,' Lauren said. 'I said I liked him, your friend Eamon, that's all, and I agreed to go with you to the movie because I want to see it. That's it.'

'Yeah, yeah, whatever,' Danny said with a laugh, 'but we need to get going, or we'll be late.'

Amanda smiled as Danny pushed the door, and they all stepped out into the night.

'I've a taxi coming in a couple of minutes. I can give you a lift,' Amanda said, tightening her scarf around her neck. The night was cold.

'No, thanks,' Danny replied, 'it's right by here.'

She watched her children walking across the car park towards the security barrier, speaking briefly with the security officer, then making their way out onto the busy roadway. She felt that sense of overbrimming love again, doing her best to ignore the small barb of guilt that was beginning to scratch in a corner of her consciousness, trying to get a firmer hold on her, that somehow, maybe, she could have done all this differently. She took a breath, upturning the sack of potatoes in her mind, watching them roll away, emptying the bag completely.

There, that's better.

Headlights swung into the car park, and a moment later a taxi pulled up next to her.

'Dr Amanda Ryan?' the driver asked. 'For Lambert's on the Green?'

'That's me,' she said, pulling the door open and getting in. Now she was beginning to feel nervous.

SHE WAS the first to arrive. The maître d' showed her to a discreet table in a dark wood-panelled alcove along a side wall. The restaurant was long and narrow, and she could glimpse through the window at the top people hurrying by, couples mostly, and gaggles of young men and women at this time of evening. She checked the time, just gone 10:15 p.m. She'd hoped they wouldn't be late: the maître d' had gently but insistently informed her that orders to the kitchen ceased at 10:30 sharp.

It was almost that time when they rushed in together. The maître d' didn't need to check their booking; they were the last diners of the day. He led them immediately to the table as Amanda stood and embraced each in turn. A waiter appeared and handed them menus, continuing to hover, pen prominently poised above his pad.

'We'd better order, or we'll end up having to go to a fast-food joint,' Amanda said.

They hastily did, and when their pre-dinner cocktails arrived and they began to sip and relax, Amanda spoke.

'I was beginning to think you weren't going to show.'

'We got stuck in traffic, sorry.'

Amanda gave Fiona a warm smile.

'That's alright.'

'The truth is,' said the other woman, 'Fiona had to coax me somewhat. I didn't think I could make it.' Emily O'Shaughnessy's tone was, just like her expression, pained. It hadn't been easy for her or her family in the aftermath. Even for a strong woman like her.

'Enough.' It was Fiona, tapping a fish fork on her glass theatrically. 'I need to say something.'

Amanda and Emily turned silently to look at her.

'This is our first time gathering together,' Fiona went on, 'and hopefully it won't be our last. But please, can we look towards the rising sun, as it were, to a new day, for us all, and make a pact?'

'A pact?' Amanda said.

'Yes, a pact,' Fiona said, placing one hand onto the centre of the table. 'Come on, join me; lay your hands on top of mine.' They did, and Fiona continued, 'Because we vow to live from this moment forward in the understanding that we carry no shame, and that although we are victims, we refuse to act as such, because we are now free, empowered in the knowledge that we can live our lives without the censure of our fiercest critic – ourselves. But we will not squander this freedom, continuously looking over our shoulders to the past, but we decide here and now to leave it behind and set our eyes only to the future, to the promises it holds. A toast, ladies. To us.'

They picked up their glasses.

'To us,' Fiona repeated.

'To us,' they said in unison.

ABOUT THE AUTHOR

I hail from Mayo in the west of Ireland, although I spent much of my life away, in the US, UK, Europe, Jersey in the Channel Islands and various parts of Ireland.

In my younger years I was incredibly restless. I left home and school at 16 and spread my wings. I've had over forty jobs, everything from barman, labourer, staff newspaper reporter, soldier in the Irish army, station foreman with London Underground, mason, and many more besides. I returned to education as a mature student in the early noughties and hold a BA in history and sociology from the National University of Ireland at Maynooth, and an M.Phil from Trinity College Dublin.

Since 2005 I've been a civilian employee of the Irish police, An Garda Síochána. However, I've been on extended sick leave since 2015 following a mystery illness which struck while travelling in Spain. It almost killed me. The doctors never got to the bottom of it and they call me the Mystery Man. But every cloud has a silver lining. It has given me the time to write. Although I've been writing all my life, most of my output languishes in the bottom of drawers.

Under my real name, Michael Scanlon, I was initially published for the first time in 2019 by Bookouture with the first of three crime novels. Working with Inkubator is another great opportunity for me. This time I'm using a pseudonym, as the style of J.M. O'Rourke books are so different, and also, I really like the name!

I hope readers like them.

ALSO BY J.M. O'ROURKE

The Detective Jack Brody Series

The Devil's House

Time of Death

A Deadly Affair

Standalone Psychological Thriller

I Know Your Secret

Printed in Great Britain
by Amazon

37951842R00199